Ayesha Harruna Attah (G at the age of seventeen, where she studied at Mount Holyoke College and then Columbia University. She received an MFA in Creative Writing at New York University. Her first novel, *Harmattan Rain*, was shortlisted for the 2010 Commonwealth Writers' Prize. She recently moved back to Ghana.

Saturday's Shadows

Ayesha Harruna Attah

Saturday's Shadows

World Editions

LEWISHAM LIBRARY SERVICE	
915 00000230077	
Askews & Holts	30-Aug-2019
AF	£11.99
	LWCAT

Published in Great Britain in 2015 by World Editions Ltd., London

www.worldeditions.org

Copyright © Ayesha Harruna Attah, 2015
Cover design Multitude
Cover credit © Angèle Etoundi Essamba

The moral rights of the author have been asserted in accordance with the Copyright, Designs and Patents Act 1988

British Library Cataloguing-in-Publication Data
A catalogue record for this book is available on request from the British Library

ISBN 978-94-6238-043-1

Typeset in Minion Pro and Calibri

Distribution Europe (except the Netherlands and Belgium): Turnaround Publishers Services, London, UK
Distribution the Netherlands and Belgium: Centraal Boekhuis, Culemborg, the Netherlands

All rights reserved. No part of this publication may be reproduced, stored in or introduced into a retrieval system, or transmitted, in any form, or by any means (electronic, mechanical, photocopying, recording or otherwise) without the prior written permission of the publisher. Phone: +31 (0)76 523 3533. Email: info@worldeditions.org.

*If you have no time to attend to your illness,
you get time to die.*
– Ghanaian proverb

CHAPTER ONE

The Crowd

We went mad after the transition. Doctor Karamoh Saturday had given up his military regime and was now president of our fledgling democratic country, but everyone knows a zebra never changes its stripes. In my household, we were going through our own changes: Kojo was away for the first time at a boarding school controlled by the same bloodthirsty thieves who ruled the country, Theo was stuck in a hole at the Ministry of Foreign Affairs, and Atsu, a meek girl from the village, had just started working for us. Me? I was wondering how long I had to live.

Either the madness seeped in from the outside, or it was a latent virus lurking in each of us, waiting for the right moment to unleash its deadly nucleic acid. I know exactly when it hit me. It was the day I was shopping for my annual Christmas party, which was a week away. I was driving to the Bakoy Market to procure the party items. A hot harmattan afternoon, the sky was shaded with grey dust, and congestion was relentless. The traffic lights weren't working, not a single policeman stood in sight, and taxis and minivans cut in and out of tiny impossible spaces.

As I inched my car forward, a migraine jabbed its way

from the left part of my skull to the right. A ball of light had formed in my peripheral vision. Nausea. Cars on the road went out of focus and street hawkers morphed into a fuzzy giant. Honks and screaming voices behind me increased in volume.

'Foolish woman, move your car!' somebody yelled.

I thought the rage was good, even though I didn't want it directed at me. Our collective anger, held back for the seventeen years of the Doctor's dictatorship, was finally erupting. People could now say whatever they wanted without fear: the fear of getting caned by the Saturday Boys, or the fear of disappearing.

A man selling torches and Christmas lights passed by me. The yellow of his shirt turned cream then white, and his head grew oblong. I closed my eyes to shut out the dizzying images. The next thing I felt was my body jerking away from the steering wheel.

Slowly, sensation crawled from the tips of my fingers into the rest of my body. My muscles felt taut, as if someone were pulling them like rubber bands.

A crowd grew fast. Sellers, other drivers, gathered by my car.

'Lady, are you drunk?' a man asked.

Another in ripped shorts approached me, hands clasped over his head, mouth hanging wide open. I wasn't given time to process what was going on.

'*Ei*, Madam, you've killed me!' he wailed. 'My boss will finish me today. I don't have money! I still haven't paid my children's school fees. Now this.'

I was confused, only beginning to realize what had happened.

'You know you did this,' he said. 'You all saw. She did this.'

I dragged myself out of the car and accidentally pushed a woman selling oranges as I tried to steady myself. I walked closer to the man's car and the crowd followed me, and even though they were at least an arm's length away, it felt as if their bodies were pressing into me. His bumper was slightly dented in the middle. My car was barely scratched.

'Oh, this isn't that bad,' I said.

'Not for you, it's not. Please, Madam, how are you solving this problem?'

I really couldn't part with my money. It was to be used as follows: four broilers, a sack of rice, a gallon of oil. The change was to be handed to Atsu to buy fresh vegetables and fruit a few days before the party. Money was tight— Theo didn't seem to be fighting harder for more respect at the ministry, and at work I was dealing with crooks who were telling me that, since the transition, palm-oil production had gone down and prices had shot up, so I had already cut back on the usual party luxuries: catered food, hired musicians, decorations that lit up the whole street, some four-legged creature roasting on a spit. If I parted with even a tenth of the money, something would not get bought.

'How much do you need?' I asked. Behind us the traffic had doubled. 'Should we move off to the side?'

'Unless I go to the mechanic, how will I know, Madam? Tell me what you're giving me.'

'Five hundred kowries?' We'd probably have to skimp

on tomatoes, garlic, and ginger.

'It's not good.'

'Let's move our cars so those people can go,' I said.

'She wants to run!' said a rough voice. Even though I hadn't thought of it, this third party was right. I could run, and nobody would ever come looking for me. I wouldn't even have to hide.

'Okay,' I said. 'Six?' My headache still lingered, but at least the nausea had left. He shook his head; he must have thought I'd be an easy target. But I wasn't about to get cheated out of my Christmas party. I said: 'Fine, I'll give you my house number.' I opened my purse and rummaged through it for my business card. I scribbled on the card with the Duell and Co. logo—the crown of a palm tree—and stretched out my hand. 'Tell your boss to call me and I'll settle this with him.'

He looked at the crowd, and I followed his gaze. Lustful for their approval, he waited.

'Take it!' a woman shouted.

'No! She's cheating you!' said another.

'Nobody just dashes you six hundred kowries these days. Someone is giving you money. Take it!'

'Don't take it!'

Their voices were rising, chanting, thrumming along with my headache: don't-take it-don't-take it-don't! They wanted me to pay. But I was the wrong person, I'd have liked to say to them. The person they should harass was up on the hill in the distance, the one who had made us poorer with oppression. Not me.

'Two thousand,' he said.

'*Massa*,' I said and laughed, 'I don't even have half of that to give you. Let your boss call me.'

'*Kai*!' someone shouted. 'Lies! She wants to get you into trouble.'

'Take her car!'

To this crowd, this is what I was: a cushy job, a nice four-by-four, a well-fed family, children in private schools, a maid, education abroad, money to take vacations, expensive diseases. They thought I was spoiled and entitled and could pay my way out of any situation, and they were going to make me pay! I was no different from the Doctor. They grew into one giant monster and marched forward, ready to chew me up.

My pride was fuel for their anger. I needed to fight back differently, so I found myself lowering my knees to the tarmac, the roughness of it poking my bare skin. I palmed my left hand in my right and said, '*Massa*, I beg you. All I have is six hundred. Call me tomorrow and I'll get you four hundred more.' My voice actually shook as I dug out the notes from my bag.

He snatched them from my hand and stomped off, leaving me with the hungry crowd. Jaundiced or alcohol-reddened eyes (depending on who you were looking at) swivelled from the departing man to me. They wouldn't stop staring, and I fixed my gaze on the girl carrying the pyramid of oranges. I couldn't tell if she pitied or envied me. Shaken, I got back into my car and willed myself to drive to the Bakoy Market.

CHAPTER TWO

Misfit

I've been at the International Secondary School for five months and three days, and everyone tells me that I'm lucky. *Not everyone gets into the ISS. It's a privilege, Kojo.* But I can't tell you what the fuss is about. In the last five months, I've been bullied, had to question my intelligence time and time again, and I've fallen in love, and everybody knows *that* is never a good thing.

'Kojo Avoka, please come and say grace,' shouts Kunle, startling me. Kunle, my nemesis and room-mate. The most annoying being on the planet. Thing. He doesn't deserve to be called a being. He snores, throws his clothes all over the bedroom floor, and every chance he gets, he punishes me.

I drag my feet onto the wooden stage, sweat sliding down from my armpits, until I am next to Kunle, who plunks the mic into my hand and strides off the stage before I can beg him to stay. That would never have happened—me beg Kunle? Never.

'Please close your eyes,' I say, and close mine.

A hush descends on the dining hall. It's funny how I can feel the silence *falling*. But now, a problem: the words I want to use for the prayer have chosen to stay hidden wherever it is words are formed.

'Dear God,' I croak, but can't remember what comes next. I say this prayer every day, morning, afternoon, and evening. Or maybe I just open my mouth whenever we're saying grace. What comes afterwards? Someone coughs. It's rough, dry, and probably fake.

'Dear God …'

More coughs. When I woke up this morning, I thought I would swallow my burned millet porridge, go to class, stare at Inaam, go for lunch, struggle through basketball, and keep on being my boring old self. I open my eyes and wish I hadn't. Half of the dining hall has their hands pressed together in prayer and the other half is gawking at me, the teachers and prefects in the back, especially. They're leaning forward, stopping short of gesturing, 'Yes, go on.' I press my eyelids shut again and pretend they're not there. Dear Lord, I pray, I know I am not the best person a lot of the time, but please rescue me. I won't think evil thoughts when an upper sends me on the stupidest errand. I won't think bad things about Daddy. Help me. I wait for God's voice for a long, long time.

'Blessed bless,' I finally say. Officially the shortest prayer anybody's ever said in the dining hall.

'AMEN!' the dining hall responds.

After lunch, as I'm slinking past Mrs. Diouf and the other teachers on duty, Kunle and two upper one boys pounce on me.

'Avoka, you don't know how to pray?' one of them says. I

can never remember his name. All I know is he's the most moronic-looking person I've ever met, jaw jutting forward, the flattest forehead in the world. We'll just call him Moron from here on. The other boy is Ayensu, and I think we're even related on Daddy's side of the family. Not that it stops him from harassing me.

'Well, we are going to show you how to pray,' Kunle says, and they start singing 'A Mighty Fortress is our God,' but their tune is so off, it doesn't even sound like a song anymore. Kunle drums on my back, and Moron beatboxes. We arrive at the boys' dormitories, and they herd me behind Tower A.

Ayensu says, 'We are going to help you remember the prayer. Tell him, Ayo.'

'Dear God, bless this food to our use, and us to Thy service, and make us ever-mindful of the needs of others,' obediently cites Ayo/Moron.

'Got it?' Kunle asks. I'm not even halfway through nodding when he twists my left ear and tries to knot it. 'Got it?'

'Yes.'

'Repeat it,' says Ayensu.

'Dear God, bless this food to our use and make us mindful to the needs of other people.'

'He's an idiot,' Ayensu says. 'A complete idiot.'

Kunle instructs Moron to repeat the prayer. I knew I'd forgotten something.

'Since you failed at your chance to get out of jail free, your punishment is to scrub the Tower A boys' toilet, shouting the prayer at the top of your voice, till you can say it from front to back, back to front, words jumbled up, helter-skelter, willy-nilly,' Ayensu says and cackles. Pure evil.

Kunle adds, 'You'll do this every day until we break for Christmas.'

'Please, I'll get it,' I find myself saying. 'Let me try it again. Please.' I can't do this for more than a day. They ignore me and shove me into the bathroom.

The boys' toilet is disgusting. It announces itself with its smell before you arrive at its doors. Water constantly overflows from three urinals, half of these boys aren't potty-trained, and don't ask me how or why, but sometimes there's poop on the floor. I douse the whole place in Dettol, which barely covers up the smell of excrement and fermented urine.

My voice goes hoarse from screaming the prayer out loud, and I'm feeling so stupid I could cry. The only thing keeping me sane is knowing that in one blasted week, this term will be over. And then I remember. Another colossal barrier exists between my current existence and my happiness: the stupid dance party. We have to invite girls to the dance. I've been meaning to ask Inaam to go with me.

Mrs. Diouf's lair. Strange math figures on the green board. There are fifteen of us in the class, and this isn't even the smallest class I'm taking. At first it was one of the reasons I wanted to come to the ISS so badly: extra attention from teachers. Now, I realize you can't hide. The nice thing about Mrs. Diouf's class, though, is I get to stare at the object of my affection.

Let's take a moment to talk about Inaam: from my description, if I've given one at all, you'd think she was unapproachable, the Denise Huxtable of the class. But no, she's Vanessa. She combs her hair into a large Afro and wears these huge glasses that cover half her face. She sits in front of the class and is the best at math and everything else, except for English, which is where yours truly excels. Although it's probably only because I'm in Mr. Mahamadu's class and he's easier than Inaam's teacher. Why am I being a wimp and not asking her out already, do I hear you ask? It's because she's managed to combine whack with cool in a way nobody does, and it's sort of intimidating:

It was orientation. The parents had been sent off to a secret room to discuss money and to be thoroughly convinced that sending us to the ISS was a worthy investment. We stood in the dining hall, new students, everyone looking shiny and fresh, some of us wearing our Sunday best. At least I was, because Mummy made me. Those who weren't controlled by motherly forces wore jeans, T-shirts, and sneakers. Not button-down shirts, slacks, and shoes polished to face-reflecting perfection. I tried not to make eye contact with anyone. Not that I was shy, but it was nerve-wracking trying to understand what each person's face was saying. I could spot the comfortable ones, the ones whose parents were paying full tuition—those to whom this school was a birthright. I also noticed those who were so smart the school had begged them to come, throwing full rides at them. And those who, like me, had made it in by a scrape, most likely on financial aid. We were the grateful ones. I especially didn't want to see us. It'd be like looking at yourself in the mirror and realizing you're ugly. The comfortable ones, they were the ones whose moms had left them alone.

The teachers numbered us from one to four and arranged us in groups: the ones together, twos together, you get the drift. I was in group two. Our group leader was my soon-to-be math teacher, Mrs. Diouf, and at that time I didn't know she was going to become one of my major tormentors.

Our assignment, as citizens of four African countries—Egypt, Senegal, Kenya, and Zimbabwe—was to elect a president and come up with a national motto. The ISS's own slogan was 'The Future Leaders of Africa,' and one of its many selling points was that we were guaranteed to graduate and become movers and shakers on the continent. In group two, team Senegal, we each had to introduce ourselves, pitch what we would do for the country, sound intelligent and cool. It seemed an exercise bent on having us sell ourselves to root out who would be popular once school started. At the end of the group assignment, the elected leaders of Egypt, Senegal, Kenya, and Zimbabwe had to battle it out to become the president of Africa. The president of Zimbabwe was this girl with a big Afro and large glasses, wearing jeans, a purple T-shirt that said 'Lost Little Girl,' and dirty sneakers. She wasn't the prettiest girl in the class—there was this one wearing red lipstick who knew she was cute—but to me she was the coolest.

And so they hilariously scrambled to become president of Africa. The four leaders tried to convince us with one-sentence campaigns. One president offered free food for all, another said no madmen would roam the streets, the Egyptian president said Africa had to become a superpower again and we had to go back to when pharaohs ruled the world. The president of Zimbabwe, in her Afro and big glasses, coolly said, 'If I'm voted president of the United States of Africa, we'll start to invent cars ourselves.' She didn't win. The president of Egypt won, but he ended up dropping out of the ISS in the second week of school.

It was the way she talked, her voice nasal and deep, and that her mother hadn't dressed her up that made her stand out. She's why I convinced my mother the ISS was the school for me. We had to become friends, no matter what. Imagine my excitement when I found out she was in my math class. On the first day of class she hadn't brought her textbook, yet the president of Zimbabwe aka Inaam ended up answering all her questions correctly even though she obviously hadn't prepared. She could be a bit of a show-off, but was still cooler than everyone else.

Now Mrs. Diouf waddles about the classroom, placing our graded quizzes face down on our desks. You can tell who's done well, because Dioufy gives them a big old thumbs up or a snappy double tap on their sheets. Those who've done averagely, she ignores. And those who've flunked, she scowls at. My throat constricts as she approaches my desk, on which I may have scribbled K+I and it crossed out (a few times). Will it be a frown or will I be ignored? A thumbs up is highly unlikely. Impossible, even.

She places my sheet down, fixes her gaze on me, and

then there's a slight puckering of the skin between her eyes. Her brow full-on furrows, her lips scrunch into a pout, and then her whole head goes from left to right. I didn't see her do that to anyone else—shake her head. This is the fourth quiz I've failed. And yet, even knowing that my math grade could affect my scholarship, somehow I'm more preoccupied with asking Inaam to the dance. Do all human beings put matters of the heart first, or is that just me?

The class ends and Inaam jets out so fast I am unable to ask her to the dance. At this point I have nothing else to lose. I see Ngozi, my dining-hall table mate and Inaam's best friend, and ask her advice on the best way to broach the situation.

'Too late,' she says. 'She's going with Kunle.'

My eyes home in on the flame tree in the middle of the school's courtyard, which becomes a blur of orange. Betrayal tastes like the bitter saliva on my tongue right now. But who's betrayed whom? When I gather myself together and ask Ngozi if she'll go with me, she says Salif is taking her. I am going to the dance alone.

CHAPTER THREE

Burned Fish

After five months of working for the Avoka family, Atsu still hasn't figured them out. It's bizarre that they're not letting her stay at their house, like other families would with domestic staff. But mostly it's their individual strangeness she doesn't get. She's never seen Mr. Avoka angry or sad, and come to think of it, neither has she seen him very happy. The son is always hiding in his room, wearing big earphones on his head, and when he surfaces all he wants to do is cook. Imagine Mama letting her brothers cook. The strangest of all is Madam. *She's* the one who's supposed to cook, but can't. Not that Atsu minds. It's a chance to experiment with recipes she sees on TV, and even though Madam draws up strict menus, Atsu takes tiny liberties, secretly working toward the chef she's always dreamed of becoming.

For today's menu of fried fish and rice with chopped cabbage and carrot stew, her special touch will be a splash of soy sauce, like she saw on Auntie Florence's *Good Dinner*. She dashes to the living room, hoping to catch a repeat of that episode, but lands on an advertisement of Protector Condoms, a man and a woman walking through a park. So many condom ads on TV. She returns to the kitchen, where she salts and flours the fish, adding a healthy dose of black pepper. She returns to the living room to allow the fish to soak up the flavour of the pepper, but on the screen is a picture of a dead woman. The newscasters repeat the image of the dead body, a deep patch of blood soaked into her blue cloth. The camera zooms in and out of the stain, and Atsu closes her eyes. When she opens them, a reporter is interviewing the person who discovered the woman's body. An old man by a kiosk that looks just like Maa Joy with its red door splashed with Maggi and Coca-Cola posters. It *is* Maa Joy. Even though she can't read, she's seen those letters so many times she recognizes them. Still she has to make sure. She dumps the fish into a pot of bubbling oil and runs out of the house. The next-door neighbour's housegirl will read it to her.

Most times Atsu avoids Ndeye, because she's constantly disparaging Atsu's village ways. Ndeye says: your clothes look cheap, you need to straighten your hair because nobody wants to marry a girl with hair that traps fingers, and the word is pronounced 'CRAB' not 'clab,' speak English. But today Atsu will suffer the abuse.

'Ndeye, please turn on the news!'

'Madam, this better be important,' says Ndeye, ripping open a packet of spaghetti. The roots of her hair are black and the rest of her hair is red like dust. She and Atsu have the same body shape, but Ndeye likes to wear tight clothes, so they look nothing alike. They walk into the living room, Ndeye wielding a knife.

On the news Ebenezer Ojo is talking about a three-day conference organized by the Doctor on malaria eradication. Atsu is sure they'll soon repeat the news about the body. The serial killer has murdered six women so far.

'The Doctor is so handsome,' Ndeye says.

'Yes, this is it. Turn up the volume and watch this. What have they written on the store? Wait, when they interview the old man. Ah ha, there. Tell me.'

'Maa Joy Enterprises.'

'Ndeye, that's right before my stop.'

When Ndeye speaks, she points the knife at Atsu.

'I'd say you could stay here, but Mrs. Freeman won't like that. Beg your bosses to let you stay tonight.'

'I can't! What if they sack me?'

'My friend, this is an emergency. Stop being foolish and just ask them.'

'My madam said those were the rules when they hired me. What if he's still there when I get home tonight? Oh God! What should I do?' Atsu is certain the serial killer only kills one woman and waits a couple of months before striking again, but you never know when lightning will strike twice.

'Ask them. It won't hurt.'

'*Ei*! Jesus! I forgot about the fish!'

She dashes back to the Avokas's kitchen, where smoke is shooting from the saucepan in round puffs. She pushes open the mosquito-proof door. The air outside is still and dusty from the harmattan. Madam will be more than annoyed. Atsu's not only burned the fish, but she's now letting in bluebottle flies, which Madam can't stand. Not the best set of conditions in which to ask for a favour.

She stops trying to fan out the smoke, and its weight settles on her, seeps into her body, and soon she begins to feel less like a body than all heart. A heart tightening with fright. Has any decision she's made in her life so far been worth it? If she were in the village with Mama, life would be uneventful. There'd be no threats. No threats of losing her job, of dying. She coughs and shakes herself out of the state she was winding into and waves out the smoke.

By evening, the smell of burned fish has diminished, but two big bluebottles are darting from left to right in the kitchen, and all her attempts to whack them dead have failed. She shudders when she thinks of the fish sitting in the fridge, charred to almost inedible levels. She turns on the TV again, because as much as she doesn't want reminders, she can't help being attracted to the gruesomeness of the whole affair. It's like watching a horrible car accident. You can't help looking.

Ebenezer Ojo says, 'A repeat of today's headlines. One more woman killed in the ritual killings plaguing the nation's capital; opposition says they've found evidence that killings are being orchestrated by the President of the Republic, Dr. Karamoh Saturday; ministers attend workshop on moving the nation forward; the Hospitality Lions and Ebony Stars draw in friendly match. I am Ebenezer Ojo for ATV News.'

Every time bad news breaks, he's in front of the camera.

She showers, powders her armpits and face, wears a clean

dress, checks that the back door is locked, and waits for Madam to arrive before catching her bus home. On days when Madam gets in after the late-night news, Atsu feels a strong urge to say something rude, because she has to wait for thirty minutes before another lorry arrives. Today, she prays Madam won't arrive till midnight.

She lies on the carpet, the TV still on. Adult education. They're talking about ways to save money if you don't have a bank account. Women can organize themselves into groups and pool their money. The carpet is hard; she has to shift her body to get comfortable. She'd like to sit on the sofa, but Madam could walk in. Ndeye told her not to let her bosses catch her sitting on their furniture.

Three loud honks cut through the room. Madam. Mr. Avoka's signature is four beeps. She goes outside, dread filling her lungs.

'Atsu, how are you?' says Madam, locking the driver's door.

'Please, fine.' Atsu is being a snail. Mama always says that although the spider rushes and tries to be first, it's the snail that ends up winning because it takes its time and doesn't make mistakes.

'I had an accident today,' Madam says and points to the front bumper of the car, hardly a scratch on it.

'Sorry, Madam.'

They walk in, Madam tall and thin, her heels clicking on the terrazzo floor, and Atsu returns to the kitchen to wipe down the already clean stove. Click-clacks on the kitchen floor tiles. Atsu asks Madam if she's ready to eat, but Madam says no, pours herself a cup of water, and leaves the kitchen. Relief floods through Atsu as she stares at the brown stain on the stove she's never been able to remove. She couldn't handle a reprimand about the fish, not today, although she's sure it will come later. Thankful she's been spared, she lets her legs carry her to the living room to address her problem. Madam is on the sofa, massaging her neck.

'Madam,' she says, 'please, they've killed another woman.'

'Terrible, isn't it?'

'They killed her in South Odor.'

'That's where you live.'

'No, North, but it's close. I'm afraid to go home.'

'Hmmm.' Madam's eyes seem to search the ceiling for an answer. 'You can stay here tonight. Sleep in Kojo's room.'

Atsu thanks Madam profusely, but doesn't know whether to keep talking or whether to take her leave. Madam is not looking her way anymore, and that must be her cue.

Windowless, the corridor that leads into the bedrooms and bathroom is the darkest place in the house. On its north wall, above the door that leads to Mr. Avoka's study, hangs a framed picture of a respectable but strict-looking old man. Mr. Avoka's father. Sometimes Atsu feels as if he were watching her, judging her every move, and so because of him she knocks on the doors of the rooms before she enters them, even during the day when no one else is around.

She knows Kojo's room well, since she has to sweep and dust it daily, although he's away at school. She pulls out a thin Holland wax print from his bottom drawer and spreads it on his bed. She lies down and stares at the ceiling, covered with two big posters of Michael Jackson and the Eastern Nuggets. Across from her stands a shelf filled with rows and rows and rows of books, words and worlds she would like to visit one day.

CHAPTER FOUR

THE DAILY POST
Monday, September 23, 1996 | We are the news! | Since 1952

Saturday's People by Theo Avoka

Some have branded me a coward. Others have called me brave. I have to agree with the first group. These essays would never have seen the light of day if Dr. Karamoh Saturday were still alive. *Saturday's People*, as I'm calling this monthly column, is partly a memoir of my life and partly a biography of the Doctor.

I still can't decide if my time with the Doctor was pure accident or fate. Even though our encounter was one I hadn't had much of a choice in making, our paths were bound to cross. Our life stories began, interestingly enough, in neighbouring fishing villages off the Senevolta River. Saturday was my father's psychologist in the 1960s, and I inadvertently worked for the Doctor when I became a civil servant in 1975.

We officially met in 1993, at a moment when I thought I would finally be quitting my job (one I had held for eighteen years) and sailing into the unknown. I was approached by my boss, the Minister of Foreign Affairs, Mr. Osei-Mintah, who told me I would be part of a team working on Karamoh Saturday's memoir. As subsequent columns will reveal, I wasn't given much of a choice. But perhaps this project began much earlier. More than one triggering moment comes to mind: my wife getting sick, meeting Courtney Steele, or maybe even long before that, when my father was kicked out of his estimable role as Minister of the Interior and executed a year later.

Some of the stories I will tell are extremely personal, others larger than I could ever imagine. I dedicate this series to the families of political persecution. My gratitude goes to *The Daily Post* for publishing these musings of mine.

CHAPTER FIVE

The Dance

The dining hall is a grey kind of dark. Light from the fluorescent bulbs outside seeps in and casts a neon glow over the dancers. I've already been around the hall twice, and I'm bored. I was dancing with Salif and Ngozi, but began to look like a partnerless idiot, so I left them and went to drink from the Kelvinator. Obviously, the point in walking around was to find Inaam, and when I did it was unsatisfying. I almost missed her, but fortunately Kunle decided to do this absurd dance move that involved tipping his body backward and kicking his legs out froggy-style, and then I saw her in a red minidress, struggling to dance. She fisted her hands and punched the air, her body moving one way, her hands another. No rhythm whatsoever, but on Inaam it was cute. Then Kunle stood upright and I couldn't see her anymore. If they had any sort of chemistry, I'd concede defeat. But they don't.

I walk to the back of the dining hall, where Mrs. Diouf is watching us. I count four seats from her and plunk myself onto the fifth. A couple makes for one of the corners near me, but they spot Mrs. Diouf and turn around. It's kind of hilarious, the way they pirouette on their toes.

Ngozi and Salif walk toward me.

'I thought everybody liked Kris Kross,' I say, sure one of them is feeling sorry for me and dragged the other here.

'Ngozi is tired,' Salif says.

'The entertainment prefects don't have any skills,' I say.

'Why? I'm enjoying the music,' says Ngozi.

'What happened to "Mr. Wendal"? To, I don't know … all the other great songs they could be playing?'

As if they heard me, the DJs put on the Eastern Nuggets, my favourite local band, but people walk off en masse and line the sides of the hall. A long queue winds toward the Kelvinator, and now that it's less crowded I can make out individuals still on the dance floor, and they include Inaam and Kunle. Are they seriously holding hands? It's dark, so I'm not sure of what I'm seeing. But they're not allowed to hold hands, if that's what they're doing. No Open Display of Affection, alias ODA. Also, I know Kunle would never be caught dead listening to or dancing to the Eastern Nuggets, so what's he trying to prove? Sometimes I wish my molecules could just break up and dissipate through the air, that I could teleport. If God were to grant me a superpower, that's the one I'd ask for. But He never listens to me, and soon I'll have to stop asking and take matters into my own hands, become a mad scientist or something.

'I'm out,' I say to Ngozi and Salif and walk to Mrs. Diouf, who is mid-yawn.

'Yes, Mr. Avoka.' Her mouth is wide open. 'What can I do for you?'

'Can I please go back to my dorm?'

'Mmmm. How I would like to leave, myself. I haven't slept well for three days.'

I wonder why she's telling me this. I don't care, nor do I want to know what she does when she's not chaperoning us or teaching math. I look behind me and Inaam is laughing at something Kunle's said and adjusting her glasses. She hasn't looked my way once. I leave the dining hall, follow the path to the two-storeyed boys' dorms.

I stuff clothes into my suitcase, after which I'm overcome with an urge to do something to Kunle—vandalize his things, something, anything to get rid of the chest-constricting jealousy I'm feeling, but he'll probably come back and catch me mid-act. Instead, I climb into bed and listen to the radio, hoping to add to my hip-hop mix tape. I haven't done this in months (an incredibly soothing pastime of mine): cue tape, hear the MC announce the song he's about to play, hover fore- and middle fingers over 're-cord and play,' and, on hearing the song's opening lines, thump on the buttons because they're sticky and sometimes pop out in the middle of recording, get the song, press stop. Usually this method is foolproof, but on 'Award Tour,' which happens to be my all-time favourite song, Radio Ivory's jingle cuts right through Q-Tip's rap. I hope they play it tonight so I can rerecord it.

Imagine I'm on an award tour, away from this messed-up school. I'm on stage with Shaheed and Abstract in Houston, Delaware, DC, Dallas. My name is Kid Kojo; I'm a sick rapper.

Scrubbing the bathroom this morning crucified my appetite. Yes, the tyrants haven't let up on their punishment. Also, the rice water at breakfast is burned. My tongue feels like a wet wad of smoke was dumped on it. So much for our school boasting the best food in the country. An upper reads the announcements and reminds us to make sure our parents get their school-fee payments in by the second of January. Mummy and Daddy won't have to worry. My plan is to sweet-talk them over Christmas, when they're nice and tipsy, and get them to send me to a new school.

Our bedroom is empty. Kunle's not back from breakfast yet, but he will be. Now is the moment to exact my revenge. Now it feels right—this morning somebody had thrown up in the boys' bathroom, and as I was holding in my breath and trying not to retch, the plan came to me. Kunle borrowed his father's Rolex and brought it to school to show off. Before I can stop myself, call off the whole revenge plot, the heavy and exquisite timepiece is between my fingers. Now I've popped open its back. Without hesitating I spit on the wheels, springs, the battery, all the internal workings of the watch. Then I snap it shut and return it to the closet. My heart is ready to burst out of my body. Voices outside. I dash to my desk and just before I pick up my Walkman, the door opens.

'How was the jam yesterday?' I can't believe I've uttered the words, but it must be guilt speaking.

'Nice. Inaam is strange. But she let me kiss her a little.'

My heart twitches, tightens, falls. In front of Mrs. Diouf?

How can you kiss someone a little?

'Are you two going out now?'

'I don't know,' Kunle says, throwing his clothes all over his bed and the floor. 'She's a little weird, but you never know. We'll see when school starts again.' A smile lifts the right corner of his mouth, and he looks so infuriating I could slap him, but my revenge calms me. From the mess in his closet he extricates a pair of sneakers I haven't seen before and slips his feet into them, and just then there are feeble knocks on the door.

'Please, Kojo's mother is here,' the voice says.

'Kojo, your mother is here,' Kunle repeats.

'I heard him.'

I drag my suitcase and leave without saying bye. I walk along the path flanked with flowerpots and get to the car park, to Mummy's Pajero. I'm glad it's not Daddy in his tired old Mazda. I will never forget the day he came to visit and smoked up the whole place.

'Oh, you've lost weight!' Mummy shouts, stepping out of the car. She hugs me, and a red car pulls up next to us as I'm hauling the suitcase into the back. She peers into the newly arrived car and clasps her fingers over her mouth.

'Obi?!' she screams. The person is not so sure, but gets out of his car.

'Zahra? Goodness, Zahra!' He's tall and looks familiar, but I'm certain I've never met him. There are three scars on both his cheeks. A girl approaches him and asks whom he's picking up. 'Inaam Majid,' he says. The horror.

'It's been years,' Mummy says.

'You're looking well!'

'I can't believe I haven't run into you till now. Not even at the kids' orientation.'

'I was out of the country for a while. My poor daughter had to figure everything out on her own. But, goodness, you're looking great.'

I'm about to get into the car when the man's large hand firmly grabs all of my shoulder and some arm. I'm going to have to bulk up over Christmas.

'This must be your son?'

'Yes. Kojo, say hello,' says Mummy. 'This is Uncle Obi.'

'Hello.' I look off to the side and see Inaam approaching, looking innocent, like yesterday she didn't stick her tongue into Kunle's mouth. She runs into her father's arms and I wonder if he can imagine her kissing a boy.

'Greet your aunt,' her father says.

'Good morning.' She pushes up her glasses with the back of her hand. Harlot, I think, then take it back. Part of me has always wanted to use that word, but it doesn't work for Inaam.

'Hi, sweetheart,' Mummy says. 'Do you two know each other?'

'Yes,' Inaam says and beams at me.

Mummy says, 'You know what?' She reaches into the car for her purse. 'I'm throwing a Christmas lunch. Obi, why don't you two come over? That's if you don't already have plans.' No, no, no! Molecules, disintegrate now! Mummy walks to her door, extracts a pen and card from her purse. 'It's nothing fancy. But it'll be nice to catch up.'

'Of course,' Obi Majid says and rubs Inaam's hair. 'Thanks. We'll be there.'

'Wow, Obi,' Mummy says as she steers out of the parking lot. 'I heard his wife died a while ago. Can you imagine? I guess it was presumptuous of me to think it'd be just the two of them. What if he's remarried? Or seeing someone. But he doesn't give off that vibe, right?'

I grunt.

'I haven't seen him since secondary school. You blink, then suddenly you've lost touch with all these people, and they start living their own lives. It always starts when the boys start growing beards ...'

She drives out of the school and picks up speed as we wind down the hill. Such a smart idea—building a school on a hill. Nothing makes me brave enough to run away even though I feel like it all the time.

'So, Kojo!' Mummy says. 'Is there a girl? A love interest?'

'No girl.'

'Come on. Don't be like that. Share.'

My silence grows fingers and claws through the air and then solidifies.

We pass by roads filled with girls and boys Atsu's age, maybe even younger, selling handkerchiefs, wall clocks, rat poison. Most of them laze under neem trees, their wares scattered at their feet, not bothered to chase after customers. A lorry in front of us stops suddenly to offload passengers. Mummy steps on the brakes in time, and we jerk forward.

I can tell she's dying to shout, 'Buffoon!'—one of the

many insults she employs on crazy drivers, but she's holding it in. She doesn't even appear annoyed. Now seems like the time, more than any, to tell her of my plans. If she didn't scream at the other driver, she'll probably go easy on me.

'Mummy? You know how expensive the ISS is?'

'Uh huh.'

'And I know you and Daddy struggled quite a bit to get me here.'

'Okay ...'

'I'm thinking of transferring schools.'

'You can't possibly be serious, Kojo,' she says. 'After all we've been through? Don't be silly.'

I'll bring up the subject again, with the other parental unit. I'm not going back.

CHAPTER SIX

Hometown-bound

People in the market square are like flies ambushing a piece of salted tilapia. As soon as one group disperses, an even bigger one replaces it. Atsu usually frequents the market to stock Madam's pantry, but today she's shopping for herself, relishing every detail—the smoky smell of river fish; the rough texture of woven cotton; young girls sitting with pans across their laps, giggling; men hauling wagons of dust-coated yams; small boys handing out pamphlets about a new political party, a party for the people. The best sighting so far has been a market mummy lovingly scooping out ladles of fried bean cakes from bubbling oil. Bean cakes will have to be on the appetizers menu for Atsu's Upscale Kitchen.

She cuts across the market square, arriving at a string of fabric sellers. It's a rainbow of colours and makes her imagine the different looks of jealousy on peoples' faces when she gets to the village and unpacks her bags of gifts, new clothes, and shoes she's inherited from Madam.

'I have the best luxury lace, straight from America,' a pimpled man says as she's passing by his stall. Atsu takes the fabric he's held out and fingers it. Silky and delicate, it feels like it's made for a rich woman, but the eyelets are too big and her mother won't wear it.

'How much is your wax print?' she asks.

'It depends,' he says, scratching his brown hair. 'Local or from Holland?'

'Of course, Holland,' Atsu says. Who wears local things? Maybe only people in the village.

'Look at this one.' He's pointing to a green-and-yellow print. It will make a good gift for Mama. 'The first lady wore something just like this last week. Fine material.'

She bargains with the man until he sells it to her for a hundred kowries, which leaves her enough to buy toys for her brothers and fish for her mother. She'd had grand dreams of buying Edem and Avah sports jerseys, imitation Nikes, and school bags, but hadn't realized how expensive things were.

She returns to the food square, stuffs her basket with four giant pieces of dried river fish, curled so their tails sit in their mouths, and the salted beef Mr. Avoka doesn't like the smell of.

Outside the market gate, the longest line in the world winds to the North Odor lorry. Atsu curses and wishes she'd left home earlier. Nobody is boarding the van. She prays that the driver and his mate show up soon, because hers is the last stop, and behind the big yellow building of the Queensway Stores, the sun is already setting.

Finally the driver and his mate surface, looking dishevelled and oily.

The mate screams, 'Yes, North Odor! North Odor, Nodor! Nodor!'

The passengers surge toward him, and the line now resembles a big crowd of ants fighting for sugar. Ants are more organized. Atsu pushes out her elbows, uses them to shove whoever is in front of her. The seats are filling up fast. A tiny space opens up between two people and she wedges herself into it. The force of the crowd thrusts her forward, then back. She feels her head graze somebody's hairy armpit, but all she can do is hope it's not smelly—she just got her hair done. She jostles forward; her arms held out like chicken wings, until she's in front, and just as she gets in, the mate pulls the door shut, leaving people banging angrily on the body of the van.

'Maa Joy, Maa Joy, Maa Joy,' yells the mate after they've made several stops and the lorry is emptier. The van pulls off to the side and as it comes to a stop, a loud crack bursts from the engine. Unperturbed, the driver and mate let people off. Atsu's gaze falls on the Maa Joy storefront and worry starts to leak from her insides, even though it's been a week since the body was found there. She stares at the red doors, closed and stamped with a Coca-Cola poster. She wonders where the dead woman's body was found. In front? Did her blood run out and stain the terrazzo floor? Who washed away the dried-up blood?

After a while, she realizes they've been in front of Maa Joy for too long. The driver attempts to start the van and what follows is nothing but the metallic tinkling of his keys. He tries again. Everyone falls quiet, and there's a click-click of the keys.

'It's not sparking,' he says to his steering wheel.

'Hey, mate!' a man in front shouts. 'My money back. I'm alighting.'

'You didn't just board. Even if you boarded at that traffic light there,' the mate stretches his hand and snaps his fingers at a green light a hundred metres away, 'there, no monies for you. Your monies is equal to petrol. We drove you from there to here.'

'Cheater! Give us our money!'

'Boss, this is not good,' the mate says. 'Every day, something happens to the van. Every day!'

'Aren't you the one who bought the plugs? I told you second-hand is better than brand new. You don't listen.'

'They told me made in America.'

People suck their teeth and leave the lorry. Atsu stares at the basket on her lap, getting more terrified by the minute. She goes over her choices, of which there are only two: walking from Maa Joy to her house, or waiting for another lorry to come that will take her over to North Odor. Neither sounds safe. She's wasted too much time, and most of the people walking in her direction have already left. By the time the van pulls away, she'll be alone. She slides off the seat reluctantly. She had wanted to start the day early. Her cousin Gloria, on her way to work, had crashed a jar of cream to the floor and begged Atsu to clean up after her. Atsu mopped up the mess and the rest of the room, because she can never do a job halfway, but that set her back immensely. Then she washed her clothes and roller-set her hair so she'd look fresh for everyone in the village. Now she wishes she hadn't been so vain. The market should have been the first thing she'd done. Ahead of her the sky is turning purple like the lotion Gloria spreads on her skin to make it bright.

Atsu clasps her fingers tighter around the plastic handle of her basket, feeling her nails clawing her palm. Somehow the pain is comforting, a small reminder that she's still alive, that nothing bad has happened. Yet. She leaves Maa Joy behind, her feet picking up the red dust of the untarred road, and hurries by the big uncompleted building notorious for being a drug-addict hideout. Maybe that's where the woman was killed. One of the drug people is leaning against a concrete column, blowing a thick cloud of smoke into the air.

'Hello, baby,' the smoker says, which makes her double her steps. Maybe she should have greeted back. Mama says it pays to be polite. When she feels like she's covered enough ground, she turns around. He's still blowing smoke and looking at her, but hasn't moved.

She nears the border between South and North Odor, a busy two-lane highway, a dividing line. People who come from Atsu's village and nearby like to live in North Odor, and those from rival groups live in South Odor. From the corner of her eye she spots a man running her way. He's not the drug man, someone else. The man gets closer. She stares at the road, which is currently impossible to cross. Atsu presses her eyes shut, her stomach churning violently, and hopes there is an accident, something to make the man leave her alone. She hears loud honks, and cars swishing by. She opens her eyes and the man is still running, away from her, going about his business. The sky is now almost indigo, and she dashes across the road.

The village feels dirty. The chickens look as if children have been plucking their feathers, trees have lost their branches, and everyone looks faded and withered. Atsu can't help feeling like an outsider.

She rolls off Mama's bed, spreads the torn faded sheet over the mattress and tucks it in. The sheet feels like it has sprouted hair. Atsu looks at the closed window, from which light seeps in slowly through cracks in the wood. She needs to get herself to church. There's a lot she's thankful for: God kept her away from harm in the city, and He brought her here safely.

Outside, the sun is high in the sky, but hidden behind a filmy cloud of dust. Her brothers are hitting the dry cracked ground with rusted hoes, and Mama is perched behind a large pot of boiling water. Next to her, flies have settled on the smoked fish from the Bakoy Market. Imagine how disgusted Madam would be.

'Good morning, Mama,' Atsu says. Mama nods back, and Atsu knows it's going to be one of those days. No matter what she does, Mama's going to find something bad to say about her. Everything she says will be wrong. She forgot about Mama's moodiness.

'Peel the fish,' says Mama, pouring millet into boiling water. Even though Atsu's now independent, she still can't stand up to her mother, but can anyone, really? She really needs to leave, but figures she can quickly squeeze in Mama's work. She overturns a stool and as she's peeling the black skin off the fish, Mama barks, 'Smaller.'

Atsu's brothers are the same size, even though Avah is a year older than Edem. It's as if he got stuck when he was nine. They never talk to her. After she handed them their gifts, they stood there, gawking at her, then walked away without saying thank you.

'Mama, I want to go to service.' A big fish bone pricks Atsu's thumb, and a drop of blood beads out of it. She wipes it on the newspaper.

'Chop the vegetables for the *okro* soup,' says Mama.

'Am I making the soup?' Atsu asks.

'Yes.'

Six days left and it's only going to get worse. It's been this way since her father left. Although there are rare moments when Mama forgets herself and is sweet. Usually it's curt answers, insults, silence.

'Don't weed too close to the tree!' Mama shouts at the boys.

Minutes go by, and Atsu hasn't even done half the bowl. Anger bubbles in her belly when she realizes that, in addition to everything, she now has to search for wood to start another fire to make the soup. The thought of going to forage for wood, of taking a cutlass to chop off branches, maddens her. Her rage, hot and burning, shows her the boys under the tree, being useless. Their digging is going to yield no results. Her rage shows her Mama's back, hunched and oppressive. It forces her to get up, to drop the knife in the bowl of chopped okra, and to face Mama.

'I am going to church.'

She marches into their bedroom, debating whether or not to bathe, but doesn't have the luxury of sticking around to make that decision—only God knows what Mama's going to do to her. She changes into a white dress, powders her face, and heads out, prepared for what Mama has waiting for her: a branch, a thick churning spoon. She doesn't care. She's protected with the blood of Jesus.

Mama doesn't bat an eye at Atsu and keeps stirring the millet paste. Atsu feels the boys' gazes on her as she leaves the compound. In all her nineteen years, she has never spoken back to Mama. And Mama has, in turn, never let her go like this. By now Mama should be shouting to the whole village, yelling that Atsu doesn't respect. That because of her, the house will go hungry. That she's a witch, not her daughter.

Atsu vaguely remembers her father. Mama doesn't own a photograph of him, and God forbid anyone bring him up. It's a subject everyone in the village knows to steer clear of. Her father abandoned them when she was four. Not even with a suitcase, was the story her neighbours told when Mama wasn't around. The man wanted to get away from them so badly he didn't even pack up his precious belongings. Whatever those belongings were, Mama probably cooked them in a giant bonfire. What Atsu does recall is Mama's pain, as young as she was then. For months after he left, Mama stopped waking up at the cock's first crow and cried for days. Her weeping was quiet, and only when you looked closely did you see tears pooling in her eyes.

When Mama recovered, she had changed, and so had her relationship with Atsu.

At a young age Atsu had to wake up early to fetch water from the village well. Then she'd clean the bathroom and sweep the courtyard, all before Mama woke up. If these tasks didn't get completed, Atsu was lashed. This went on until Atsu was eight, when Mama met Edem and Avah's father, Mr. Tenu. He lived in the next town with his wife and children. Atsu doesn't know how that affair began, but after years of being treated like a slave, suddenly she was cut some slack. Mama started wearing her best cloth, applying powder over her breasts, and cooking sumptuous meals for this man. At first Mr. Tenu was in their village every other day. Then Mama had Avah. Barely a year later the frequency of Mr. Tenu's visits declined. By the time Mama gave birth to Edem, Mr. Tenu was only visiting twice a year. At that time Atsu was ten, and an adult in Mama's eyes. Once again, Atsu was doing all the work, including taking care of her brothers. When they started going to school, the jealousy she felt when she pulled up their navy-blue shorts in the mornings and brushed their little pearls of teeth was indescribable. Maybe if her father hadn't left she'd have gone to school.

Mr. Tenu has barely visited Mama or his sons these last couple of years, and Atsu can't remember the last time she saw Mama powder her breasts or wear her Sunday best.

When church service ends, to delay having to go home she stops by her friend Josi's, who had twins while Atsu was away. When they are caught up, Atsu has no choice but to return home. In the courtyard, balls of millet have been wrapped with clear plastic bags and placed on a large aluminium tray. The pot of okra soup is boiling. Palm oil slides over the rim of the cauldron and into the fire. The flame grows bigger and then returns to normal.

Mama's in her room, sitting behind her sewing machine, not sewing but staring at the ceiling, her lips pulled down at the corners.

'I'm sorry, Mama,' Atsu says, but gets no response from her mother.

CHAPTER SEVEN

THE DAILY POST

Monday, September 30, 1996 | We are the news! | Since 1952

Linus by Theo Avoka

We lived in fear of my father, Linus, especially after my mother died. A reserved man to begin with, he curled more into himself when he was left to raise my five siblings and me on his own.

Ours was a well-heeled but strict upbringing. We lived in a colonial-style house, two children to a room, under my father's rule. We called him 'sir' and would wake up at 5.30 a.m. every day except Sundays, when we could sleep in before church. On other days my father would have us gather in the dining room, instruct us to open the *King James Bible*, and we'd hold an hour-long Bible study. We older children would recite a passage he'd assigned us to memorize, then we'd all go around talking about lessons we'd learned from these passages, after which Linus would correct our pronunciation or call out statements he thought we hadn't drawn out enough. On Sundays, he'd make sure our house help dressed my brothers and me in smart bow ties and shorts and my sisters in frilly white frocks with lacy gloves. We sat, lined up in the third row of the Faithful Shepherd Methodist Church, the virtuous Minister Avoka and his children.

From the upbringing I had, I know if Linus Avoka were still alive he would not have approved of the kind of household I ran with my wife Zahra. He would have been appalled to learn that I let her handle the finances. Or that she earned more than I did.

It wasn't always grave, however. We could let loose in my father's small fishing village, which we went to quite often; Linus shipped us there during school vacations, and it was where he sent my mother in the last trimesters of all six of her pregnancies. He felt so connected to the land there that he wanted every single one of his children to be brought forth in the same place. My mother and her enormous belly could barely stay still as my father's Plymouth bounced on the rocky road from the city to his village. Her sixth journey was her last, as she died giving birth to my youngest brother.

We were in the village for the first anniversary of my mother's death, and I was at the age when I thought I knew everything about the world. I'd made friends with Didier, an eleven-year-old boy, the son of a fisherman. Didier had taken to getting us into all sorts of scrapes—stealing guinea-fowl eggs, setting grasscutter traps, watching young women bathing in the sea. The siblings weren't allowed to come with me, not even Alexander, who believed he was just as old as I was. Didier said he had a surprise for me, and I thought he was finally going to steal his father's canoe to row us down to the estuary, that magical place where the Senevolta River met the sea. But when he picked me up, we walked in the opposite direction of the river.

Didier strode ahead of me as we twisted around our usual paths—the chicken coops, the Methodist Church with its bright white walls, past the school building. Soon we arrived at the village outskirts, the point where wild grass grew tall and danced to a strange whistling. I pleaded with Didier for us to turn around, but he pushed through the dry grass, and I had no choice but to follow him. I sensed that if I turned around and went home, Didier would lose whatever morsel of respect he had for me. Then I would be stuck with my siblings for the rest of the vacation.

Blades of grass nicked my skin whichever way we turned. The field came up to our shoulders, and I staggered along. Finally we arrived at a tall mango tree. Didier wordlessly climbed up it, and so did I. From the top of the tree the whole village was spread out to one side—thatch huts, scattered aluminium roofing, the house we lived in, the Senevolta and thickets of mangrove along it, the river kissing the sea. Didier pointed away from the sea, to a rocky patch where a man was seated and another stood above looping circles in the air. The seated man was my father, and the man standing was Efo Komla, the resident healer and rumoured juju man.

'Juju,' Didier said, and broke a piece of bark from the branch he sat on. Efo Komla stopped the looping; he began to inhale and exhale while my father sat still. I didn't understand what I was seeing. Didier said Efo Komla was giving my father powers. The thought chilled me. I grew scared and didn't want to see anymore. In my panic, I lost my grip and fell into the grass, which cushioned my fall. Without it, my accident would have been worse—fatal, even.

Efo Komla was the one who set my bones, and as he stretched my arm to attach medicated sticks to it, he told my father that it was my friend who'd landed me in trouble, that I'd just been following the fisherman's son. He stood next to my father with his wizened body and red eyes. Then my father loomed over me and slapped me.

'If you surround yourself with the wrong people, trouble will come looking for you. Stay away from trouble,' he said.

His words haunt me every now and then, yet he was guilty of the same, staying in a government he didn't believe in, allowing himself to get framed, and then executed. Why didn't he heed his own advice? Did he want to die a hero? Was he like me, foolishly blind and hopelessly positive that he could change the status quo, but only from the inside? He was full of too many contradictions, like going to church yet keeping Efo Komla as an important part of his spirituality.

Linus was a man I looked up to, a man whose shadow I lived under for most of my adult life. And maybe that led to my making the same mistakes that he did. But, as they say: like father, like son.

CHAPTER EIGHT

Mma

Mma came down for Christmas. Atsu had gone to her hometown and I couldn't manage the household by myself, especially with the rock of a headache knocking about in my head. When she arrived, Mma said that I looked gaunt, that Atsu hadn't been cleaning the house well, that I was neglecting Theo, that she could see the unhappiness in his eyes. And I wanted to tell her that her cloth looked faded, to let her know that this wasn't her house, and that my relationship with my husband was none of her business, but the rock in my head ricochetted faster and I could only wonder if I'd made a mistake in asking her to come.

It was always strange having her over for Christmas, a holiday she didn't believe in, even though we'd been doing this for so many years. After managing to convince her that Theo wasn't condemning my soul to hell by making me a Methodist, she was slightly placated, although she let me know that my father in his grave would never forgive me, that I had broken his sweet heart. I wish I'd stopped listening to her earlier. If I had, I'm convinced my life would have been different.

Obi and I met when I was in my third year of Senevolta Secondary School and he was in his seventh, with one foot already out in the world. He was the prefect in charge of grounds, and had punished my class by assigning us to clear the football field of weeds after we'd been caught talking during quiet hours. Our instructions were to trim the field to exactly half a centimetre. Midway through the task everything blacked out, and when I came to I was in the German-run hospital next to the school, a fat bandage wrapped around my head. I'd fallen on a rock. I didn't think the nuns would let him in, but in the three days I was kept in the hospital, Obi visited twice a day to check on me. When he asked me out a few weeks later, I couldn't tell if it was guilt or genuine interest.

Our relationship lasted into my fifth year of secondary school, when a few months before he was to leave for university in England he came home to meet my family, to drop hints of marriage. It was the three scars on either side of his face—marks that I'd run my fingers over many times under the baobab tree behind school—that were the problem. Mma said no way was I marrying a man from an ethnic group that had made it its due to steal our livestock, burn our houses, and rape our women. She was, of course, referring to the Black Cattle War, which happened decades before she herself was born. In 1837 somebody from Obi's ethnic group (the three-scarred) or Mma's (the unscarred)—who the culprit was depended on who was telling the story—stole a black cow from the other, and for ten days both sides went at each other, inflicting damage on women, livestock, and property. Mma told him he wasn't welcome in our house, and for the entire three-month vacation, she kept me indoors or chaperoned me wherever I needed to go. I hadn't heard from him since then, only getting snatches about his life from former classmates. When I eventually got to England, I spent my first year searching street after street, hoping I'd find him, looking at every face I encountered, hoping one of them would be his. It was futile.

'Your city is getting uglier by the minute,' Mma said, looking out the window in my kitchen, her fingers submerged in water-soaked corn grains. She wasn't letting me cook; it had been established that my food was always insipid or the wrong texture. And Mma blamed herself for letting my father treat me more like a son than a daughter.

'Dirtier than before the transition?' I asked.

'Soldiers keep things neat.'

'You might be right.' Then I said, 'You won't believe who I saw when I picked up Kojo from school.'

'Who?'

'Obi Majid.'

Mma's face registered no recognition. She puckered her lips, and her irises rolled to the left. She shook her head.

'Who?' she asked. I couldn't believe it!

'From Senevolta. The one who went to England, the one whom you wouldn't let me see?'

'Oh! That one with the three marks.' She sucked her teeth and smiled. 'I did the right thing. Your father was so relaxed about the whole affair. If I hadn't put my foot down, the man would have ruined your life. Being Christian is better than having those horrible marks. Just look at what a beautiful child you have today, thanks to me.'

'Mma, they don't mark themselves anymore. Well, he's coming for our party.'

'Does your husband know about him?' This said in an almost conspiratorial whisper.

Luckily Kojo walked into the kitchen just in time and I didn't have to respond. Mma wiped her hands on her long skirt, walked over, and wrapped her arms around him.

'Big boy!' my mother said. 'You still haven't told me about your glamorous new school. And where's your father? Why does everybody in this house like to stay hidden?'

'I'll go check on him,' I said, because I could see judgment in her eyes. I let the eyes carry me to our room, where Theo, bare-chested, flipped a page of *The Daily Post*.

'Mma wants to know why you're always hiding in here,' I said.

'You two haven't started squabbling yet.'

He tossed the newspaper onto my side of the bed and walked over. His hand reached under my T-shirt and he danced his fingers on my belly, then settled them behind my back. He whispered, 'Now that Mma's here, we should go away, take a quick trip somewhere.'

'Hmmm,' I said, unsure of what to do with his hand on my back. It was warm but didn't feel like an extension of my skin anymore, not the way it used to. Now it was foreign, like having a stranger touching you, and I wondered when it had come to this. The last time we slept together was five months before, after my boss Somto's fiftieth birthday party. The alcohol-addled sex had been messy and embarrassing, and I had to take a shower as soon as we were done, when some of the alcohol had worn off. I couldn't say exactly when I lost interest in Theo. I still thought him good-looking; I loved him; and he was smarter than the average Kofi, but I just wasn't physically, emotionally, or intellectually turned on by him anymore.

'Let's think about it,' he said, rubbing his fingers along my hips and between my thighs. The air in the room thickened. I was annoyed at my body, that it was betraying me by responding, growing wet and warm and hungering for more than just his hand on my back.

'Theo,' I said, as he pressed closer to me. 'What are you … What is this, Theo?'

'What is what?' he said.

'I can't do this. I've had a migraine all morning.'

It felt like I was being suffocated. Then he said, 'Sex is proven to cure headaches and other ailments. But you should get it checked out. You keep getting them.'

'It will pass.'

'Zahra.'

'It's fine,' I said and walked out to lie down on the living-room sofa, unable to shake off what had happened. I'd never flat-out refused his demands for sex. Usually I played along, and luckily he hadn't been very needy these last couple of months. The rock of a headache didn't care about me or Theo or sex, it was swimming from its nest in the middle, bounding left and right. Mma came and hovered over me.

'Zahra,' she said, 'I've thought about it and I don't think you should let that man into your house. I'm not comfortable with it. On top of his being three-marked, wasn't he the one who didn't believe in God?'

Mma's memory was terrifying. She didn't remember his name, but she remembered a comment I'd made in passing about Obi's agnosticism?

'At least you go to church. You have a religion,' she went on.

What Mma didn't know was that, like with sex, the last time I went to church was not a choice I had made on my own. It was my friend's baby's baptism. Our attitude to church seemed to be the only thing in common Theo and I had left. Theo started questioning God, I started questioning God, church faded into the muddy brown areas of our lives.

'It's better than having no religion at all,' Mma said. 'Like that politician who got into trouble with the white woman. It's because he declared himself an atheist.' Mma's monologue was boring. More and more, Theo seemed like a better option that Sunday afternoon.

'Where did Kojo go?' I asked.

'Said he had to read for school. He's quieter than I remember, Zahra.' I don't know what she wanted me to say. The boy was an adolescent, a strange time for most people, as far as I recalled of my own teenage years. Mma looked comfortable in her seat, and just when I thought she'd never leave, she said, 'Time for prayer.'

I waited for the sound of water hitting the bathtub, then

dashed into our room with such speed that Theo turned to regard me. I switched on the air conditioner, pulled my T-shirt over my head, peeled off my leggings. His eyes were fixed on me as I climbed onto the bed. I pegged my thighs around his waist; he wrapped his arms around my bottom, pressing his nose into my belly. He dug his fingertips deeper into my flesh, massaging circles into my skin. A slice of pain jabbed in my left temple. He was stiffening between my legs. I knew what would come next—he'd turn me onto my back, and we'd get him satiated. I didn't want to go on, couldn't go on. I stopped moving. He stopped moving.

'What's wrong now?' he asked.

'The headache.'

His body pulled away; all that was left was the cool, electric breeze of the air conditioner.

CHAPTER NINE

THE DAILY POST

Monday, October 21, 1996 | We are the news! | Since 1952

University Years by Theo Avoka

I'm sure this will make me sound like a fossil, but university students these days don't know what it means to be in university. For us, the university wasn't just a launching pad into the real world; it was the real world. Campus politics were real and nasty, and all too often what was going on in the country spilled into our dormitories.

At the end of my third year of university, I decided to run for office, for president of the Student Representative Council. I had never held office before, but I was a confident young man: I was well read, eloquent, doing well in my literature concentration. It was a move that would please my father, who wasn't terribly smitten with my literature focus. It seemed natural for the son of a politically important man to enter into politics as well.

It was around that time that I met Zea, who would become one of my lifelong friends. He'd worked in the SRC for two years, as treasurer, and when I started frequenting the SRC office we hit it off right away. Ours was one of those easy friendships in which, without speaking, we understood where the other was coming from even though we couldn't be any more different. Zea was the first in his family to attend university. I was the son of the Minister of the Interior. We'd spend hours at Auntie Khadi's, perched behind big bowls of plantain and cassava-leaf stew, waxing on about politics, music (classical versus popular), and literature. In those days he wasn't yet 'Zea.' He was still Koffi CONDE, and always wrote his last name screaming. Zea had earned his nickname from a fourth-year agricultural-science student, because he was always going on about how corn would revolutionize the world. He insisted that corn was why wars were being fought, and corn would save the world. Zea now works as a businessman who imports rice, oil, and other provisions into the country. None of his products is corn-based. He is also the owner of a number of opposition newspapers, bought when the ban on a free press was lifted, but this also meant he spent most of the early nineties battling libel suits filed mostly by the Doctor and his cronies.

For my SRC presidential campaign Zea helped me print my posters, stopping short of distributing them with me across the various dorms around campus because he had to be seen as neutral. I took the black-and-white posters printed with my face, half-serious, half-friendly, and posted them anywhere I could find space. I remember stopping in the middle of a postering errand to marvel at how beautiful the campus was. In those days the university was green and pristine, not the red-sand-and-plastic-bag-infiltrated place the whole city has become.

I went up to students, telling them my vision for the SRC,

for the university, for them as individuals—we were there to study, I told them, so the university policies should put that first. I became a minor celebrity, and freshmen would point at me, impressed.

By the time April 1973 rolled around, there were two clear candidates: a man called Kouyate Santos and I. His father was a big-shot lawyer in the opposition. There we were: the son of a minister, and the son of a person considered a nuisance, a man calling for the secession of two ethnic groups when the country had been independent for less than twenty years. Santos was a chip off the old block. I saw him trying to canvass voters once. His was a scary approach: yelling at people and making them feel bad for not coming to SRC meetings.

I felt confident a week before the election was to be held. I'd already won the presidency, I was sure. Then scandal hit and shook everything I had been working for. My father was accused of embezzling funds meant for the building of a network of railroads, and of a conspiracy to destabilize the country. His picture was splashed all over this newspaper's pages, as well as other rags that operated in those days: *Morning Sunrise*, etc. I tried to get a message sent home, wrote the old man numerous letters, but received no response, until I returned to the village a few weeks later. Eventually, he was placed under house arrest and executed by firing squad a year later.

The day of elections came and we had to deliver fifteen-minute arguments. Looking back, that's when I lost any delusions of grandeur that my father may have planted in me. That day any big ambitions I'd harboured were killed. Kouyate

Santos went first, his speech vitriolic, peppered with personal tirades—'The son of a thief and coup-maker is not fit to lead our student body!' After he strode off the stage, the applause that followed in his wake is a memory I haven't been able to shake.

I stood behind the podium and the room grew quiet and cold. I don't recall any words coming out of my mouth, and when I was done I saw only Zea clap, and, I think, my girlfriend at the time. Kouyate became SRC president and I spent that holiday in the village, surrounded by soldiers who monitored my father's every move. My father retreated into himself, developing all sorts of ailments—he grew grey overnight, his blood pressure shot up, and he suffered loud nightmares that sent my younger siblings and other village children scurrying into my room, where I tried to calm them, telling them stories to make them fall asleep again.

My father was killed in 1974, a year before I started working as a civil servant when the Doctor overthrew President Adama Longman in a coup. My father would have called me foolish for joining the government, but I felt I owed it to him. It was my turn to make things right. In some small way. How? I wasn't exactly sure yet.

CHAPTER TEN

Cooking

Christmas snuck up on me. I didn't even have time to buy a decent T-shirt or get a haircut. Not that I'm trying to impress the girl. It's just that she's coming to *my* house, so things have to look good. I have to look perfect. Show her what she's missing out on. But of course nothing is working. Inaam has seen all of my clothes and they look worn out and faded, and on top of everything else, because I'm helping Mma cook, I'll have no time to go groom myself properly.

I've set up my radio and tuned in to Radio Ivory. Hip hop and soul hour: check. DJ Onesandtwos: check. Mummy tried to protest, but I saw her swaying to my music when she came to ask us what she could do to help. I don't know why parents pretend they don't do things like dance.

Mma hums along to every single song. It's so annoying. First of all, if she understood half the things they say in those songs, she'd be horrified. Second, her voice is gravelly and louder than the music. She even hums along when there's rapping. And she loves to talk. Non-stop. I love her, though. Thanks to her, I can hold my own in the kitchen. At first she didn't want to teach me when I asked her. She would say under her voice, tell your mother to learn it herself, or have a girl, then we can talk. But when it became clear that Mummy wasn't having any other kids or learning how to cook, Mma gave up and started to teach me. Mma wanted lots of grandchildren because she could only have one child, but Mummy said she wasn't put on the planet to be living someone else's failed dreams, even if that person was her mother. Mma showed me the way to boil rice without measuring, how to make three kinds of soup using the same base. And I owe my skill, speed, to her. I'm extra-super-fast at slicing onions, even though I hate cutting them. Right now, I'm sure I stink of onions and raw chicken. We've seriously deplumed twenty chickens.

Mummy comes back into the kitchen, a confused expression on her face. Then she comes to me, pulls my cheeks, presses them to her breasts in a hug.

'Any woman would be lucky to have you,' she says and kisses my forehead. On her breath is some kind of sour alcohol. It's not even noon. She never drinks this early. When I was in primary school, our math teacher always gave off funky alcohol breath, even at nine in the morning. Those who sat in the front seats suffered the most. Guess where my assigned seat was? Smack in row one. Maybe it's why I don't like math. I go back to slicing onions. If she's drinking this early, something must be wrong.

'Do you have your father's Eastern Nuggets' "So So Chop Chop" tape, Kojo?' she says. 'I'm making sure we have all the music we need.' I tell her it's in my room, and she doesn't send me for it. Somebody else (read: Theo Avoka) would have had me stop what I was doing just to get the tape, even if what I was doing were more important than his silly errand.

'Got it!' she says, brandishing the tape.

Too legit, too legit to quit, woowoo!

I can't help it. I start doing the MC Hammer running man. Mummy laughs and says I'm silly and leaves the kitchen. Mma thrusts a pot of stew into my hands and has me take it outside. After I've gone back and forth over a hundred times, my T-shirt sticks to my back, I reek, and the guests should have arrived over two hours ago. I escape from Mma's clutches, tiptoe into my room, and shut the door quietly. My room is a mess. Okay, I don't know why I'm so concerned with the way things are looking here. One, girls aren't allowed in my room—Mummy's rules—and two, Inaam kissed somebody, somebody who wasn't me, so it's not like there's anything I can do. I lost. The clock catches my eye. I have twenty minutes.

I'm barely done showering when I hear loud voices from the hall. Men's voices. Daddy's. And Uncle Zea's high-pitched laugh. And maybe another voice I don't know.

I decide on a purple shirt. Purple seems festive enough. I put on the shirt, jeans, and Obsession. Lots of Obsession.

Outside, a few people have arrived. Daddy and Uncle Zea are uncorking wine bottles, the neighbours are seated and already chewing the chicken Mma and I fried. I don't know why the sight of them annoys me, but it does. Maybe it's because of their uncouth daughters. Their girls are in school in Switzerland and come down for the summer holidays, but they can't be bothered to return a simple wave or hello. I don't know if they think I'm interested in one of them or what, but I don't find either of them cute. Their parents are perfectly nice to me, but they are guilty by association.

'Kojo!' Uncle Zea says. 'Merry Christmas, young man!'

'Many happy returns,' I respond.

I don't want to go into the kitchen because my clothes will smell of food, but Mma probably needs help, and it would be super-boring to be stuck here as Daddy and Uncle Zea go on and on about the Doctor and politics and how the country is decades behind Malaysia even though they won independence after we did. They don't realize their conversations are dry. Once, Uncle Zea knocked over a glass of red wine into Mummy's white dress as he was trying to make a point, as he was trying to 'land.' She wasn't amused one bit.

Another group walks into the house. Daddy's boss, Inaam, and her father. My heart actually skips. No. Wrong reaction. I don't like this person anymore. This person is awful. Mummy goes to them and I guess I too have to go say hello. Inaam hands me a present. I didn't think to get her anything. Was I supposed to?

'I cooked the food you'll be eating,' I blurt out.

'That's impressive. My dad cooks, too. He baked apple crumble,' Inaam says. 'Open it?'

I unwrap the red-and-black wrapping paper and inside is a book, dog-eared and yellowed with years of sitting on a shelf in old-lady Inaam's house: *Choose Your Own*

Adventure #2: Journey Under the Sea.

'It's not new,' she says. Who gives someone a used book as a present? 'But I think you'll like it. You haven't read these before, have you?'

I shake my head. We're even, I think, as Mummy herds us to Daddy and the other adults. A used present equals no present. All the grown-ups make these '*Ei!*' sounds and nobody can hear what anybody else is saying. I look at Inaam and it seems like we're thinking the same thing: escape.

Uncle Zea says he's met Inaam's father before, and they're both trying to figure out where that was. I honestly don't think Inaam's father remembers Uncle Zea.

'You said you were at Senevolta with Zahra? Not Malisec?' Uncle Zea says, his face squeezed as he ponders and ponders.

'Yeah, he was my senior at Senevolta,' Mummy butts in. 'Always punishing me.'

Ah, it must run in the family, being the persecuted.

Inaam's father nods and says, 'My father had us live in the Eastern Sector for three years. You didn't happen to live there?'

I signal to Inaam and tell her, with my super-power eyes, to follow me. We walk out and it's nice how all the cars have lined up on our street. It makes me feel important. The music coming from the garden is faint, but you can hear the boom-boom-boom of the bass of whatever song's playing.

We walk past the minister's shiny Benz, Daddy's beat up Mazda, and get to Inaam's father's Datsun, parked by our neighbour's gate. It's just as ugly as Daddy's. They are both so ugly, the only way they'll be saved is if they're spray-painted orange and turned into taxis. I lean against it, and Inaam presses herself to the Freemans's cassia tree. There are usually ants on the tree, but I don't tell her. Maybe I want them to climb over her. At least they're not the biting kind.

'Have you heard the latest Tevin Campbell song?'

She shakes her head and says, 'Your house is so beautiful.' Okay, not interested in music. Minus twelve points, Inaam. You're already in the negative zone thanks to Kunle. Sheesh, it's not like I hit her with something hardcore or obscure.

'It's old and belonged to an English brigadier back in the day,' I say. 'Now we live here because my father is a civil servant.' How does she not know Tevin Campbell's song?

'Mine is an engineer,' she says. 'And that's what he wants me to be.'

'Is that what *you* want?'

'I don't know,' Inaam says and flicks an ant off her arm. 'He's a chemical engineer, but it seems terribly boring. He always comes back home tired. I want to be an aerospace engineer.'

'Cool. So you'd go to space?'

'That's the whole point. Leave the earth.'

'You know something funny?' I say. I know I'm going to sound foolish, but whatever. 'My mother told me when she was young she wanted to be an air hostess so badly. She'd see them on TV when someone had flown in to visit the president, and they looked so sharp and proper with their little black hats. Now, she realizes they're just ... she says they're glorified bar girls.'

Inaam doesn't laugh. I guess I have to finish my point. She should let me land, like Uncle Zea says, and stop widening her colossal eyes at me.

'So, maybe one day going to space will be just like visiting another country. And spaceships will be like aeroplanes. Then astronauts will be glorified drivers and bar maids.'

'Funny,' she says. 'But wouldn't that be amazing? I'd rather live in space.'

'Me too,' I say.

'Earthlings are horrible,' she says. Here it comes. She's going to cry and talk about the people starving in the world, and all the wars. 'Have you heard about the rumour Kunle is spreading?'

'No. What rumour?' Of course I'm the last to hear of anything. 'What?'

'Calm down,' she says and pushes up her glasses. 'It's not a big deal, but it is. Okay, so after the dance, he tried to kiss me, like really tried.' But wait, he was successful. Kunle said he kissed her. 'I didn't let him, and he apologized for being pushy. I told him I wouldn't kiss him if he wasn't my boyfriend. He laughed in my face and said he'd never be. And that was that. At least that's what I thought. And then yesterday I was speaking to Ngozi on the phone and she asked me about my kiss with Kunle. By the way, she really likes him, so she could be lying, but I don't think she'd make up something like that, but isn't that horrifying?'

Her eyes widen and close, her hands roll about in the air with every word. I could kiss her, right now, right here for saying those words. Should I? I lean forward and press my lips to her cheek. But then meddling Mma sticks her head out the gate, and we have to go back in. Inaam looks scandalized.

'What was that?' she whispers.

'Nothing,' I say. She just told me the best news to send off my horrible year.

CHAPTER ELEVEN

Christmas Lunch

By the time Christmas rolled around, I had completely lost my appetite and was more nervous than a baby bird about to fly. I went into the kitchen and found Mma and Kojo outside, plucking the feathers off mounds of chickens. Flies wove above the carcasses, settled on them and then looped about, disappeared, and magically reappeared. I appreciated Mma being here to help, but she was teaching Kojo bad habits. What was wrong with working in the kitchen? I didn't want my guests getting food-poisoned.

I asked the cooks if they needed my help and Kojo snickered and Mma waved me away. I walked back into the kitchen, preoccupied with having invited my former lover to the Christmas party. What had possessed me? Every time I did things impulsively there were invariably consequences. But it was too late to cancel on Obi.

Mma had prepared a spread of sauces and soups: *mafe*, okra stew, cassava-leaf stew, pepper soup, all of which made my stomach lurch. The smell of food was so nauseating I had to fix myself a glass of ginger and rum: ginger would cure the nausea, and the rum would calm my shot nerves. Glass in hand, I walked outside to the Indian almond tree, where we'd arranged chairs borrowed from the neighbours; Mrs. Freeman owns a party-rental company. Their watchman and help—the one Atsu had taken an annoying liking to—had brought in and laid out the chairs in an arrangement not dissimilar to rows in a church, so I set about creating four circles of six. In my circle I would seat Obi, Theo, Anna and her husband, Zea (Zea and Mabel had quarrelled and Zea wasn't bringing her along, which was unfortunate, because only she knew how to temper him), and myself. I needed Obi and Theo in the same circle so I could manage the conversation. My bosses (if they showed up), Theo's minister and his minions, and the neighbours could have their own circle. They all belonged to a nouveau-riche world and they could share tales of the new cars or vacation homes they were planning on buying. I spread a tablecloth on the dining table and began to feel bad about the hierarchy I was creating, but that's the way things have always been done. Elders sit at the high table; children are lucky if they even get seats. Christmas wasn't the time to challenge the status quo, as much as I wanted to. I turned on the music and Salif Keita's voice floated over the empty garden.

In true African fashion, the first guests appeared two hours after the scheduled time. It was the neighbours, Mr. and Mrs. Freeman. I tried my best not to giggle as I led them to their seats. Mrs. Freeman had coated her face with foundation three times lighter than the shade of her skin, which she'd combined with thick blue eyeliner and blood-red lips. Next, in walked Theo with Zea, lugging boxes of

Don Simon wine and crates of beer. Zea hugged me and seemed happy to be free of his wife, and as much as I wanted her there to babysit him, Mabel could be a bore, always talking about their last trip to Europe and the US, how she'd gone shopping at Bloomingdale's or Saks or this or that boutique. Anna came with her family in tow, and her boys immediately started running the length and breadth of our small compound.

Osei-Mintah walked in at the same time as Obi and his daughter, each clutching a gift, and my stomach flipped. Earlier, I had told Theo that Obi and I were old schoolmates, that his daughter and Kojo were now classmates, wasn't that uncanny? I learned early in my marriage that sometimes it was better to omit certain aspects of my life. I didn't, for instance, need to tell Theo the exact number of people I'd slept with, but I learned the hard way after how scandalized he was by the truth.

After a number of guests had trickled in, Mma, gleaming in her white veil, lace top, and gold wrapper cloth, summoned Kojo and me over. It was time to bless the event.

I said to Kojo, 'You'll say grace for us, okay?'

'But—' he started. 'Mummy, can I not?'

'Just say thank you to everyone for coming and say a blessing. Be a sweetheart and do this for me. Thank you.'

We stood by the spread of food—three generations: Mma, Kojo, and myself—and looked at our guests. Obi and Theo were speaking, and my mouth went dry. Slowly, they and everyone else turned their attention to us.

'Welcome to our annual Christmas party,' Kojo said, his

chin raised to the sky, his eyes not focusing on anyone. I was going to have to work on his confidence. 'We hope you enjoy the food we've prepared for you. Shall we pray? Blessed bless, amen.' Smart cookie. Short, sweet, and inoffensive.

Mma's *dawadawa*, not unlike the smell of old damp socks, wafted from every single stew, and I knew I couldn't help her serve. It didn't matter that I'd told her countless times not to use the spice. She was disabled without it. I could usually get over the odour after a while, but my nausea was worse than it had been in the morning and everything was off-putting. I walked to my little circle.

'Obi,' I said, and couldn't help glancing at Theo. My guilt was trying to make itself known. Perhaps a part of me wanted to get caught. 'Where are you working these days?'

Theo, Anna and husband, and Zea looked at Obi, who said he was a chemical engineer with Unilever. He'd asked to be posted here after his wife died. I kept an eye on the serving table, where Mma was scooping a giant piece of fish into Osei-Mintah's bowl. I supposed the right thing to do would be to have someone make a plate and take it to the minister, but I couldn't keep up with all these mores.

I looked at the three scars on either side of Obi's face. He'd grown into a handsome man, but he was clearly aging—crow's feet, hints of grey at his crown, laugh lines. Then it only seemed natural to turn to Theo, to conduct a compare-and-contrast of my past and present. Theo, skinnier in comparison, still had a boyish air and could pass for a twenty-something if he really tried.

'Anna, come,' I said. 'I have presents for the boys.' Bad timing on my part, especially since Zea had just started talking about crooks he was dealing with, a topic dear to my heart, but like a schoolgirl (a drunk one), gossiping about Obi seemed more interesting.

I added more rum to my glass, we went into my bedroom, and I handed over her gifts.

'The boys thank you,' she said. 'And your party is a success despite all your worrying.'

'It's going well? It's not as good as the other years. Funny that I could throw a bigger party when we under a dictatorship. Isn't life supposed to get better?'

'We grew used to the regime. And we'll soon get used to this. Human beings are resilient. Besides, sometimes simpler is better. Can you believe *I* am saying that?' She laughed.

'Live music would have been nice, though,' I said. 'Anyway, listen. Remember I told you about the man I almost married when I was in Senevolta?' She nodded. 'Obi!'

'No!' she said, scrunching her nose. 'With those marks? I was wondering who he was, but it was obvious you weren't going to introduce him.'

'There's nothing wrong with his marks.'

'What's he doing here?'

'Nothing. Absolutely nothing. Anna, I don't know why I invited him. It's strange that he and Theo are sitting across from each other.'

'I love the coming together of worlds,' Anna said, picking a thread from her drainpipe jeans. Ever the slave to fashion, she made sure she was always up to date with what people were wearing in New York. 'Funny. I remember when I first met you ... you were talking about Obi. It was with such wistfulness, such beautiful nostalgia. You made me wonder what *I* was doing wrong in my relationships. I didn't miss or long for a single one of my exes. Then, before I knew it, you were with Theo. Any regrets? Want to reset the clock?'

'If only life worked like that,' I said, shrugging. 'We should probably head back.'

I stopped by the kitchen to add ginger juice to dilute my rum. Anna's questions ate at me, but I let the rum wash them away. Mma was spooning blobs of cassava-leaf stew into a clear casserole dish.

'Zahra, you haven't eaten a thing,' she said. 'It's not good for your guests to see that you're not eating. They'll think you want to poison them.' She kept looking at my glass.

'I'm going to have soup,' I said, trying hard not to roll my eyes.

Mma looked at me accusingly, her eyebrows high on her forehead, and I knew she was criticizing everything about me: the eyes which looked just like hers, only now probably reddened with alcohol, my friends with their cigarettes and foreign ways, everything about me. She knew I had been drinking but couldn't complain. The first times she'd visited, we'd pretended we didn't drink, but when Kojo turned five I told Theo I was tired of pretending, so we had wine at the table. Mma was shocked; she wouldn't sit with us. I put my foot down and insisted she'd have to get used to my being Christian. I watched her purse her lips as she realized there was nothing she could do. I'd seen her pull that face countless times, because she almost always lost. My father always took my side, although the only time she won was when it really counted: with Obi.

'Be careful with that fellow,' she said, as if she'd read my thoughts.

I ignored her and walked out with my drink, my body lithe, my limbs looser. Theo was talking to his boss who had wound his way into our circle, and Zea and Obi were biting into chunks of chicken. Mma joined the younger crew, my co-workers, some of the secretaries at Theo's ministry. It's funny that she felt more comfortable there than she did with the 'elders.'

'Obi!' Zea shouted. 'I have finally figured it out. This was years ago. I believe you were visiting the country with your wife and daughter. I was clearing goods at the harbour for my business, and you were getting some things you had brought down from England.'

'Ah, yes,' Obi said. 'Great memory!'

'Zea never forgets a thing,' I said.

'Your daughter was small like a dot!' Zea went on. 'We were working with the same clearing agent, the biggest crook in the harbour. He was such a bastard! Remember, if you had two of anything, he would take one and place it in a bag he had on the side.'

'How on earth did you dig that up?' Obi said. His voice was deep, rounded and full. A man's voice.

'It's your daughter's face. She looks just like your wife, who was not giving the guy an easy time at all. She wanted him to break down everything you were being charged for. And when he tried to pull the "You have two" trick on her, she gave him a good lambasting.'

Right then, I wished I could kick Zea in the shin. If I'd lost the person I loved the most I wouldn't want any reminders of the past. Or maybe Obi was already over his grief. The rum was beginning to warm my head. Maybe I wouldn't care. I was losing my grip on the conversation.

Theo and Osei-Mintah were very involved in their private chat, and when they reinserted themselves into the larger conversation, Theo seemed troubled. It didn't take much to ruffle his feathers, so it could be anything. Something the minister said about the house could push him to the edge, make him bite his nails. He just seemed even more coiled into himself than usual. He could try to be festive.

Anna's husband asked Theo, 'How's that Malaysia project going?'

'Slowly,' Theo said, and took a furtive glance at his boss.

'As with everything in this country,' Obi said.

'Nation building takes time,' Osei-Mintah said, a smile curling his lips. 'Minister Osei-Mintah.' He introduced himself to the group, title and all, as if to warn us of who he was and what he could do. I felt nervous, in a bitter, grey kind of way. These nerves weren't the butterflies of the morning, when I'd been expecting Obi. This was a reminder of who was running the country and how we could go back to the military era if one person willed it so.

I wanted to steer the conversation away from politics,

but had to do this with finesse, so I asked Theo to tell us the details of his project, which I thought were non-political enough. Big mistake. Our government was partnering with the Malaysian government, so every year, students from our country would be sent there for school and a year of work experience. He'd been working on it for the last five years, and the project was still in planning mode. Now that we weren't in a military dictatorship, he was convinced that things would pick up, but nothing had changed, though he didn't mention this last statement to the group.

Obi boomed, 'It's a pity that such a project shouldn't be seen to fruition. Don't you think so, your honour?' He stared at Osei-Mintah but didn't let him respond. 'Things are worse than they were in the seventies, before I left the country. I remember when I finished secondary school I had the option of getting a job or going to the university. I could actually choose. Now, kids go to university because they can't find jobs.'

'Africa,' Osei-Mintah said, leaning forward, 'is on the build-up. After all, they say Rome wasn't built in a day. Ten, twenty years from now you'll be singing a different tune.'

Zea, who had been surprisingly quiet all along, shouted, 'Well, Rome will never be built if our money keeps going into senators' pockets.'

Our circle grew quiet, and I looked behind us, at Osei-Mintah's minions. One or two were no doubt Saturday's Boys, sent to spy? Their muscled arms bulged out of the shirts Osei-Mintah had probably lent them. Luckily they hadn't heard us, or if they had, they didn't know what we were talking about. Osei-Mintah's face lit up, as if he'd been programmed to smile through it all.

'I know things are still hard,' he said, almost beaming. 'But think of Europe through the industrial age. The Americas. Don't forget being sent to the Americas was a death sentence at one point in the world's history. These places were worse than what we're living through. Europeans bled us dry and used our resources to get out of their poverty. But we'll do it by ourselves. Our country is still rich in resources. Rebuilding Africa will just take time.'

'Respectfully,' Zea shouted. Theo and I locked eyes. Zea used 'respectfully' when he was feeling the least respectful. 'Is that the bullshit they've been feeding you?'

At this point conversations all over the garden hushed down, and Miriam Makeba's voice floated over the silence that was growing. I looked at Osei-Mintah's thugs, peering our way. I wasn't sure what they would do or what they could do, but I was really frightened. The rum wasn't helping.

'Zea gets very worked up,' Theo said, patting Zea on his back, as if to apologize on his behalf. I also needed to do something to help. This was a Christmas party, not a political rally. People had to dance. It was the only way to make us forget or not make us dwell on our pain. After Saturday's coup, a curfew was installed. Theo told me the only way things could seem normal is when he and his cronies went out to nightclubs in the afternoons and stayed overnight till the curfew was lifted in the morning.

I walked to the sound system and slotted in one of Kojo's

tapes. Those in Mma's circle were the first to hit the dance floor. No one in Osei-Mintah's circle danced. The floor spun slightly. If I sat down, I would get even dizzier, so moving was good.

'Anna,' I whispered. 'Get your husband and I'll get Obi.'

'You know he doesn't dance,' she said.

'Even better, get Zea, and I'll get Obi. That way they'll both stop antagonizing Osei-Mintah.'

'I'm doing this only because I love you. Zea is so clingy.'

Obi and I loved to dance in secondary school. It wasn't allowed on the school grounds, but we stole away to the seedy bars not too far from Senevolta. There were three of them, but our favourite was a nameless hideout covered with palm fronds lit up with blue Christmas lights. There would be twenty or so bodies on the dance floor, each competing for space, as the loudspeakers boomed out The Ramblers, King Sunny Adé, S. E. Rogie, or Osibisa. I was immensely jealous of the women we saw there. Unlike mine, their bodies were full, shapely things. When Rogie belted out 'Easy Baby,' their hips would bop to the left, hover in the middle, and loll to the right. It was a sensual laziness. Easy Baby, left, middle, right. I tried to keep up, as much as my bony hips would allow me. Lucky for me, those women didn't interest Obi, and we'd spend the whole night wrapped in each other's sweat.

I got Obi onto his feet. We began with a wide berth between our bodies, but slowly they inched closer. His hand, even though it hadn't been on my body in eighteen years or so, felt surprisingly comfortable, normal. Our legs scissored, and I attempted Easy Baby, left, middle, right. It felt so freeing!

'I think we're making your husband jealous,' Obi said, his deep voice vibrating against my head.

'Well, I'm saving his job by keeping you away from his boss,' I said. I was always well behaved. But now, here I was, swinging my hips in front of Theo's boss, my family, my co-workers. My breasts brushed Obi's chest and I closed my eyes and imagined we were the only ones on the grass.

'Bathroom break,' I said. Of course I wanted to keep dancing, but I knew I was bordering on being an embarrassment. I stepped into the house, floating from room to room, trying to stop myself from going back into Obi's arms. Anna found me, not long after, and told me Theo stared at us the whole time but didn't say a word.

The rest of the party was a blur even though I had stopped drinking, and when Kojo and Mma brought in the last of the plates and cutlery from outside, I was lying on the sofa, not in the mood to talk to anyone, so I pretended to be asleep. Theo hovered over me, with Kojo standing nearby. I could feel their auras: Theo's heavy, Kojo's light and tall, still waiting to solidify. Mma's feet shuffled into the kitchen.

'Should we carry her to your room?' Kojo said.

'I'm not sure your mother would like that,' Theo said.

'I don't think she'll be happy getting bitten by mosquitoes in here either,' Kojo said. 'Let's just wake her up.'

'No.' Theo's voice was distant; I tried to figure out what was going through his mind. He probably didn't want to touch me after the way I had behaved in front of everyone. He wanted me to be bitten by malaria-bearing mosquitoes, to suffer. I opened my eyes and he was staring out the window.

'That solves things,' Kojo said. 'She's up. Do you want us to carry you to your room, Mummy?'

'You're too kind, young man. But no, thanks.' Theo still would not look at me.

'Are we still going to the market on Monday?' said Kojo. 'I desperately need blank cassettes.'

I nodded and kept looking at Theo. The room was spinning, and my head felt like it had been snapped off my body and glued back on sideways.

'We almost had a mini civil war today,' I said, trying to get Theo's attention. 'What was Zea thinking?' Theo grunted and moved closer to the window, as if answers to whatever ailed him lay on the lawn. 'What's wrong?'

'All right, folks. Good night,' Kojo said and left us. He always managed to free himself from uncomfortable situations just in time.

'After fourteen–fifteen years of marriage, you do things that completely trip me up,' Theo said. 'Did you have to drink so much?'

I could have apologized, but my spirit would have been angered that I succumbed, and if I kept quiet it would be the same thing as being contrite, which I wasn't. I wasn't sorry I got drunk, and I wasn't sorry I danced with Obi. I just wished Theo hadn't been there to see all that, because it gave him the upper hand.

'I was letting loose,' I said. 'You should try it sometime.'

Theo made for our bedroom.

'Especially around the holidays!' I shouted as his back disappeared into the corridor. I stared at my reflection in the TV screen, not really paying attention to it, but aware of it. Obi and I never closed our chapter. And now he was back.

CHAPTER TWELVE

THE DAILY POST

Monday, November 18, 1996 | We are the news! | Since 1952

Zahra by Theo Avoka

I was twenty-four. The Ministry of Foreign Affairs had sucked dry two years of my life, but I could still walk out. I could find a lucrative, prestigious job and maintain my dignity. Anyone who stayed past twenty-five truly became a civil servant—a person frightened of new furniture, technology, anything that changed.

One day in July 1977, I was looking for jobs in this very newspaper's classifieds. Sports reporter was the only position that was open, and I didn't even like sports. But, I told myself, I could develop the passion. I had seen it, red-eyed and real, in my friends who gathered on Sunday afternoons to cheer at matches in which grown men pummelled each other to blood and flesh. I could develop the obsession, the physical heartache that came with a favourite team or player losing a game. But all thoughts of leaving the ministry vanished when Zahra strutted into my office, demanding that the minister interview her. She was young and slender; strands of hair had escaped from her tight bun and stood at attention above her forehead. The minister didn't even know my name, I told her, and he sure didn't do administrative work of any sort.

'Are you interviewing me then?' she asked. Her accent was clipped, her T's stark, the epitome of posh. But something about her hair sticking out told me that under her severity, under her Britishness, hid a roguish side.

'No,' I said. 'But before you get interviewed, maybe you want to brush your hair, fix your face. The ladies' room is that way.'

She patted her hair down, twice, stared straight at me and said, 'I'm here for my National Service interview. Could you possibly tell me whom I'll be talking to?'

'His Excellency the Deputy Minister,' I said. She listened as I gave her convoluted directions to his office at the end of a long brown hallway. Her nostrils flared, her expression hovered between impatience and amusement. She turned on her heel, walked toward a set of pasty-blue double doors, and muttered under her breath, 'His Excellency.'

At this point in my life, I wasn't single. I had been seeing a girl called Mercy. Mercy and I were going on our fourth year; she said it was becoming increasingly embarrassing for her. Young women needed to be married before twenty-two. We should have already had a child, or had one on the way at least. I remember thinking of how I should set her free, but like the job, it had become a thing I wasn't doing anything about, an incessant buzzing in my ear that I'd simply grown used to. There was nothing wrong with Mercy, except for her insistence that I follow her to Christian Fellowship, and all the traits that came with her being an evangelical Christian—her trying to make me born-again even though I was already

Christian, her praying for the nation's soul, her belief that everyone else was going to hell. But she was loyal, the kind of girl who would drop everything to go shopping for curtains with you. And she cooked. Hers is still the best food I've ever had. I suppose a part of me held on to that relationship because I had seen several of my friends leave good women and end up with heaps of regret when it was too late. But then the woman who'd walked into our dowdy offices at the ministry made me realize I didn't want to be with Mercy. She wasn't enough. She would suffocate me down the line with her loyalty; she was the kind of person who would cling to me even if I went astray. So when Zahra came out of her interview and said, 'People here are impossibly stiff. Where can a young lady get a meal and a drink?' I didn't hesitate. I took her to our canteen and kept badgering her until she accepted a proper date with me.

I loved going to the Panama Hotel in those days, when it stood tall on the coast and wasn't a crumbling network of concrete and steel. Visitors to our country were always first sent to the Panama Hotel, to assure them they had indeed come to paradise. I took Mercy there on our first date and, ever a creature of habit, took Zahra there as well. She arrived wearing a bright-pink miniskirt, one that Mercy would have balked at and gone on about all evening if she'd seen Zahra. When Zahra sat down and our waiter surfaced, she ordered a vodka tonic.

'Just don't tell my mother,' she whispered and laughed. There was something naughty and playful about everything she did, which I hadn't seen in any woman around me. 'And now that you've lured me here,' she said, 'what plans do you have for me?'

'We'll eat here, go for more drinks downstairs, and then, if it's not too unposh for you, we'll go to the Orange Tavern in the Bakoy Market.'

'Don't let the accent fool you,' she said. 'I've been in places you'd be scared of going to.'

'I don't believe you,' I said. I could see Zahra's whole life in front of me: only child, running up and down the corridors of a large house, maid chasing after her to get her to eat; secondary school in a private school before she was shipped off to England. Her mother probably never worked a day in her life and was disappointed that Zahra was taking the proletarian route. 'Have you even been in the Bakoy Market before?'

'Don't insult me,' she said, still smiling. 'And you? Don't think you don't look like you just stopped drinking your mother's milk. I'm more hardened than you are.'

'Don't bet on it.'

'Where did you grow up?'

'Here. Where did you grow up?'

'In the north.'

I was taken aback. Still, her family probably owned the nicest house in a sea of mud houses, which is what I pictured the north to be before I made the trip up there to ask for Zahra's hand.

'Your face says it all,' she said, and picked up a piece of chicken with her hands, as if her confession about where she was from freed her and she could peel off the layers covering the true Zahra. I wondered if she'd soon put her feet up. 'You made a snap judgment about me and you were wrong.'

'Touché. But you probably did the same.'

'You were once privileged and suffered some big trauma,' she said, still sucking on her bone.

'Not bad,' I said and watched her mouth curl into a smile.

'I'm intuitive about these things.' The bone was pointed at me, then: 'I haven't chewed a bone like this in public in years! But with the look of horror you gave me, I suppose you people down south think you're too good for that.'

'No,' I said unconvincingly.

'I left the north and went straight to England, so I need someone who can show me how things are done down here.'

'You might be asking for more than you can handle,' I said, growing more enamoured with the woman sitting opposite me.

We spent the whole night dancing at the Orange Tavern, me flailing about and struggling to keep up with her as she outdanced the women on the floor. Her power was wild and electric, and it was in that moment that I knew I wanted to spend the rest of my life with her. Something in her spirit seemed free, and I wanted in on that.

Zahra didn't last long at the ministry. Within six months she'd landed a marketing-assistant position at a textile-manufacturing company. Over the years, she seemed to magically acquire new and better jobs every so often, while it's taken me fifteen years to shake off being a civil servant. I married Zahra a year after we met, and we held the reception at the Panama Hotel.

And then, fifteen years into our marriage, three days after a Christmas party Zahra throws annually, I found myself seated with my family at the dinner table for the first time in a long while. Our house help was still away for the Christmas holidays, and my mother-in-law, who had been running our house in her absence, had gone to visit some relatives. My son Kojo had served us dinner and we sat at the table in silence. After an incident at the Christmas party, I tried to wage a Cold War on Zahra but I was failing at that, so I resorted to passive-aggressiveness and terse replies to questions. On Zahra's plate were two tablespoons of rice specked with a drop of stew, and a morsel of meat. She forked through the meal, hardly eating, and making small talk with Kojo about what her mother had cooked for us. I asked Kojo how his classes were going and he responded with one word: fine. I wondered when we'd become this disconnected family, and I felt like bursting into tears. Instead I persevered and thought about asking him if there was anyone he was interested in—a question that would never even have crossed my father's mind, but one that I thought would bridge the gulf between us—when the room went dark. Zahra swore, and Kojo said he'd get candles and fumbled out of the dining room. And then it was just Zahra and me.

'Typical,' I said, and she snorted.

'Are you still angry with me?' she said, completely tripping me up.

'Why would I be angry?'

'Now, we're going to pretend?'

'Fine. I just want to know why you did that—humiliate me in front of everyone.'

'I didn't plan to,' Zahra said, her voice betraying no contrition. 'I had been drinking. Sorry for making you look bad.'

I didn't know how to respond. And didn't say anything till Kojo returned with a candle, a wisp of black smoke rising up from its flame. He set it in the middle of the table, and I caught Zahra glaring at me. She'd managed to shift the dynamic in the space of a five-minute conversation. And just like that I wasn't angry anymore, simply amazed at the power she held over me, and how untamed her spirit had remained all these years.

CHAPTER THIRTEEN

Lights Off

Our power was turned off for three days. On the first day we thought it would be quick, simply a minor inconvenience the higher-ups who controlled electricity, water, and our brains had waited till after the holidays to inflict on us. We were even granted a short reprieve when the electricity returned for an hour, and then off it went again. By the third day it became clear that I was the only one suffering: Theo, when he was home, seemed content to work by candlelight, Mma was happy to beach-whale herself on the living-room couch, fanning herself dramatically but still not doing a thing. (Granted, she wasn't comfortable in the city and could really do nothing.) And Kojo had batteries for his radio and didn't care. I was the only one going out of my mind. My typewriter—an electronic contraption my bosses had foisted on me—didn't work, the house was hot, and the Christmas leftovers were sprouting all kinds of fungi and mould.

I walked into Theo's study, dark even in the daytime. Two candles stood on his desk, burned to half their original lengths. Hunched over a stack of papers, he barely glanced my way. I rued the days when I was still a surprise, a person to be paid attention to, yet here we were, familiar and contemptuous. After a long wait he finally acknowledged my presence with an impatient nod.

'What are you working on?'

'Osei-Mintah's organizing a meet-and-greet with some ambassadors and has asked me to prepare his speech.'

'Do you enjoy working by candlelight?'

'What's that tone? This is a drag for all of us. Did you have to put it so unpleasantly?'

'This same Osei-Mintah you work for is most likely not sitting in darkness, so why are you suffering when you do all his work?' He was about to say something, but I didn't let him. 'And we all know this same Osei-Mintah has got Karamoh Saturday's ear, so I just don't understand why nothing good ever happens for us.'

'You make it sound like it's the easiest thing in the world. And I love how you've changed your tune. Usually, you never want to have anything to do with the Doctor, now it's, Theo, why don't you use your connections? You're not consistent.'

'Maybe you're right, but I came here to ask what you're doing about the electricity.' I conceded because the argument would be drawn out and nothing would be solved. Theo loved to stretch things out, mull them over. I liked quick decisions. His expression hovered between impatient and annoyed, one that was manifested in a slightly furrowed brow, cold eyes, and a firmness of the lips. Marriage, relationships, taught you to learn to read other people's unspoken desires. Theo just didn't want to deal with me.

'What exactly do you think will fix things?'

'Anything. Perhaps going to ElecCorp. I'm taking Kojo to the dentist and Mma to the market before she heads up north. Besides,'—cue the baby talk—''you are better suited to handle these government things than I am.'

'I don't think any of that will make a difference and I have to get this speech in shape. I'm sure it will be restored soon. The power usually doesn't stay off past three days.'

If my chest could literally swell in anger it would have. He returned to his papers and added: 'Since you're on your way out, ElecCorp will just be one extra short stop.' Then he shrugged. The most exasperating gesture in the world. *The shrug.* Helplessness and nonchalance carried in the movement of one's shoulders up, then down. A lack of desire to help.

'Jesus!' I shouted. 'I can't do everything. This would benefit everyone in the house. Yes, even you, and you just shrug?'

He pressed the softened wax pooling on the plate that supported the candles and didn't look my way. I would get him.

I dropped off Kojo at the Teaching Hospital and went with Mma to ElecCorp. Its lightning bolt of a logo was barely visible on a warped slab of wood above the entrance. This was the institution controlling the distribution of power to the whole country, and even some neighbouring ones? It was falling apart. Inside we were greeted with an infuriatingly huge framed photo of Karamoh Saturday, and below that, three booths: Pay Bill Here; Buy Meter Here;

Claims. No one was in the Claims booth, so whom did I talk to for customer assistance? I grudgingly joined the slow-moving Pay Bill Here line, while Mma made herself comfortable on a bench in the reception area. When it was my turn, I told the cashier about the three-day blackout.

'So what do you want me to do?' she said, and I almost screamed at the collective disinterest.

'To whom can I speak?'

'Madam, I went without power for almost two weeks, once. It wasn't easy.'

'Can I speak to the manager?'

'*Ei*, who are you?'

'An unhappy customer.'

'You sit there and wait.'

The line behind me was snaking out the door, and I began to feel bad about holding up everyone else, so I exhaled, didn't respond to the inane exchange I'd just been subjected to, and obediently went to sit by Mma.

'Theo should have come to handle this,' I said.

'Ah, you know men. Things don't really bother them.'

'Oh, he was bothered. I know he wasn't comfortable straining his eyes by candlelight, but he just doesn't act. Mma, I'm tired of doing everything.'

'Theo tries. You don't know the number of things I did to keep our house running smoothly. Your father was only worried about his farm.'

My father could do no wrong. That was admittedly one of my faults, holding the man in such high esteem, but it's extremely hard to let go of childhood beliefs. Yet Mma was right. I never saw him lift his plate after eating; Mma was there for that. And for a child like I was, so drawn to power, it made Mma come across as weak. Enter Theo, years later, a man very different from my father. A man I usually wouldn't have considered, but he had this persistence and potential, which I found so sexy. But now years had passed and that potential still hadn't become kinetic. His inertia in situations like this one drove me crazy. I became the one making all the decisions, and I was exhausted. I wanted to be doted on, to feel feminine, and to have someone else take charge.

We waited, and I eavesdropped on a conversation two men were holding behind us. One man was convinced that the Doctor would do everything to stay in power, rigging one election after the next.

'We've slapped on the democracy title just for show,' he said.

'Ah, but my brother, but you know Africans don't understand democracy. Let me put it this way: if you keep trying ill-fitting clothes, then you must be mad. It doesn't work for us.'

'It's African leaders who don't understand democracy. If I became president, I swear, I would serve my term and leave.'

'That's what you think. Wait till you taste the sweet seductiveness of power.'

Their conversation was refreshing. Only two years earlier they couldn't have dreamed of talking so openly, especially not in a public institution such as this one, with

Saturday's Boys on the prowl.

'Mrs. Avoka,' shouted the cashier.

I went over, and after I gave her the coordinates of our neighbourhood, she made calls and found out that a power line had been knocked over, but no one had reported it. How misguided we were. People were willing to suffer a lack of basic amenities in silence, but if our national football team had lost a game, they would be calling for blood.

I took Mma to the Bakoy Market to prepare for her trip back, and by the time we got home, the house was still swathed in thick darkness and Theo's car wasn't in the driveway.

CHAPTER FOURTEEN

Mama

Atsu can sense things before they happen, in her dreams. She dreamed of a chicken with ten yellow chicks the morning before the Avokas hired her to work for them, ten being her lucky number. Then there was the dream the day she became Christian: she was standing atop a high hill, below which water from the village river rushed by, when a voice told her to jump. She did, and awoke feeling that something in her life had changed.

This morning, however, her dream was disgusting. She woke up angry with herself, quietly got off Mama's bed, set her knees on the ground and prayed for having thought such satanic things.

Now she tries to banish the dream from her head by keeping busy. She starts with washing the pile of clothes on Mama's floor, with soap that doesn't lather, singing hymns to keep her mind off her sinful thoughts. She flings Mama's white cloth into the sky, and her mind, always connecting one dot to the next, drifts back to the dream. Standing in the Avokas's bedroom—only in the dream the room was hers—curtains blowing with the gust of a thunderstorm, but outside the sun shone as brightly as ever. Into the room walked a tall man, skin the colour of loam, a handsome man she didn't know. He walked to her, didn't speak a word, and proceeded to remove each layer of her clothing. She had been wearing a dress, a petticoat, and a bra and panties. They all came off. It was strange to her, the way dreams worked, how she was both participant and viewer. She was in the body, dancing a strange dance with the man. And yet she saw everything in detail, as if she were outside the window staring in. The worst was right after the dream, when she'd put her fingers down there: hot and wet.

Mama comes out of her room holding a bundle in her hand. It's the bed sheet. She dumps the ball of scrunched material at Atsu's feet and heads back into her room. Atsu is mortified. Was she moaning so loudly in the dream that it seeped into real life? She stares at the sheet in shock. Now Mama's going to think she's a hypocrite, only pretending to be a good Christian, and Atsu won't be able to convert her. Slowly Atsu peels apart the sheets, dumps the first cloth in the murky water, and begins to unfold the other to see what she left behind. She's halfway done when she notices a big red splotch on the sheet. She bursts out laughing in relief. Her period. It figures, she thinks as she goes to the bathroom to clean up; it's only around her period that her body betrays her with these disgusting dreams.

Edem comes out, wiping sleep from his eyes with his little hand.

'God is good, Edem!' she says, glad he's alone, not tailing Avah as usual.

He carries himself over to sit by her, and she dunks the

stained sheet in the soapy water, picks up his hands and coaxes them into the clear water in the basin by hers. Soon Edem is rinsing as she suds the sheets with the useless soap.

'Why do you always go to church?' he asks. It sounds like he's been dying to get the question off his chest, because his face, at first serious, suddenly relaxes.

'Because it's the only way to get into the Kingdom of Heaven.'

'Me and Avah and Mama won't get to heaven?'

'I pray for you every day, so God being good, if you become Christian, you'll be saved. I could save you.' Atsu smiles as she remembers how she herself was saved two years before, the day the voice told her to jump. 'Remember when a Christian revival group came here?'

Edem shakes his head. He was seven then. Atsu was going to the river to fetch water for Mama and came upon a baptism ceremony. Five or six priests in white robes pushed people into the water, and when they came back up, they didn't look like their heads had been dunked into water for an uncomfortable length of time. Instead they appeared brand new. Then they'd walk out of the river, cross themselves, and peer at the sky. They all seemed peaceful and happy, and whatever it was they'd gone through, she knew something made them different from Mama, from half the people in the village who were sick and poor. That's what the voice in her dream must have meant. She had to jump into this thing. Later, she snuck into the revival camp, and by the end of the two-week session, she was saved.

'I'm hungry,' Edem says, drops the blouse he was rinsing

and walks back into his and Avah's room.

At the drying line, Atsu scrunches clothes together to make everything fit. As she returns to the basins of water, she sees three figures approaching their compound. Their outlines become more solid, and she realizes it's Mr. Avoka, Kojo, and Avah, whom she'd assumed was still sleeping.

Avah goes into Mama's room. Mr. Avoka shakes Atsu's hand and then releases his grip too quickly. Maybe her hand is still wet, or too wrinkled from the washing. She tries to hug Kojo, but he seems to be taking in the state of her mother's hut, the dry caked ground they live on, the leafless trees, the poverty.

She isn't sure why they're here but lists the possibilities: she's being sacked, they are about to accuse her of stealing something—Madam's jewellery, or the coins she leaves lying on her dresser, which Atsu has never touched.

Avah and Edem come out with stools and set them under the tree in the courtyard. Mama shuffles out of her room and Mr. Avoka springs up and shakes her hand. Mama nods and sits on a mat on the ground.

'Atsu, you haven't offered our guests anything?' she says, staring at the sand between Atsu's feet.

'Oh, thank you, Madam,' Mr. Avoka says. Atsu can tell he wants to say no, but he can't. They don't have ice water. Their water has been sitting in the big pot for the last four days, and Atsu likes to think it's the best-tasting water there is, but now, with Mr. Avoka present, it seems backward. They should have a fridge, they should use proper glasses, not the fat plastic mugs she's pouring the water into.

Mr. Avoka, looking uncomfortable, presses the cup to his lips, but she doesn't think he actually drinks the water. Kojo's cup sits on the sand before him. She isn't certain if her heart is aching because they're putting down her life here, or if it's because she wishes she could offer them better. Probably both. Her brothers hover behind Mama, sizing up Kojo and his clothes, the watch on his wrist, the school bag on his knees, how his skin is unblemished. They have the same skin tone, her brothers and Kojo, but his looks creamier, softer. She did the same when Madam came to the village to pick her up: stare and stare.

'Ms. Akakpo,' says Mr. Avoka. 'I have come to make a big request. You're welcome to refuse it, in which case I completely understand.'

Atsu looks at Kojo. He rolls his eyes and somehow that sets her at ease.

'I was wondering if Atsu could come back with us today.'

She hasn't committed some unforgivable crime? She's incredulous, but keeps her excitement hidden in her belly, under her cover cloth, and lets it rumble there. Then she wonders why Mr. Avoka is here, not Madam. Madam is the one who deals with her. Insecurities form in her mind: does Madam not want her back?

Then Mama talks: 'We also need her here. This year has been difficult for us, no rain since August, and I'm not as strong as I used to be.'

'I understand,' Mr. Avoka starts, but Mama is not done.

'My boys are in school and can't spend the whole day on the farm. In fact, I'm happy you've come, because I was planning to tell Atsu to let you know she wouldn't be coming back.'

'Madam, if you will let me speak …'

Kojo is cleaning a line of red dust on his left sneaker. Her brothers are as stiff as straws.

'Madam, I realize that I'm burdening you. While I can't promise to increase your daughter's salary, I have an offer to make her. We will provide her with a room in our house.'

Atsu wants to clap and beat her chest and stomp her feet. Jesus *is* good!

'And that should cut her rent and transportation costs. That way she can perhaps send you more money to help? I don't know if this will help you make your decision?'

Insulted, Mama spits.

'Yes,' says Atsu, not looking at anyone. 'I'll pack my bags.'

Walking to Mama's room, she feels bad about Mama growing old and needing extra help, but she's more annoyed than sad. Mama was trying to trap her here? She stuffs her clothes into her Ghana-Must-Go raffia bag, and remembers that in the bag is an envelope of money. She takes out half of what's in there and places it on Mama's dressing table, by the tin of dusting powder. She loves Mama, Avah, and Edem—if any of them were to die, she would tear her clothes and mourn for years. And yet when they're around, she doesn't feel like they're related by blood. She takes out the rest of the money, adds it to the pile on the dresser. She wants to write Mama a letter explaining why she needs to make something of herself, but she can't write and Mama can't read.

Outside, after hugging the boys and giving each a kowry, she nods at Mr. Avoka, who digs in his pocket and pulls out his wallet. He tries to shake Mama's hand (obviously with kowries balled in his fist), but she frowns and refuses his money.

Atsu sits in the back of the car, dozing for the first half of the trip, the Eastern Nuggets lulling her into sleep filled with Mama and the boys and the man from the dream. Each time he appears, she sits up straight, discreetly crossing her chest. As she makes uncomfortable eye contact with Mr. Avoka in the rear-view mirror, she realizes he is, in this very moment, at her mercy. He owes her one, for having made her disobey her mother. He'll do anything she asks him. She's going to learn how to read and write.

CHAPTER FIFTEEN

The Tutor

Mrs. Diouf is going on and on about F's and X's, and I'm completely lost, but I'm not minding being back at school. So far I haven't said anything stupid to anyone, the upper boys haven't rolled me in a barrel, and it just feels good to be out of the house. Something is going on between Mummy and Daddy, and it doesn't smell pretty. And what was with that busybody Atsu, following me everywhere I went? Why did she have to come and live with us? Mma had to rush back to the north and all, but we could have managed just fine. Atsu's so pushy, with her big breasts: *Kojo, why did you leave your shorts on the bathroom floor? Kojo, Madam said you should wash your own plate. Kojo, blah-di-blah blah.* And she doesn't even let me cook. Style-cramper.

Mrs. Diouf is not shutting up. I badly want to understand her, but she's speaking a foreign language and it's frustrating. Since Christmas I've had a change of heart and strategy: before, I just wanted out. Now I need this. If I pass all my subjects I can get a scholarship to go abroad to continue secondary school. America is best; England, maybe; here, no way. Fine, I also have another reason to stay at the ISS, for at least another year.

Inaam's hand goes up, and my heart beats fast. I haven't seen her since the Christmas party. She asks a question that I can't repeat, not even if you offered me ten thousand kowries, because it's in the same weird language. And as Inaam's voice goes higher and higher, I realize what I need to do. It's the perfect plan and Mrs. Diouf is going to help me get it done. I must be smiling, because Mrs. Diouf is now looking at me and smiling back, her mouth is opening and she's asking me a question in slow motion. Obviously I have no idea what the answer is, so I stare blankly at her like the biggest fool in the class, then she leaves me alone. She assigns us a bus-load of homework and says it should be on her desk tomorrow morning. She's pure evil, that Mrs. Diouf. The bell rings loudly, adding to my distress.

Inaam is forcing her textbooks into her bag. I beg her to come with me.

'Mrs. Diouf,' I say, 'I didn't understand today's topic, and you've given us homework and I don't think I can—'

'Come and see me,' she starts.

'I was thinking Inaam could be my tutor,' I say, explaining how Inaam can break down the f of x stuff easily, how we'll do our homework together, and how I can also help Inaam with whatever subject she's struggling with. At which point Inaam looks at me like I'm crazy—she thinks there's nothing I could teach her, but how wrong she is. This is someone who doesn't even know Tevin Campbell.

'Hmmm,' Mrs. Diouf says, but writes us a permission slip. 'You can meet between sports and dinner. In the girls' common room. Wednesdays and Thursdays only.'

I almost hug Mrs. Diouf as she waddles out the door. Inaam looks bemused.

'You could have asked me first, Kojo,' she says. I thought she'd be warmer, after the moment we shared outside the Freemans's gate at Christmas. I guess I thought wrong. 'I'm so busy. And—' She pushes up her glasses with her fore- and middle fingers. 'Sorry. I'm just really stressed. Are you all right?' Her eyes grow bigger behind her glasses.

'Yeah,' I say. 'You?'

'Fine, thank you. How's your mother?' she says.

Why do we have to bring up the party? No one missed the way Mummy was all over Inaam's father. The way she was embarrassingly drunk.

'Fine.' And even though I don't want this conversation to drag out any longer, I say, 'Your father?'

'Travelling, as always. Listen, I can't meet you on Thursdays. I have flute.'

'You don't even like music.'

She winces, hoists her bag on her back.

'I like classical music,' she says. 'And electronic music. I just don't know what's new in rap.' Her gaze darts to the floor. Strange girl.

'Anyway, can we meet today to go over differences?'

'Differentials.'

'Yes.'

'I want to help you, Kojo. Just next time, please don't ... I don't like things being sprung on me. And everyone seems to like springing things on me.'

She looks so cute when she's annoyed. I pick up my bag

and prepare for French class. *Professeur* Drone. Next to him, Mrs. Diouf is a hoot.

I wanted to leave sports early, take a shower, and then go meet Inaam. But as I was trying to sneak away, Kunle saw me and shouted my name, which made Mr. Ba punish me. I ran two laps around the field and did twenty press-ups, and by the time I was through with all of that, I was already ten minutes late. So here I am, sweaty and disgusting, approaching the girls' common room, this strange place with pink curtains and frills and a new TV. Our TV is black-and-white, and sometimes we have to bang the side of the tube to get rid of staticky images. Girls get everything. And we get their seconds.

Inaam is already seated behind the large table, reading. When she sees me she presses together the pages of the book and stashes it in her bag.

I'm so nervous that my palms sweat as I pull out my notebook. I drag my chair closer to her, but leave enough space for a thirty-centimetre ruler to fit between us. I think that's appropriate, given her frost this morning. Still, it's enough for me to get a whiff of her smell: coconut cake.

'Do you want to go over differentials or start with something else?' she asks.

'The stuff Mrs. Diouf taught us today.'

In addition to being late, I left my textbook in my room. Inaam, looking cross, is about to tell me off when two girls walk into the common room. They ignore us and plunk themselves in front of the television.

'Hurry, hurry,' says one of them. 'I hate when we miss the beginning. *Alejandro y Ernestina.*' She rolls both *r*s and waves a hand in the air as if she really speaks Spanish. The other girl presses the remote and the TV set zings to life with an Omo commercial: *Omo washes brightest and it shows.*

'Kojo, I just want you to know, before we continue, that I'm doing this for you, only because ...'

'Why?'

'Because ... it doesn't matter.'

The whiniest song I've ever heard comes on, and the girls croon along. Three more girls burst in and rush to the sofas. '*Alejandrrro y ErrrnestinAAA!*' A big chorus of noise. It's hard to concentrate.

'I know you're doing this because I put you in a tight spot. Sorry.'

She's quiet, then adds, 'I'm not doing it just because of that, but can you please focus?'

'Okay,' I say. 'Let's do this. Just, please go slowly.'

Inaam is behaving as if she has a household of grand-children to go back to and feed. I lean in closer to my note-book and watch her fingers work. They dance over the page quickly. Coldly. Maybe she doesn't like me at all. A possibility I hadn't, till now, considered.

'Now you solve this,' she says, pursing her lips.

It's a jumble of dy, dx, and numbers: d jumps to its homie y and sometimes down to its dog x. And all this is equal to a simple answer, which is not simple at all. How will I ever make it? I look at her example. The ds have disappeared and now there's an S-looking thing that's not d or x or y, but it's chilling with the simple equation. Confusing?

'Oh! Alejandro is such a fool. Always going for stupid, beautiful women, when the love of his life is right there!' a voice says.

After I swim in mild confusion things begin to connect, and Inaam and I finish our homework. We leave the common room, and before she heads to the girls' dorms, I wrap my arms around her and squeeze. She looks at me, confused. Then, for what feels like the first time today, she smiles, then pushes me away. Very playfully, she tells me I stink of mouldy bread. Her fingers shoot up to her glasses, and she gets serious again. I think she likes me.

'Next Wednesday. Same time?' she says.

'Thank you.'

As she walks away, I think, Atsu's body is better. And then I freeze, in disbelief that I thought of Atsu. I look around and pray no one can read my thoughts.

CHAPTER SIXTEEN

Pie Dish

I wasn't usually the kind of woman who needed excuses to do anything. I didn't have patience for indecision: Theo couldn't decide what shirt to wear, I picked out one for him; Atsu was given a monthly food menu she had to stick to; Kojo was wishy-washy about his school and what to study, I picked his school and subjects for him. He could have one creative subject (literature), but he was doing math and science. Yet, since the Christmas party, I found myself hesitating, constantly weighing pros and cons. Whether to tell a doctor about my lingering headache; what we should eat for dinner (I still hadn't come up with a menu for January); what to do with the farm cooperative that was taking me for a ride. The major debate brewing in my mind, however, was Obi. Whether to see him or not. Of course I wanted to see him, but I told myself to be an adult and let it slide. That way I wouldn't hurt Theo, because it seemed inevitable, given my strong connection with Obi, that something would happen. On the other hand, reeled my mind, I could exercise control even if I saw him. Yes, we were human, but we were both rational, and he and I would know better than to muddy things. I would just return his pie dish, which I'd stashed in my car after the Christmas party, and instead worry about myself and my failing marriage.

When the holidays ended I drove to the trouble-causing farm cooperative. Before Christmas, I'd tried several times to reach Mrs. Ouedraogo, its caretaker, but she was always conveniently absent. I liked Mrs. Ouedraogo. Not only did she make me happy, she made my bosses happy. Also, she was full of entertaining stories about her grandson. One time the two-year-old woke her up and told her that one day he'd buy a car so the lady (me) wouldn't have to keep driving over to steal and sell *her* palm oil. Children are the most honest people until they learn how to lie.

When I arrived, I could tell my presence wasn't welcome. Mrs. Ouedraogo didn't show up until three different girls went in search of her, and when she finally surfaced, her face registered shock, then feigned politeness. She led me to the palm-nut tree where we held meetings, and as she arranged four stools by the tree, she talked about finding her grandson, hoe in hand, hacking away at its trunk to get palm wine. I chuckled, although unable to fully commit to laughing at her story. And when two other women in the collective arrived, I wished I could split into two. One part, the active thinking brain, would climb up the thorns of the palm-nut tree and settle at its crown, peering down, while the automated part did all the legwork. I was tired, and I could already tell this wasn't going to be a smooth meeting.

I went around and shook each hand, all calloused, all stained orange.

'Long time no see,' I said, and asked about their various

families, their health, and fielded questions about my family and health. All fine, I lied. Then I asked why I hadn't heard from them.

'The fruits are growing smaller and smaller,' Mrs. Ouedraogo said. 'We haven't been able to harvest a single bunch yet. The rains aren't good.'

'In September that's what you told me,' I said. 'What's really going on?'

'In fact, since July last year we haven't seen any good harvests,' Mrs. Toure said. 'The rains aren't good.'

Each woman played a role. Mrs. Ouedraogo was Mother Hubbard; Mrs. Toure was Mrs. Ouedraogo's parrot, if only she were as smart as a parrot.

'It's the manure you brought us,' said Binta, Mrs. Ouedraogo's niece, chewing hard on a stick and staring straight into my eyes. She fit nicely into the role of the bitchy one.

'Mrs. Ouedraogo, you will tell me the truth. We've worked together all these years. You'll tell me if you're selling to somebody else? Somebody has come and offered you more.' I had to control the pitch of my voice. I never screamed at my clients, and I think it's how I managed to retain them. But now I wanted to stand and tower over them.

'*Walai*!' she said. 'You're my first and only customer.'

'It's the manure!' Binta said and dug the chewing stick behind the top row of her teeth.

'Stop using it then. For goodness' sake!' I said, instantly sorry that I'd raised my voice. I had to remain as calm as possible before these illiterate cheats. 'Will you let me know what happens next month? When you stop using the manure?' Binta's claim was hogwash. USAID had sent the country sacks of plant food in February, and we'd applied to the Ministry for Food and Agriculture for a share. We received a two years' supply for both farms. The other farm had seen bigger harvests since they started using the manure. I stared at Binta. Her red-and-yellow cloth looked shiny-new, and above that she wore an indigo moiré top. Separately, her clothes worked well, but together, Binta was an eyesore. What I would do to give them all makeovers. Binta would be stunning—not that she wasn't already beautiful, but I was a firm believer in dressing sharply, and Binta could learn a stylish thing or two from me. Her mahogany skin glistened in the sunlight; her hair, coiled into thick cornrows, radiated indifference. That day she looked particularly well fed. Someone was paying them more.

'Mrs. Ouedraogo,' I said, and exhaled. 'I don't like bringing this up, but you haven't forgotten that we signed a contract, have you? If you're selling to somebody else, this is over. I'll have to terminate the contract, and I don't think that will be good for any of us.'

'No, no, no,' Mrs. Ouedraogo said. 'I'm insulted that you'll even say that. Don't say that. Everything's fine.'

'No problems,' Mrs. Toure said.

Binta sucked long and hard on her teeth. 'Let her go! Just comes to drain and leave us poorer.'

Mrs. Toure bent forward, unfolded her cover cloth, exposing flat breasts, striped with marks that told of children pulling on them, sucking her dry, a husband biting her. Kojo was a biter. I threatened to stop breastfeeding him, but Theo begged me. He said the reason why African babies were stunted is that their mothers didn't feed them enough breast milk. Theo could make me do things then. Mrs. Toure retied the cloth around her chest. In a way, I couldn't disagree with Binta. I was the evil middleman, and sometimes it bothered me, and other times, like in that moment, I didn't care.

'Can't we just sell to both of them?' Mrs. Toure asked under her breath.

The other two glared at her and avoided my eyes. Anger simmered in my belly. Mrs. Ouedraogo and her pet were probably only a decade younger than Mma, so I couldn't utter the words that were lined up in my mouth: useless, profiteering, good-for-nothing, flat-breasted bitches. Behind them, people came and went with bowls of palm wine, pans pyramided with coconuts, women peddling second-hand clothes.

'Well, you know what this means,' I said, standing up. 'We'll be in touch with termination proceedings.' They said nothing. As I drove from the village, I was sure to leave a fat plume of dust in my wake. As much as I hated to admit it, the Doctor and his military government kept people like these in check. Mrs. Ouedraogo and her friends were probably so petrified of Saturday and his boys that they stayed on the straight and narrow. Now that we were no longer under a totalitarian regime, they were free to do whatever they wanted with impunity.

I was still annoyed when I arrived back in the city. If I went to the office, I would probably continue to seethe. I should go home. Or, it occurred to me, this was the time to return Obi's dish. He'd always had a way of making me feel better, of making every worry seem trivial. I called him from a phone booth to announce my arrival.

Obi answered the gate himself, and I was disappointed. I was hoping he'd have made more of himself than I had. Here we were, two been-abroads, who opened our own gates. At least I had Atsu. When he hugged me, the familiar flooded back: Senevolta, the baobab tree, millet porridge, buckets of brown water, the nuns next door, dance floors, palm-fronded fences, pain, disgrace, long separations, Mma, England, searching every face looking for him, and then moving on. And yet he was different from the person I associated with those memories. Now he seemed a man with something to lose, not the one who could get up, go anywhere, and leave me behind.

He'd made a pot of chicken soup. What if I had waited to find him? A man who cooked, who was raising his daughter by himself.

'Obi,' I said, after I'd drunk more soup than I'd expected to. It was the first meal I'd had in a long time that hadn't made me queasy. He sat across from me, his fingers crisscrossed into a ball, his brows raised, waiting for me to go on. 'About last time ...'

'I'd forgotten how feisty you were with alcohol.'

'You haven't seen me drink. I didn't drink at Senevolta.'

'But I have. But you did. Don't tell me you've forgotten that night at Nameless.'

'We went there several times.'

'When you wanted to try palm wine and you had two calabashfuls. Before we could stop you, you were dancing with this huge woman.'

'I don't remember getting drunk,' I said. Obi leaned back, cradling his head in his hands. 'My tolerance has gone up since.' I was annoyed he remembered me losing control.

Obi dredged up the past: one time a fight broke out and somebody threw a punch so close to me, I swore it was the last time I was going to Nameless. Yet the next week, we went right back. My heart warmed with the memories, and I wondered where love went when two people couldn't be together through no particular fault of their own. I couldn't tell, with Obi, if our love had disappeared or if we'd both interred it under new spouses, children, our occupations. Our relationship then—so real and raw—was unbridled energy between two bodies, and energy doesn't just disappear.

'Can I get you something to drink?' he asked.

'Look where that got me last time,' I said.

'Well, I have orange juice, ginger, *bissap*, wine.'

'*Bissap*. Did you make it yourself?'

He shouted no as he left the living room. Glass clinked on metal, metal on metal, his feet shuffled about the kitchen. A vein pulsed somewhere on my temple. I stood up and looked at his room divider. Trinkets, shot glasses, a snow globe of Big Ben and a red double-decker, a picture of Inaam, toothless, and then his wife, the spitting image of

Inaam. I heard that the woman killed herself, but I couldn't ask him. We didn't kill ourselves, people like us. What could push a person so far? An imbalance? Or did she have something to hide?

Obi returned with the hibiscus juice. We sat on the sofa, and our conversation stayed on old, safe topics. I asked him if he got lonely. Okay, not exactly safe.

'Who doesn't, Zaza?' he said. Nobody had called me that in years. He stared at the ceiling and then said, 'I think people *are* meant to be lonely. No one can explain to me why we have to face loss. What is the point in having something, losing it, then experiencing a bottomless emptiness that nothing can fill?'

His dead wife was more present in the room than before, and I felt cheap for having thought of seducing him—yes, the thought had been there all along, also another presence that sat between us, uncomfortably close, daring us to deny our attraction.

He was still talking. 'I didn't have any toys, and yet I was happy. I knew what to do with myself. When I got to England and started buying things, I couldn't be happy unless my life was filled with stuff. I'm prattling, Zaza. I just think if we all stayed alone, we wouldn't have to deal with loss.'

'You can't isolate yourself,' I said, a part of me disappointed that the visit hadn't been the lust-filled reunion I was hoping for, yet grateful that I learned that Obi hadn't dealt with his problems. He could be an interesting project—everyone needed to be healed once in a while. And I thought I could help.

CHAPTER SEVENTEEN

English Lessons

Evening classes, Madam's decided. There's no working around that. Not that Atsu's tried to put up a fight. She can't. Maybe with Mr. Avoka, whom Atsu could blackmail using the image of her poor mother in the village. But certainly not with Madam. Everything she says is the final word.

So, with eager and frightened steps, Atsu walks to the junction to catch a car for her first day of English. She squeezes into a battered blue taxi and gets off at the Queensway building at the Bakoy Market. Vendors still mill around, some leaving, some setting up stalls with kerosene lamps, some unloading canoes of beef ribs onto grills. In the air waft smells of fried fish and paraffin oil. People are going and coming non-stop. The commotion comforts her. No chance for the serial killer to strike with so many people around.

Her classroom is at the end of a long school building, its door marked with the number six. Posters of the Doctor flank the classroom door. On one, his head is crowned with a pair of horns, on another it's a halo. She wonders if children did that.

Inside the classroom sit about twenty students, mostly

men, but the front-row seats are all occupied by women, one of them looking as old as Mama. At her age, Mama is not teachable, nor would she put herself in such a situation, so Atsu admires this woman for wanting to improve herself. As she makes her way toward a seat she realizes what a blank page the room is; she can reinvent herself, be mysterious, pretend she's already a restaurant owner, not a housegirl. She decides that just because the women have flocked together in one place doesn't mean she has to join them. Instead, she picks a seat by a man in an orange uniform.

So many different people, trying to be better. There's a man in a long robe and a small Turkish cap, another in a black suit, a woman with long dreadlocks who scares Atsu with her hardness, like she can beat up all the men in the room and more.

A tall thin man stoops into the room, his skin dry, his lips chapped. Atsu removes her exercise book and pencil, and just the act of touching a book that's hers, a book that will soon contain her writing, makes her heart skip a beat and she lets out a gasp. Thankfully no one notices, and she concentrates on the new entrant who's setting his briefcase on the table in front. He makes for the blackboard and writes four letters. She recognizes an S, because it's in her name.

'How many people can read this?' he asks.

A few hands go up, then more. More than half of the class. Three-quarters of the class. Atsu's happiness quickly retreats into her stomach. Of course people know more than she does, like the ones in suits who are probably here just to brush up on their spelling and reading. She doesn't know a thing, but not wanting to look foolish, she lifts her hand too. Within the sea of raised hands, only two or three people have theirs down. The brave ones. They put her to shame, these ones who aren't afraid to show their ignorance.

'What does it say?' the teacher says.

'Mr. Sy,' says the dreadlocked woman loudly.

'Good. Most of you seem to know your alphabet, so I'm going to skim over letters, and then we can start reading.'

Cross with the teacher for saying they'll rush through the alphabet, but more so with herself for not being honest, she watches Mr. Sy scrawl on the board, annoyance pressing against her chest. Is he not going to take care of the brave two or three who couldn't read at all? He writes out twenty-six letters, and she takes solace in being wicked with numbers, her mother having taught her to count, add, multiply, how to manage money. Once she gets this English business sorted out, she'll be unstoppable.

The class sounds out the letters, and Mr. Sy writes the words 'cat,' 'dog,' and 'snake' on the board. It's so exciting that after an hour she can recognize more letters than those in her name, and roll them on her tongue. Each new word is a delight, and saying them out loud is like when she swallows a piece of perfectly done condensed milk toffee: smooth and velvety.

Mr. Sy hands them dog-eared books that look as if he and his wife stapled them together one afternoon on their living-room floor, cups of tea or coffee close by. The book contains pictures and corresponding words. Their homework is to learn the spellings of all the words. After the class, adrenaline-high, Atsu's not ready to go home. What awaits her is a bed in Mr. Avoka's quiet study. When Madam and Mr. Avoka are home from work, she can't watch TV, and even though she occasionally drops by Ndeye's to gossip and watch *Alejandro y Ernestina*, she feels bad leaving the house at night, because Mr. Avoka likes to lock up early. By ten, the house is a prison no one can leave or enter. It gets boring, staying by herself in the study, so even though she's sorry for inconveniencing her employers, and still frightened about a lurking serial killer, she decides to linger, to take her time.

She follows a man in a suit and his friend, both from her class, keeping enough distance between them while taking in the night's offerings. It's naive to trust them just because they attend the same class, she knows, but having that connection, however tenuous, is comforting. She catches whiffs of burning kerosene, plantain and ginger sizzling in oil, cigarette smoke, palm wine, urine, meat browning on a grill, incense. Since she moved to the city, she's become scared of the night, but she's more alive at night than during the day. The two fellows from her class stop in a line of people buying plantain and she decides she'll have some too.

'Boy!' says the one in the suit. He's beautiful. 'It *has* to come here. Then we'll show the whole of Africa how it is done.'

'Ho!' the other says, chomping on gum. 'We've become useless at football.' He's one of those people you don't look at twice because there's nothing different or interesting about him: he could be from her village, he could be the shoemaker who comes to the Avokas's house every two weeks, he could be a butcher or a fisherman. When she looks at the suited one, on the other hand, he could be a bodyguard, like the ones that surround Doctor Saturday. People say the Doctor screens his bodyguards, and if they aren't attractive he doesn't hire them, because every time he gives a speech, the camera captures them too. She can't disagree with the Doctor.

The weight of somebody's gaze on her grows strong, and she realizes the bodyguard's less interesting friend has caught her staring at them.

'Did you enjoy the class?' the friend says, his voice warming and scaring her simultaneously. His voice is rich and soothing. She nods and stares at her feet, wishing it was the other one who had talked to her.

'I'm Nasar,' he says, and reaches out his hand to shake hers. 'This is Harry.' Harry the Beautiful also shakes her hand, but doesn't engage her in conversation. A lorry zooms by blasting a song by Gita Divine, one Atsu has never heard.

'Ah, Auntie Mounas's line is too long,' says the beautiful man. 'Can't keep the wife and baby waiting any longer. Boy, see you later?'

They snap fingers, he salutes Atsu, and she watches him march away, legs spread apart, fists balled and barely touching his body. Of course, all the beautiful ones get taken fast.

'You didn't tell me your name,' Nasar says. Nasar, of the uninteresting face and crooked teeth. Yet when he smiles she notices his dimples and his almond-shaped eyes that press together—almost as if he needs a second to appreciate all he's seen—and she thinks she judged him too quickly. He seems like a nice person, and that makes him beautiful.

He tells Atsu he can read but dropped out of school years ago, so he needs to get a certificate from Mr. Sy's class to land a job at a printing press. He and Harry work security in the meantime. She was right! He doesn't seem to mind that she's not that talkative, and when it's their turn to be served, he pays for her plantain and groundnuts, then they walk together to the bus stop.

Apart from Ndeye, she's never made friends who aren't connected to her through family, and certainly not male friends. So she doesn't know what to say. She's not even sure if it's premature to be thinking his having bought her food automatically makes them friends. She's uncertain what her body should do, how she should hold herself. It would be nice to have someone to talk to after class, so she won't have to hurry home. And he might come in handy for when she has to walk home late.

'Do you want to eat in the lorry station?' he asks. At this time, the station is filled with empty benches and ghostly lorries and taxis. It's a cemetery and she doesn't know if she can trust him yet. She would say yes, but that's probably how those stupid women got killed.

'I have to go home,' she says. 'You'll come to class next week?'

He says yes. They nod at each other, and he still walks into the lorry station while she waits for her ride home. She hopes he's not a ghost. When she can't see him anymore, she realizes that she's been holding her breath, and she finally exhales.

CHAPTER EIGHTEEN

THE DAILY POST
Monday, December 18, 1996 | We are the news! | Since 1952

The Doctor by Theo Avoka

When Doctor Karamoh Saturday ousted President Adama Longman in 1975, he completely overhauled and restructured the parliamentary system and every single ministry in the country, and the Ministry of Foreign Affairs, where I worked, probably benefitted the most. In December 1977, we were moved out of a crumbling building in the middle of the noisy Bakoy Market to a behemoth by the sea. At eight floors, the MoFA could easily have been the tallest structure in the city, but the Doctor wouldn't have felt right unless he was looking down on all of us, so he converted an old fort on top of the city's highest hill and made that his headquarters.

With a new MoFA home and a new head of State came a new minister. Our old minister disappeared, and I've always wondered if he escaped the country, or if he, like several politicians, businessmen, and regular people the Doctor just didn't like, is buried somewhere, new developments sprouting atop his bones. The new minister, Osei-Mintah, was boisterous. In those days he was a skinny man with a penchant for bowler hats and thin cigarettes. He has since abandoned the hats and adopted Cuban cigars. He studied political science and graduated from the Nigerben University, which I also attended. We got along, and he treated me more like a colleague than a subordinate.

I have to admit I was completely taken by the Doctor's message in those days. Politicians in the previous regime had failed and murdered my father, people he'd considered his friends, and I was looking for some kind of retribution, so I applauded the Doctor's coup. He promised change, better spending, and most importantly, 'payback for the cockroaches who emptied our national coffers.' Our freedom fighters were disappointments, growing fat and sending their children to expensive schools abroad, while my father, who had educated every single one of us locally, who had lived in the same house he'd bought before he became minister, was the one who'd been disgraced and killed. I don't have to repeat the story of my father's fall. Most of you are old enough to remember. I empathized with the Doctor. He once said in a speech that it physically hurt to see one founding father, his own mentor, because the man had grown so fat that he couldn't fit through the doors to his office and larger doors had to be built. The country had no need for a person who used national resources to feed his obesity, said the Doctor, and to his credit, he was probably the only African head of State who didn't put on weight during his tenure.

1978: The Doctor had been in power for three years, and at the MoFA we had settled into our castle by the sea, positions in the building commensurate with one's level. My first office was on the second floor, and by the time I left the ministry I'd only made it up to the fifth floor. The eighth floor was not a place most people visited often—they went there twice, on their first and last days—but once Osei-Mintah learned that I had studied literature at the university, he called on me for advice on his speeches, which I ended up rewriting. Everything about the building reflected the superiority of the eighth floor—the air up there smelled less salty and musty, and the ministry's one elevator only rode to the eighth floor. It was a place that made you feel important, and I enjoyed being summoned there. Osei-Mintah's writing projects could sometimes take weeks, and I relished those moments as much as I could.

Those early years were exciting. I remember driving to the office with a sense of purpose, feeling like we were moving the country to a far better place. I, like most in the country, believed the Doctor was Jesus reincarnated, the black saviour. He could avenge my father's wrongful death. He was young, educated, eloquent, and wanted the same things we did—jobs, accountability, and equality for all. The fervour with which Doctor Saturday rallied the youth and got us involved in politics and reshaping the country was unprecedented.

Years later, even after I had grown disillusioned with the Doctor, I still couldn't shake off that initial infatuation I'd had. So when, in December 1993, Osei-Mintah informed me that the Doctor had chosen me to be one of his biography writers, my first emotion was pride. Never mind that he told me in the middle of my wife's Christmas party! Then I thought of how I would tell Zahra. I wasn't being given a choice, and if I quit my job, the only way I'd get a new one was in another country.

The day I met the Doctor, we were at the beginning of the

rainy season. The air was damp, yet somehow my hands felt dry. I'd been let into the presidential mansion and seated on a raffia mat on a freshly mown lawn. I'll never forget how terrified and awed I was, sitting on a hill that looked over the whole city, a different view from Osei-Mintah's. This was the king's view. Saturday could see every single part of the city, and I couldn't help thinking that, at night, he got his boys to sit exactly where I was, each armed with a pair of binoculars, ensuring that his citizens were being upstanding. I imagined my emotions weren't unlike Marco Polo's before he met Kublai Khan or Queen Scheherazade before King Shahryar. To the east was the MoFA, right by the sea, looking like a sardine tin turned on its side. To the west, North and South Odor were laid out as corrugated-iron sheets piled in rows and rows. Home was in the middle somewhere, but it was hard to tell which house it was exactly. One of Saturday's assistants had brought me a calabash of coconut water and a pipe and snuffbox. The Doctor kept me waiting for half an hour.

I wiped my now-clammy palms on my thighs when I heard the front door of the Ashanti stool-shaped house swing open. First out walked a muscular man, then the Doctor in his trademark smock and woven hat, trailed by another bodyguard. I stood up as the trio approached. The first bodyguard stopped in front of a heliconia bush and the other stood off to the side once the Doctor was before me. It was the most of out-of-body experience I've ever had. Standing face to face with the man who had snatched power for seventeen years and was now president. He was more commanding, and yet strangely accessible, in person.

The Doctor picked up his pipe and snuffbox and stuffed leaves into the pipe's bowl. He lit it and inhaled.

'Welcome, Theo,' he said, sitting on the raffia mat and crossing his legs under his body. 'Sit, please.'

Lithe and taller than I realized, there was not an ounce of fat on the Doctor's body, even though his face was round and moustached. He was also older than I'd imagined, probably in his seventies. As the Doctor took drags from his pipe, his bushy eyebrows shot up and down.

'When Osei-Mintah mentioned your name as a possible writer,' the Doctor said, 'I didn't even have to think twice about it. You know I read your senior thesis?'

I didn't know how he got his hands on my thesis, *Meditations on Fathers and Sons in Oral African Literature*, which I thought bordered on sentimentality since I wrote it after my father died. But I couldn't ask the Doctor what his source was, since I couldn't find my voice.

The Doctor said, 'The resemblance to your father is uncanny. I'm sure you know he was one of my clients. And one of my personal heroes. Ugh, what a brilliant mind. His ideas about government and what our country could be—such beautiful ideas. His horrible end at the hands of Longman and company, of course in addition to many, many other factors, was why I decided the country had to go in another direction. I borrowed some of his ideas. Like his dream of opening more secondary schools in the interior of the country, so not everyone would be forced to go to the big cities to be educated. But you're probably wondering how I came across your thesis?'

I nodded, my throat dry. My father was the Doctor's hero?

My father was partly to blame for the Doctor's coup?

'He showed me the letters you wrote him from university. He said you were a strong writer, but hoped you'd go into law. Then, when his scandal hit, which I saw coming by the way ... He told me people in the government were out for him. When the scandal hit, I decided to find out even more about him. I knew that he'd been wronged. And being in the position I was, I had access to a lot of people, including some of your professors. One of my good friends, Dr. Nyarko ...'

'Professor Nyarko?'

'Yes. Your advisor gave me your thesis because I was always talking of your father. The sly dog didn't let on that you were his student until I was at my wit's end. Your essay gave me a lot of information. I make it a point to learn from great people. I read about who they are, where they come from, their dreams, their mistakes and weaknesses. You'll soon see my library. I have a biography of almost every great figure in history.' He took a drag from his pipe. 'I myself toyed with studying the letters in military school, but psychology was my first love.'

Nothing was sacrosanct. I tried to think of everything I had written in university, but my memory failed me.

'I haven't written anything creative in years,' I said, finally.

'I've read the speeches you've written for Osei-Mintah. You're lyrical, which is just what I want, and I'll guide you. Tell you exactly what I want. This is a political memoir of sorts. You know these journalists we have. They can't speak or write English. Osei-Mintah couldn't recommend you enough.'

I wanted to tell him: You know why you can't hire a professional writer? Because you put fear in our artists' hearts and the good ones have left. But all I could do was nod. Besides, there he was, defending my father. The tide of emotions coursing through me!

'You'll work on this project two or three times a week, and then we'll see about increasing your hours.'

'Should I bring a notebook?' I asked.

'We'll get you a typewriter.' The Doctor turned to look at the macho man behind him. 'Call Pape, will you?'

The two macho men exchanged non-verbal signs, and the other one who'd been standing farther away replaced the other and stood behind the Doctor.

'I'd like this book to be written and published in the next year, so we must make haste.'

Saturday's assistant skittered over. His head, that of a boy's, nodded as the Doctor asked him if he'd ordered flowers for his wife. The boy took notes, the Doctor listing off what I would need: typewriter, A4 paper, yellow foolscap, a box of pens, a desk, and the most comfortable chair out there.

'Sir,' the boy said. 'We have the furniture the Danish embassy sent.'

'Right, right. But I want Mr. Avoka to have something that's his own. I suppose you're right. But get the typewriter and other things.'

The boy walked away, still scribbling violently. I wondered how he had come to occupy that role, and what secrets he held. He probably knew the brand of toilet paper the Doctor preferred.

'My nephew,' Doctor Saturday said. 'He failed all his exams, and my sister came crying. You know family.' He sighed deeply and then looked out at the city before him. 'Next week, Mr. Avoka?'

'Yes,' I said, and stood up faster than I'd intended to.

After that first visit, I was more perplexed than ever. The Doctor seemed normal. Take away the last seventeen years and he was a wealthy man who took care of his family and his workers and treated them with respect. Yet this was the man under whom hundreds had disappeared. This was a man who controlled a band of thugs who enforced the rule of whatever law suited them, or made up their own if they found the country's constitution lacking. Who could forget the 'No suits on Saturday law'? I have several friends who were flogged after coming home from weddings or church. Land was seized and distributed to his ministers.

My own wife, Zahra, had suffered at the Doctor's hands. Her family had owned rice farms in the north, and after her father died, her mother survived with earnings from these farms. But two years after the coup, Saturday's boys seized their farmlands, and to this day they haven't been returned. Overnight, her mother grew dependent on Zahra in a way she never had been, in a way that was embarrassing to both of them. Zahra would never forgive the Doctor for this. The hardest part of being assigned this job was having to convince her that it was for the better, even though I wasn't sure if it was.

CHAPTER NINETEEN

Private Eye

There was nothing Theo could hide from me because he was obvious when something was wrong. I had lately begun taking pleasure in unravelling his problems, digging at them like a private eye, and solving them with a magician's ease and flair.

Take when Kojo got accepted into the International Secondary School. Theo stopped sleeping. The man would shuffle about and sneak into bed at dawn. His appetite, not large to begin with, diminished. He would go around the house turning off all the indoor lights, and at dawn he would switch off the outside lights even though it was still dark. His showers became quick affairs, and he glared at Kojo if the boy spent an indulgently long time doing the dishes, or at me if I fell asleep with the TV on. I figured that he was trying to save money because of the fees we'd be paying at Kojo's new school: one semester cost the same as five months of his salary.

We'd talked about the cost of the school long before Kojo even applied to the ISS, but said we'd cobble together something if Kojo got accepted. But I understood his worry. Theo was taking care of Kojo's education because I handled the running of the house. It was *his* problem. It also didn't help that Kojo really wanted to enrol in the school. He kept on about how he didn't have to get stuck in a big dorm; that he could have a radio or Walkman in his room; that there'd be fifteen students in a classroom instead of the fifty-students-to-a-teacher situation he was leaving behind. Theo could tell how heartbroken Kojo would be if we told him he couldn't go to the ISS. But he was taking out his helplessness on us, snapping at everyone, and not doing concrete things to fix the situation.

So one day I skipped work and drove all the way to the ISS, perched on its little hill, and walked into the atrium of the administrative office, where a thin man in a slender necktie whispered that Mrs. Bobole, the principal, was in meetings all day.

'I'll wait,' I said.

I'd brought work with me and flipped through stacks of paper while I watched the thin man walk in and out of Mrs. Bobole's office, getting more flustered by the minute. I could tell he hadn't had the balls to tell her that I was there. When he made for her office the hundredth time, I followed him. He looked at me with horror, shaking his head with worry—whether out of concern for me or for himself, I couldn't tell.

'Madam,' I said, brushing past him, 'Mrs. Bobole, good morning. You don't know me. Sorry to barge in like this. I'm the mother of one of your newly admitted students.'

Mrs. Bobole didn't smile, but she dismissed her secretary and let me in. Her office was dark and cold. An air conditioner whistled and droned behind her.

'I just want you to know how grateful we are that you admitted our son, Kojo Avoka,' I said, sitting across from her. 'We are so, so proud.'

'He did the hard work. He deserved it. Now, how can I help you?' Mrs. Bobole said. All this while, her features (large globular eyes, round nose, big leonine hair) remained placid.

'Mrs. Bobole, let me repeat how honoured we are that Kojo got in.' I studied her impassive face, her little finger drawing curls on her mahogany desk. She was not the kind of woman who responded well to grovelling. I had to play her game, so I said, 'But the truth is, I'm here to withdraw him. We can't afford to send him here.'

Under her breath she said, 'Why did you apply, then?'

I was taken aback, and then grew impressed. If she was this no-nonsense, Kojo had to come out of this school fearless.

'*He* wanted to,' I said. 'If I had my way, I'd ship him to the north, send him to Senevolta.' Not true. It would mean Kojo would have to spend vacations with Mma. 'I had a stellar education there.' Senevolta's status had plummeted after the coup. Most of the public schools in the country, really.

Mrs. Bobole sighed and rested a fat palm on her forehead. Her eyes shifted right, then left, and I watched her think. She couldn't just turn me away. Especially when I was seated right across from her, completely reasonable, intelligent, with a legitimate concern. It was basic, decent human behaviour for her to consider my situation.

She finally said, 'I'm sorry, there's nothing I can do.'

'My husband's a civil servant,' I told her.

'We have scholarships reserved for the poorest students. Students from villages, where neither parent works, places which don't even have running water or electricity. Your son has two working parents. It's just impossible.'

I stared at Mrs. Bobole. Her face was aggravatingly smooth. I'd have preferred a face peppered with moles I could count while I thought up some insult for her.

'I appreciate your time, Mrs. Bobole,' I said, with a strong desire to reach over and slap her. But I kept it together and walked out. At least I had one more option: Osei-Mintah.

I called the Ministry of Foreign Affairs and got one of Osei-Mintah's secretaries on the line. She told me the minister had no openings for the next three days. This, I knew, was just a tactic used to make ministers seem busier than they were. I had worked there. She couldn't fool me. The best solution was to show up at the ministry, head wrapped babushka-style with Jackie-O sunglasses, and badger the secretary until I was let in, but there was the risk that Theo might show up. I ran through other options: pretending I was calling from the British High Commission and heightening the British accent—enunciating more, increasing the haughtiness, insisting that I be given a private meeting with the minister. Or I could impersonate Osei-Mintah's wife, but I was sure she called his office regularly, and honestly, I couldn't imitate her—she had a breathy, high-pitched yet motherly voice that middle-aged women took on when their spouses became important.

'It's urgent,' I said to the secretary. 'It concerns one of his employees.' I hesitated. 'Theo Avoka.' The secretary was quiet, but the rhythm of her breathing changed, from impatience to interest. Sick, gossip-filled interest. 'I'm his wife and this is important.'

'Please hold on,' she said. 'I'll see what I can do.'

Within under a minute Osei-Mintah was on the line.

'Zahra,' he said.

'Honourable!'

'You know it's already halfway through the year and I'm still dreaming of your mother's stew from the Christmas party,' he said, and burst out laughing.

The secretary had obviously not briefed him on the nature of my call, and it was sad that the only point of intersection between my husband's boss and myself was my mother's stew. I was sure we had more in common than he probably let himself see, but maybe it was good he kept our relationship light.

'How can I help you?' Osei-Mintah said. I pictured him, massive body reclining further in his seat, hands clasped on belly.

'Honourable,' I said, 'before I say anything, please, please promise me you'll keep this between us. You can't tell Theo.'

'Indeed,' he said. Picture him leaning forward now, with his blue silk shirt that his stomach's folded into three pleats.

'We need a little favour. Well, it's not little. It's a big deal—for us. Kojo got accepted into the International Secondary School.'

'Congrats!' he said. He's able to relax a bit now. It's not as dire as he thought, but still … Am I going to ask for a raise for Theo? He's not quite sure yet. He could do with a glass of whisky, though he hasn't eaten lunch yet, so it's not a great idea. His Canadian doctors have told him if he doesn't cut back his drinking they'll have to do a liver transplant.

'Yes, thank you,' I said. 'The thing is, as you probably know, the school is terribly expensive, but that's the school I want Kojo to go to. In fact, I can't recommend it enough when your daughter is thirteen.' He was probably thinking, my daughter's going to school abroad. End of story. 'I was hoping you could help us get a partial scholarship.'

'Oh,' he shouted. 'Done! Zahra, you know how I appreciate the work Theo is doing. This is nothing. In fact, hold on. Catherine!' he screeched in my ear. 'Come here!'

A patter of feet. Catherine stands in front of the minister, probably in a red trouser suit. Not overweight, but hasn't lost the belly after having three children. The minister annoys her, but she's borderline in love with him.

'Catherine,' Osei-Mintah said. 'What's the deal with your children's scholarships? How do they work?'

It was unfair that the secretary's children got subsidized education and not Theo. It was unfair that I had to go through all this grovelling. The secretary mumbled something.

'Okay,' said Osei-Mintah. 'They have to maintain B+ averages or something like that. Right, right. Just for public schools. I see. Thank you, Catherine. And please bring me a cup of tea. Zahra, what's the name of the contact at Kojo's school?'

'Gertrude Bobole.'

'So,' he said. 'What are you going to do for me?' His tone had dropped a lascivious notch. My heart twitched. Was altruism dead? Did he want me to say to him: let's meet at the Panama at 4.30? He must have sensed my concern because he immediately said, 'You better invite me over for your mother's stew this Christmas!'

Kojo was able to enrol in the International Secondary School as a partial-scholarship student.

Now, a year later, Theo was at it again. At the Christmas party, besides my flirting with Obi, Theo's surliness had probably also stemmed from us blasting the radio on high, from all the gas Mma had used for cooking, from the petrol he'd burned in going to buy drinks to entertain his own boss. Everything we did must have upset him. His bad habits had returned—not sleeping, not eating—but now he'd added a few more—leaving home early, coming home late. And for the life of me, I couldn't figure out why. Kojo was struggling in math, which should bother me, because he could lose his scholarship, but I hadn't even told Theo about that. If anything, our expenses had gone down now that Atsu had moved into the house, and I was the one paying for her English classes, because everything to do with Atsu was a 'domestic expense.' If anybody had worries to mull over, it was me. I still hadn't found a replacement for those crooks of old women after ending their contract, and my health was no better.

I decided to stop playing detective and ask him. I left work at midday and drove to his office, where an inept soldier insisted I show ID, which I couldn't produce, because we still hadn't been issued national IDs and I was not carrying my passport around. I had to wait in the heat of midafternoon while the soldier sent someone to fetch Theo. The bureaucracy of the ministry seemed to have worsened since my six-month stint there in the seventies.

We drove to the Green Onion, the closest decent restaurant around. I ordered golden fried shrimp for appetizers, shredded beef and rice for Theo, and sweet and sour chicken for myself, and billed everything to the company account. This was work-related. If family life wasn't good, work life would be no better.

'What are we celebrating?' he asked.

'Nothing. This seems to be the only way to get you, especially with your new work schedule.'

He wiped his eyes, then his lips, and set down his plastic spoon. We had a long way to go if one of nicest restaurants in the city used plastic tableware. I looked around the restaurant, and each table was covered with vinyl tablecloths with red-and-black Chinese characters. From the kitchen, loud, unintelligible music emanated from a crackly sound system. Our lives were not only tacky but imitative. I wanted to live truly, wholly. Since I'd come back home I felt like I'd been play-acting. For fourteen years!

'What is going on?' I asked him. 'And no lying, please. There's something wrong.'

Theo covered his eyes with his left hand and massaged

his brow. His wedding band glistened. He said, 'Osei-Mintah has taken me off the Malaysia project.'

'When? When did he do this?'

'Christmas.'

'What's his reason?' I said.

'You won't like this,' he said. 'The Doctor wants me to write his memoirs.'

'Huh,' I said, totally confused. The angry monster disappeared. The Doctor had always fascinated Theo, even when I wanted to find a way to assassinate the fellow. 'Why you?'

'He read my university thesis and decided I was one of the people he wanted on his writing team. So …'

'I'm sorry. I'm really flummoxed and still trying to connect the dots.'

'It's Kojo I'm worried about. If it were just the two of us, I would quit and find a new job.'

'It's too dangerous. You touch that man and you might as well be dead. The blood that's on him! Is he going to tangle you into his lies?'

'I know. But I imagine I'll just be writing down his rhetoric. It sounds like he just needs a typist. But think of when I write that book I've been dreaming of. All this could be put to use. And, get this, the pay is twice what I am making at the ministry.'

A waitress came and cleared our plastic plates, leaving an oil-stained bill on the table. I paid for our meal and stood up.

'I have to go back,' I said, annoyed because Theo had already made up his mind. He'd been losing sleep about how to tell me, at the moment when nothing I said would matter. 'Do me one favour. Ask him why he never returned my family's land.'

I drove him back to his ministry by the sea, and as he walked toward the gate, I shouted, 'What happens when he decides he doesn't like your writing anymore? Or when the volatile bastard wants to work with someone else?'

'Shhh,' Theo said, glaring at me. 'We'll discuss this later.'

'Think about it seriously.'

Theo was one of those stubborn people who spent forever making up their mind, but once they did, there was no budging. Yet it was more complicated. We didn't have a choice. Theo had to work with the Doctor.

CHAPTER TWENTY

Rain

Our first midterm break is here and I didn't go home. The problem lies with the person called Atsu whatever her last name is. Without warning she pops into my head at the worst possible moments. I'll give you an example. The other day, during craft hour, my palms were moulding clay on the pottery wheel, innocently pressing into the soft doughy mix, when all of a sudden, what did I think of? Atsu's breasts. I was so embarrassed I immediately had to make sure no mind readers were around—they exist, I swear. Truth is, this makes no sense because apart from the ride from her village with Daddy, I haven't spent that much time with her. She started working for us a month before I left for boarding school. So, anyway, when I finally call Mummy to schedule a time for her to pick me up for break, I say I'm staying, and she asks if I'm okay, if she should come visit with food, and I say no, the food is supposed to be better over break, and I have to stay focused and study for the big math exam that's two weeks around the corner. And since she doesn't want me to lose my scholarship, she acquiesces.

All right, all right, I'll come out with the whole truth: I

found out that Inaam isn't going home, because her father's travelling. I would rather spend time with Inaam than Atsu. It's not even a choice to make.

Those who stay over midterm break are usually poor, or students whose families live too far for them to go home. But I've decided they get to experience the school in its best state: calm, Kunle- and teacher-free. We'd usually be in class by now, and *Professeur* Drone would be doing *quelque chose* so boring we'd be sleeping. Instead, I just woke up and I'm strolling on the lawns we're never to walk on, and taking in the heavy grey sky and the smell of wet soil, just taking it all in.

The cracked basketball courts are empty and above them, thick clouds are crawling towards the sea, trees swaying forward and backward. Rain is on its way. Behind the fencing of the basketball court is a gate I've never noticed. A small, dull, brown wooden gate next to a milk-bush shrub. I'm usually worried about getting hit on the head by the basketball, so it's absolutely passed me by. I wonder where it goes. Probably a secret passage straight to Mrs. Bobole's office. I plod on and head for the dining hall, where a handful of students are settling down to breakfast. I am expecting a bell to ring, something to drag out everyone else, but people are already digging into their toast, omelettes, and sausages. Sausages! At a table with four students who are already eating, I serve myself and look around at the emptiness. Maybe I should have gone home. Maybe I'm not the introverted genius I think I am. Maybe deep down inside, I'm a loud person who needs people around to be happy.

But before my depression grows deeper, the kids drag me into a conversation.

'Kojo,' says Nina, one of the girls at the table, 'what do you think? These people think the Doctor sleeps in a coffin.'

I freeze, unsure how to answer. Mummy just told me about Daddy's sweet new gig, which I kept to myself. But did someone else find out and tell everyone?

'Why are you asking me?' I say.

'Just guess. Do you think he does? Fred over there says the man does everything by juju, including sleeping in a coffin to get his powers.'

'In by juju, out by juju,' says Fred, biting into a chunk of sausage. 'My father says that's the only way the man will go out. If someone does juju on him.'

'Why hasn't it happened yet?' someone else on the table shouts.

'Kojo, what do you think?' insists Nina.

'I have no idea,' I say, and she moves on to the next person. Sounds like she's just taking a poll of everyone at the table.

'You just love the Doctor,' Fred says to Nina.

'I just don't understand how he got in by juju. How can you do juju to a whole country of how many million people?' says Nina. 'He's done more for us than our first president did.'

Have I told you how much I hate politics? Inaam walks in just in the nick of time and sits by me, and I am able to angle my body away from that conversation.

'You didn't tell me you were staying,' she says, bag-less, book-less, still wearing her glasses. This is the first time I've seen her not look stressed out.

'I need to study for the math test.'

'Sure,' she says. 'Why didn't you go home? Really, truly.'

'Honest. I'll get more work done here. You should eat. This is better than anything the kitchen staff's ever made us.'

Thunder rumbles and the room grows darker. Inaam shudders and rubs her arms. Some people burst out of the dining hall, leaving their dishes behind. What special treatment! Where's Kunle to drag them back and make them scrub the plates *and* the dining hall?

As her fork hovers mid-air, a sliver of omelette on its tines, Inaam says, 'It's great, isn't it, being here for break? We can go to each other's rooms. There's no curfew. People can watch their *Alejandro y Ernestina* till the cows come—'

'We can visit each other's rooms?' I say. Inaam swallows her egg. 'Nice!'

Wind flings one of the dining hall's trapdoors wide open. More kids storm out, screaming when they get outside. Pellets of rain drum the tin roof above us.

'Should we leave?'

'The black man is afraid of rain,' she says, and when I frown at her, she adds, 'Something my father says. No, let's finish eating.'

She cleans everything off her plate, and we take our plates to the drop window, which is usually disgusting when everyone else is around. We leave the dining hall and the rain is so heavy it looks like a sheer curtain. Inaam runs into the waterfall, and I'm hesitant, but soon I follow her. I'm assuming we're headed to the same place, otherwise she'd have said bye. The rain pounds every inch of my skin. A flash of lightning splits the sky in two and a thundering boom follows. Inaam shrieks.

At her dorm Inaam stomps on the terrazzo floor, as if that'll dry her clothes. We're both soaked. She wipes her glasses with her wet T-shirt.

'Wait here,' she says. 'I'll change and find something for you to wear.'

I almost burst out laughing, picturing myself in her T-shirt with the cat eyes and a flowery skirt. She comes back out and tells me she left clothes on her bed.

Her room is neat and smells like coconuts. I can tell which bed is hers—the upper bunk. Her room-mate's is piled with stuffed toys of every member of the animal kingdom—there's even a lobster in there. On Inaam's bed are books, a black T-shirt, and her PE shorts. After I'm dressed I walk back out, feeling ridiculous, but I pretend it's no big deal.

'Want to come in?' she says, and we go back into the room.

As she places her foot on the first rung of the bunk bed, I blurt out, 'I also have the top bunk!' I don't have to tell you that this is the first time I've been alone in a room with a girl who wasn't my kindergarten playmate. It's going to be extremely difficult to keep playing cool Kid Kojo.

'I like it better,' Inaam says when she's halfway up. 'Especially with a room-mate like Maa Grant. Only God knows what kind of things she'd drop on my bed.' She stares down at me. 'Oh no! I'm being mean, right?'

'Inaam, you can't always be nice,' I say. I take my time up the rungs and settle by her. There's a good chunk of space between us. A whole human being could fit there. A three-year-old. Both our legs dangle out of the space underneath the wooden railing. My belly flutters as I stare at the wardrobe opposite the bed. This could be my room if it didn't smell of coconuts, which is a semi-comforting thought.

'Do you have a radio or boom box?' I ask. She shakes her head. 'Seriously? No Walkman? How do you study?!'

'I can't study with music.'

'Music is my life.'

'My mother liked music a lot.'

I don't know what to say to her. We all know Inaam's mother died and there are all sorts of rumours weaving around the school—suicide, murder, she just disappeared—but I don't like uncomfortable topics, because very soon I'm going to say something wrong, so I steer the conversation back to the boom box.

'Can we use Maa Grant's?' It's a small blue radio, the antenna broken in half. I don't even wait for Inaam to say yes or no. It's the nerves. I spring down and struggle to find a signal. There's no getting DJ Onesandtwos, so I settle for a station playing Whitney Houston, just at the part where she stops and yells, 'AND IIIII-Y-I, I will always love you. Love youuuu!'

'Did you know my father and your mother went out in

secondary school?' Inaam says. Why does she keep bringing up uncomfortable topics? That explains Mummy's behaviour at the Christmas party.

'How do you know?' I say, and put my hand in the three-year-old space.

'My dad tells me everything. They even almost got married.'

I think of Mummy and Inaam's father; I picture them kissing and a shiver runs through me. I could see how they'd work out, but it's weird. He's Inaam's father, Uncle Obi, not the man who could have been my father, which is an inappropriate and bizarre thing to be thinking since I want to kiss Inaam. Still, I wonder why things didn't work out, but this subject is uncomfortable, and I realize I have my foolish thinking face on. I can feel it. My lower lip sort of hangs and one corner of my mouth curls up. I look like a complete idiot, and I can't help it, and Mummy hits me every time she sees me like that, but it just happens.

Inaam tucks her hand under my palm. God! We look at each other and she smiles shyly. I want to tell her I like her and ask if I can kiss her, but that's not how it happens: I just have to lean in and kiss her. I grip her hand and pull her toward me. Our foreheads touch and her glasses press against my cheeks. And then I just do it. My lips touch hers, which are soft, with a faint taste of mango. Our heads separate and we look at each other. I always wondered what kissing with glasses would be like, and it was fine. Yet I pull them off her face, fold them, and put them on her pillow. I wonder if I'm the first person she's kissed. Probably not. Kids who grow up in England and places like that start doing things when they're seven. She makes the first move this time, and her tongue pushes into my mouth. She definitely knows how to kiss, because her tongue is circling mine, flicking it up and doing things that are making me feel warm all over, and yet I'm terrified.

'Ina—,' I start. She shushes me and lies down, pulls me on top of her. Oh nervous, happy day! I had no idea she could be this in control. I don't know what to do with my hands and legs. She grabs my hands, leads them to her breasts—soft round things—and I press them gently, trying hard to banish Atsu from my head. Inaam places her hand over mine and makes me pinch them harder. Her eyes are barely closed, the whites still show—and slowly I close mine, too, breathe, and listen to the faint sound of cars on the highway below the hill.

CHAPTER TWENTY-ONE

THE DAILY POST

Monday, January 6, 1997 | We are the news! | Since 1952

Courtney by Theo Avoka

Happy New Year to all the loyal readers of this column. Hope this year brings you happiness and prosperity. Just to recap for those now discovering *Saturday's People*, I first shared my childhood as the son of the former Minister of the Interior, then I chronicled my early years at the Ministry of Foreign Affairs, and began to write about how I was recruited to work with Doctor Karamoh Saturday. I'll now continue with how things began to spiral out of control.

There are people you encounter who end up moulding your life in ways that seem the stuff of movies and fiction. If anyone had told me that I'd meet a white woman who would reshape my relationship with the Doctor and my family, I'd have called him or her a liar. Apart from the white people I occasionally bumped into at work events, I really didn't have any use for them, but Courtney would become one of the most influential people in my life until she was forced out of the country. We met under what I thought were the most banal circumstances.

About four years ago, I was at a reception at the American

Embassy with Minister Osei-Mintah and his cronies. It was probably also around the new year. As usual, I stood off to the side, watching the man and his sycophants making fools of themselves, filled with dread and jealousy, feelings that had been sitting with me for a couple of months. The former persisted because I had still not committed to working for the Doctor. The latter was simple: I never felt like part of their circle, and hovered on the outside as they clung to every word that came out of the American ambassador's mouth, bursting into laughter when he as much as smiled. Each of them sported a middle-aged paunch—ball-like bellies that bounced up and down with each outburst.

On this occasion, two bars had been set up at the embassy, one inside, the other outside. I made my way outside and ordered a whisky. The smell of the harmattan was thick in the air. In a few days, dust would cover the city, and all of us would suffer cracked lips and dry, scaly skin. A white woman walked to the bar and ordered a drink from the barman, a red bow tie tucked under his chin. I stared at the golden liquid hitting the tumbler and I remember my exact thought: I should talk to her. She might give me a new job. Who knows how the mind makes such connections, but it does. The woman grabbed her drink and raised her glass to mine. At the same time Osei-Mintah and his friends erupted into laughter.

'Courtney Steele,' she said, shaking my hand. 'I've seen you around a few times.'

'Our city is really a small town,' I said.

We all make snap judgments when we meet people. I'm guilty of doing this often. These were mine: this woman is one of those types who came here straight out of college, trying to save the world, one developing country at a time. She's been around for a while, probably for five or so years, since Doctor Karamoh Saturday lifted his ban on foreign-run NGOs. She's a woman who destroys marriages. The last thought was not because she was particularly striking or beautiful, but because in her eyes shone a certain fierceness and fearlessness, which I found very attractive. Zahra also wore this brand of womanhood.

She asked me what I was doing at the reception because I didn't seem to be enjoying myself, and I told her I was there with the Minister of Foreign Affairs, that I was usually invited to functions in which Osei-Mintah had to make a speech, and that I'd rather be at home.

'That makes two of us,' she said, staring at the orange rectangle of the Ambassador's house. 'I used to be so fascinated by these events when I first got here. It seemed glamorous, being invited to the Ambassador's house or to this or that MP's cocktail party. I wrote to everyone back home, boasting.'

'Where's that?' I asked. She was American, that much I knew. 'Back home.'

'I grew up in Boston. Have you been?'

I shook my head. There was something about her (striking, despite my initial claim), and I found myself thinking up questions to keep talking to her. How long had she been in the country? Two. What was she doing here? Monitoring elections and the transfer of power from military to civilian rule. The little man in my head was on high alert, reminding me of a rumour about Saturday keeping a white mistress. Could this be her? Instead, I asked why was she still around since the elections had ended. She said she was monitoring how the country was coping with the transition.

'Were our elections free and fair?' I asked.

'Smooth,' she said. 'You showed the rest of the continent how it should be done. People arrived on time, there were no skirmishes, no attempts at voting twice.'

'Really?' I asked. I could point to several instances where thugs, Saturday's Boys, intimidated people trying to vote; ballots also went missing.

She paused, looked around, and studied me for a long time. Then she whispered, 'You and I both know they had problems.' She shrugged and finished her drink. 'I know you're judging me for having lied, but I've learned the hard way that your world here doesn't exactly run on honesty.'

'I'm sorry. My world?'

'You know what I mean.'

'No, not really,' I said. I never got worked up about anything, so I don't know why she was riling me. I was also secretly impressed by her candour. *I could have been a major Saturday sympathizer for all she knew.* 'It's your people who like Karamoh Saturday. He can do no wrong in your American eyes. I'm sure you were given specific orders to lie about the elections.' Now my loose tongue could cost me my job. I changed the topic and asked her how she was adjusting to the food, to our love for titles, our love for mediocrity, and to the chaos of our daily lives.

She exhaled, laughed, and said, 'You're in the wrong camp!' She told me about her photography project, an exhibition she would be putting on soon, and handed me her business card.

'I enjoyed our chat,' she said. 'I would love to talk more in a friendlier setting. I have some friends you might like.'

'Likewise, Madam.' I took her outstretched fingers—soft, delicate—and shook her hand. I was tempted, for a second, to press my lips to the back of her hand. When I was growing up I saw my father do these things and cringed, promising myself I'd never be as pretentious. Yet I found myself unconsciously repeating his tics.

She walked away and I looked at the card, flattered and rattled. The right thing to do would be to throw it away and not entertain any unnecessary thoughts. But she might be important, especially if I wanted a new job. Americans paid well.

When I got back home I didn't tell Zahra about my encounter with Courtney. I thought it'd be nice to have a benign secret peppering my marriage, a marriage that was beginning to feel very one-sided.

CHAPTER TWENTY-TWO

Nightlife

Atsu is plagued by these city friendships. She isn't sure if she should say hello to Nasar because they talked last time or if should she pretend nothing happened, even though she's sure that will be rude. Ndeye has put too many ideas in her head. Almost everybody is sitting in the same seats, which places Nasar at almost two o'clock from her seat and she can't avoid greeting him. She decides to wave.

'Atsu, how are you?' he shouts back. He hasn't forgotten her name, but now everybody must be wondering why he knows it.

Mr. Sy walks in late, a large oil stain on his shirt, and teaches a lesson on vowels and consonants. He makes them read words that have only consonants, like d-r-y. But to Atsu *Y* is like *I* so she's sure it should be considered a vowel, but Mr. Sy says it's a consonant. That, and *H*. English, like life, is not making a lot of sense, but she has to learn the rules. Mr. Sy, who's behaving as if he left the iron on at home, says he has to cut the class short. What a trickster. First he comes in late, now this. He better not repeat this disappearing act, because they're paying good money to be here. Sure, Madam is paying on her behalf, but this is unacceptable. As she's stuffing books into her bag, Nasar comes over so fast, she doesn't even have time to think of something to say so people don't get suspicious.

'I'm glad we're done early,' he says. And here she was thinking other people would be just as annoyed with Mr. Sy's laziness. Everyone's walking out of the classroom, Mr. Sy is long gone, and the beautiful man, Harry, lingers too.

Nasar invites her to Club Amnesia, apparently a real nightclub, which she's never been to before. She only knows that sinful things go on in them, and even though the thought of being away from the Avokas's is tempting, she's not sure this is the night she should witness sin being committed. Also, she'd have to explain that she doesn't live in her own house, on her own terms, that she has to be back home early. And that, the fact that she has to expose that she's just a housegirl, makes her decline their offer.

'Not tonight,' she says and snaps her bag shut. Her refusal should make her come off as mysterious. 'Why are you going out on a Wednesday anyway?'

'Wednesdays are ladies' nights,' Harry says, and winks at Atsu.

'Why don't you come?' says Nasar.

'Maybe next week.'

'What if it rains next week?' Nasar says. 'Don't be boring.'

Atsu watches them about to exit the room and suddenly realizes she'll be left alone, so she speeds up and walks out with them. She wishes she were braver. She could have gone for half an hour, and Madam and Mr. Avoka would never have found out. She's always lived her life scared of what would happen. Scared to say no to Mama. Scared to live. Other people seem to take risks and nothing happens to them.

By the time she gets to the Avokas's house, she's worked herself into such a state of agitation that she needs to talk to Ndeye, who has such a simple way of looking at life and is sure to have a solution.

Ndeye is in bed, her face, neck, and cheeks powdered white, her TV blasting *Alejandro y Ernestina*. It's nice that Ndeye has a TV, even if it's black and white, and small. Atsu sits and watches the screen flash in greyscale, impatient to talk, but once *Alejandro y Ernestina* is on, there's no making sense out of Ndeye. Omo saves the day: *All your brights sparkling white. Omo! Omo!*

Atsu asks Ndeye if she's been clubbing before.

'Many times,' Ndeye says. The moons of her breasts are also covered in powder. She is lying. She's probably gone one or two times, and probably felt out of place. Atsu absolutely relishes moments when the village girl in Ndeye peeks through.

'These two boys in my class said I should go with them.'

'*Ei*, Atsu, what boys?' *Alejandro y Ernestina* is back on.

'Wednesday night is ladies' night.'

'Let's go. Let's go. Now!' Who knew Ndeye would get so excited about boys she's never met?

'We can't go today. What would I say to Mr. and Mrs. Avoka? Maybe we can plan for next week?'

'Why won't your bosses let you go to a club? Mine don't

care what I do, as long as I cook and clean.' Another lie.

'What should I do?'

Ndeye reaches forward and her cover cloth drops to her waist, revealing a lacy bra.

'Bosses only understand sickness and death. You have to say someone is sick or someone died.'

'I can't kill someone, oh!' Atsu says.

'You could use me.'

'That doesn't make any sense,' Atsu says. 'Wait, what about Gloria? I'll tell them that Gloria is sick, that I'll spend the night in North Odor and be home early in the morning to prepare their breakfast.'

'That's it!' Ndeye says. *Alejandro y Ernestina* is over, and she hasn't even noticed.

It's every village girl's dream, *Alejandro y Ernestina*. Ernestina is a poor girl from a Mexican pueblo who moves to Mexico City to work with a rich baroness. Alejandro is the baroness's handsome son, who is in love with Ernestina but hasn't realized it yet. Sometimes they get close, but the baroness interferes, and poor Ernestina is left heartbroken. Atsu knows, though, that Alejandro and Ernestina will end up together.

The club, in the Bakoy Market, is not too far from their school. It used to be called Liberty in the sixties, then Orange Tavern, then it closed down for a long time, and now it's Club Amnesia, Nasar tells them.

Ndeye has been ogling Harry all the ride over and is beginning to annoy Atsu. At the door of the club, Atsu's bad mood is slowly replaced by excitement and fear. Lately, many things that give her pleasure make her question if she's doing the right thing. Like while watching Saturday-afternoon movies, she finds herself drawn to the sex scenes, glued to the TV screen and tickled in the base of her belly. Then when the scene is over, she's overcome with such unbearable shame. Likewise, this night is going to be pleasurable, and she's not sure if she should even be there.

Nasar puts his hand on the small of her back and leads her into the smoke-filled room. Disco balls throw red, green, and yellow rings of light on the walls and the twisting bodies of the dancers. He herds them to a table in the corner. Atsu would have thought Harry would be the leader, but she's impressed that Nasar's the one in charge.

'What would you like?' he asks the girls. She asks for a Coke.

Atsu wonders what it is about newness that inspires both fear and wonder in people. Maybe it's that anything can happen to you, the outcome of which will be either great or terrible. And that possibility is exciting. When Madam first brought her to the city, she had a constant heaviness in her chest, that anything could happen. Standing in the club, the feeling is so strong.

The music is loud, and she doesn't feel like dancing, but when Nasar asks her, she goes anyway. He moves fluidly. His waist seems to circle around itself, and his hands pick up hers as 'So So Chop Chop Mr. President' belts out of the club's speakers.

'Harry is not going to do anything with Ndeye, is he?'

she asks, watching her friend and Harry get onto the dance floor.

'No,' Nasar says, pulling Atsu close, humming and palming her back. He feels warm, and she fits perfectly in his arms. But then she realizes her breasts must be pressing into his chest, that the closeness is probably not good, and even though she'd like to stay there for the whole night, she pushes back and breaks the embrace.

'Where's Ndeye?' she asks, suddenly panicked.

He points to Harry and Ndeye, plastered to each other. Ndeye is a grown woman, she reminds herself and tries to enjoy the music.

She would like to leave now, but she can't go without Ndeye. And even though she wants to ask Nasar why it's okay for a married man to be sticking his thing into the backside of her friend, she doesn't. The whole thing unnerves her, and she's not sure if she's mad at Ndeye or herself, because if she's really honest with herself, a part of her is mildly titillated, and that's what disturbs her. Which is why, before she can stop herself, she leaves Nasar behind, walks over to Harry and Ndeye, and informs Harry that she and Ndeye need to have a moment.

Women are squashed into the bathroom, several in tight dresses. If Atsu is sure of anything tonight, it's that half of these women are prostitutes, women her mother admonished her to steer clear of when she left for the city. Two of them are sharing a tiny mirror, spreading brown face powder on their foreheads. She's not sure how to confront Ndeye.

'It's too hot in here,' Ndeye says. 'What? You want me to fix your make-up?'

'No,' Atsu whispers. 'Why are you dancing with him like that?'

'Like what?'

'Like one of them.' She lets her eyes walk to a woman in a black tank top and red miniskirt.

'You're not serious,' Ndeye says. 'Don't bring your village things here. Everybody is free to dance how they like.'

'He's married.'

'So? Have I said I'm going to steal him from his wife?' She sucks her teeth and stomps out of the bathroom.

Atsu follows her, and not long after they leave the club. Their ride home is quiet. Atsu wonders if there's something wrong with her, and why, in trying to do the right thing, she ends up alienating everybody. Mama and her brothers, and now Ndeye. She won't be surprised if Nasar never asks her out again.

CHAPTER TWENTY-THREE

Broken Machinery

I hadn't been in Dr. Mamby's consulting room in over two years, the last time being when I'd had food poisoning. Since then I'd been avoiding hospitals as best as I could, only going there for Kojo's sake. Dr. Mamby, whom I affectionately called DR, sat across from me, his chair much higher, which rendered him godlike. His head appeared to brush the ceiling, which, along with the walls, had been painted a sickly deep green. He'd refused to talk to me when I arrived because he thought I'd found a new doctor.

'Oh, DR,' I said. 'If ever I find a new doctor I'll be sure to come and personally rub it in your face.'

He laughed and said, 'Good. I'll expect nothing less from you. What can we do for you?'

'That paint, DR? I'm sure you chose it.'

'Go into every office in the hospital, and you'll see that your government has decided to invest in buckets of forest-green paint instead of stocking us with more equipment. Apparently green is associated with health and vitality. What can I say? *Ei*! You're married to a civil servant, so let me keep my mouth shut.'

'Huh,' I said. Then, 'I should have probably come earlier.

I've had a headache for the last four or five months.'

'Zahra!' he said, stood up, and ordered me to lie on the hospital bed.

He looked down at me with furrowed, bloodshot eyes, biting back words. He pressed his stethoscope to my chest, stuck a cold thermometer under my tongue, did a ton of doctorly things, then sat me up and asked me to describe the headaches to him.

'They're not like any I've had before, and I've *had* headaches. These feel very different. How do I describe them? They make me feel nauseous and badly affect my eyes. It usually starts with this aura. The world becomes a bit like an abstract painting.'

'Trust you to see your condition so poetically,' Dr. Mamby said. 'Go on.'

'Everything seems less focused, more mottled, and I get dizzy spells, too, but they don't last very long. What's wrong with me?'

'I'll have to do tests. Usual run-of-the-mill things—malaria, pregnancy …'

'Oooh, no no no!' I said, too vehemently. Theo and I hadn't had sex in months. It wasn't even possible.

'Just to cover all our bases,' Dr. Mamby said. 'I'm sure it's nothing you have to worry about. I'm going to send you to the lab.'

'You know I hate injections,' I said. 'Must you put me through this?'

'Big baby.'

If only Dr. Mamby were attractive and tall.

Later, I sat in a waiting room and watched as vials of blood were moved from room to room. The dark crimson liquid made my belly lurch in a way that I didn't expect. I wasn't usually squeamish about blood.

A technician took me into a small green room, stuck a needle in my arm, instructed me to urinate into a beaker, and gruffly sent me back into the waiting room, but I couldn't handle the suspense any longer, so I left the lab area, half-wishing I had a smoking habit that would take me outside. I walked through two sets of double doors that opened to a large ward. A tiny old woman was seated on her bed, slurping loudly. She sucked at whatever it was with her whole body. I prayed that whatever was wrong with me wouldn't land me in this place. I left the ward and walked back out the way I came.

'Madam,' said a technician, 'our machinery just broke down.'

'What does that mean?'

'You have to come back at the end of the day.'

I tried not to scream at him. It wasn't his fault. He was just a little man in a white coat working with the stupid equipment our government had purchased—if purchasing is what they had done. They'd probably inherited it from a defunct hospital in Russia.

'What time?' I asked him.

'Anytime, Madam. Just don't come after five, because no one will be here.'

I drove to Duell and Co., trying not to insult anyone who committed the slightest traffic error. It seemed lately that my anger lasted longer and, like the headache, became this untempered spirit impossible to check. A couple of days before, Atsu had hand-washed one of my silk blouses and stained the white thing pink. I gave her a piece of my mind and told her to throw it away.

Sectioned in two, the Duell office was in the boys' quarters of my boss Somto's house. The bosses, Emma and Somto, shared the smaller room, and the rest of us—me, Lizzie the secretary/treasurer, and Mr. Adamu, our agricultural consultant, who was meant to come in once a week but showed up behind his desk every day—split the larger room. That afternoon, Mr. Adamu was immersed in a newspaper, laughing and repeating unintelligible phrases, and I wanted to hit him.

Lizzie walked to my desk.

'Three calls came in for you,' she said. 'Kojo, Vasily Farms, and Obi Majid. Also, Emma said to remind you of the review in two months.'

I wondered why we still bothered with reviews. Emma and Somto were practically friends of mine at this point, and they had nothing to say to me.

'Did Kojo leave a message?'

'He said he needed your advice and would call again tomorrow.' How cryptic. I was shocked to hear Obi's name. I had been thinking about him a lot. He said to call him at his office, and I wanted to return his call immediately, but privacy didn't come with our office.

'Hahaha! Bean sprouts,' Mr. Adamu exclaimed.

I would call Obi on my way back to the hospital from

a payphone, I decided, and instead plodded through paperwork and studied the accounts of three possible new farms. Mr. Adamu's chuckling was louder; Lizzie and I had learned to ignore him, but that probably only encouraged him. I liked Lizzie for the most part, since she minded her own business, but sometimes everything became a chore for her, especially if *I* was doing the asking.

I couldn't concentrate. The numbers on my financial sheets jumped into each other, and when I tried to read them out loud, Mr. Adamu's gruff voice was stiff competition. I watched time click away. At four, I picked up my keys and went to the General Post Office, where I found only one of three payphones working. Obi's deep voice was instantly soothing.

'Long time no speak,' he said. 'I was beginning to think I'd done something wrong.'

'It's been busy.'

'Same here. I've been travelling a lot. I hope it was okay to call your office.'

'Of course.'

Silence.

Then he said, 'Zaza, can I see you again?'

The right words.

'Well,' I said. 'Yes. Sure.'

'So when?'

'Let me call you back. I have to run some errands.'

Fantasies are meant to stay fantasies, and when they're made real, paraded right before you, they change; they morph into tangible objects you actually have to deal with.

You have to flip them over, consider them, weigh their benefits and detriments. I'd never had an affair. Yes, I'd fantasized about sleeping with many people over the course of my marriage, and I'd even had a few close shaves—for instance, working late one night when Somto tried to make a pass at me. I know that story might have ended differently if I were attracted to him. (Also, his wife was in the main building. Also, Somto chased anything without a Y-chromosome.) Obi, I wanted so badly. And now he was real. He wasn't a dream, he was real, breathing temptation.

Back in the hospital, Dr. Mamby was in the lab and he and a technician were embroiled in a bitter argument about Mrs. Saturday's family history. Dr. Mamby said Mrs. Saturday was first cousins with former president Longman, and the technician was incredulous, but said if it was the truth, then Mrs. Saturday was a wicked woman, that she'd allow her husband to overthrow her own family member.

'Ah, Zahra,' Dr. Mamby said when he noticed me hovering. He stretched his arms above his head and turned to the technician. 'No lie. They're related by blood. Miss Wonder Woman, come into my office?' He picked up a grey manila folder and strode out of the lab. I braced myself for bad news. Was I cancerous? Whatever I had, would it give me enough time to make sure Kojo became a solid man? Theo had lived without his mother, and while he'd turned out well adjusted, I know it's only because his father was no-nonsense. I couldn't say with confidence that Theo would do the same with Kojo. Also, the thought of Kojo growing up without me around just pulled at my heartstrings.

I watched Dr. Mamby's short, gnomish body and pictured him at home with his wife. She probably dwarfed him. He had me lie down on the twin bed in his office. I closed my eyes and listened to him shuffle pages.

'So far,' said Dr. Mamby, 'we can't detect anything. It's not malaria. You're not pregnant or HIV-positive. You will have to come back next week for the other test results. But I can say, without a shadow of doubt, that there's nothing physically wrong with you.'

'The headaches? I've been throwing up.'

'Zahra,' he said and paused. 'Sometimes taking time off clears the mind and body. Tell me, what's going on at work? Everything okay with the husband?'

I couldn't believe it. I sat up. The green ceilings lent a pallid glow to his doctor's coat.

'Dr. Mamby, you, of all people, should not patronize me. Are you telling me this is all in my head? I'm not a mental case.'

He said nothing. Then, after I'd stared him down, he added, 'I'd suggest talking to an ophthalmologist. For the headaches and auras, sometimes it's eye-related.'

I didn't even bother asking him for a referral. I kept my tongue firmly pressed between my teeth. I didn't want to say anything to ruin our relationship—he was the only doctor I trusted—but I left the hospital fuming. His asking about Theo was unnerving because it could be connected. But if there was physically nothing wrong with me, why did I feel like the world was crashing? I knew my body well, and it was failing.

The city didn't have any parks, any spaces one could slink into to hide and cry. The only green space I knew of was tucked under the Doctor's armpit. I needed a quiet safe place, and a confidante, someone who wouldn't belittle what I was going through. I took Obi up on his offer to see me.

We met at the Miracle Mile Resort, a run-down hotel where former president Longman used to meet his ministers. After the coup, Karamoh Saturday had made the place a no-go zone. It contained little coves sectioned off with dwarf palms, the perfect place to be incognito. Obi ordered us beers, and I told him about Dr. Mamby's diagnosis.

In the dim lighting I studied him. It felt like no time had passed at all. Back in school, when we went out, he would get me a Fanta, go chat with the kebab men, charm the socks off the bar ladies, and return with a plate of the best cuts of goat meat. I didn't have to do much with him. I could let him take charge of whatever situation we were in. And now, the man before me seemed calmer, less youthful, yet still in control. We ordered grilled snails, and when it seemed like the people in the kitchen were now going snail-foraging, Obi got up to investigate. He came back with a heaped plate.

'I'm sorry about our last conversation,' he said. 'I didn't think I'd get so melancholy. When you left, I knew I'd blown it.'

'Blown what?' I asked.

'I don't know, Zaza. I was hoping you'd stay longer and that we could properly catch up.'

It wasn't just about catching up. Those weren't the words I wanted, and it was annoying that we were both being coy. Weren't we both adults?

'Obi, just say what's on your mind.'

'I haven't been able to stop thinking about you,' he said. 'I know it's easy to say our shared history will always connect us, which it will, but I really can't get you out of my mind. It's almost childlike, the fixation my mind's had on you.'

'I'm married.' I don't know if this was said out of duty or as a disclaimer. *But you knew I was married, Obi.*

'As I'm well aware. I just thought … I don't want you to act on it or anything. I'm just putting it out there because it's been sitting on me. And, of course, I wanted to apologize for my sullenness. I get that way once in a while, ever since … Look, I know I'm not the best person to be around then.'

'Let's go to your house,' I said.

It was like sliding into a pair of old moccasins. At first it felt funny, like almost too perfect a fit, and with perfect the only way left to go is down. Then I let myself settle into the familiar—everything felt the same despite the weight gain (on Obi's part) and the aging. With Obi, I lost myself completely. I didn't worry about my belly fat, about how I smelled, about how I moved. We just dissolved into our own universe, one with absolutely no rules, just laughter and comfort and silliness.

'Exactly what is your problem with Theo?' he asked me one day, my nipple pinched between his fingers.

'That came out of the blue. Doesn't feel like the right time to—'

'No. I need to know that you have a legit reason for doing this.' He flicked at my nipple, gently.

'I don't know,' I mouthed.

'Seriously, Zaza. You've thought about this.'

I had and I hadn't. I'd thought about my marriage not working and not being attracted to Theo anymore, but I hadn't yet sunk my teeth into everything. What was wrong with Theo? Maybe it was that, while we'd built our own world, we'd never really found that synergy to make it mind-blowing. I found him too serious. He took the world too seriously, and I could never lose myself within his rigid walls. Another theory I toyed with was that Obi was my true love come back to me, if such a thing existed, although I didn't want to admit that, even to myself.

'We're different,' I said. 'And I know people make those differences work, but this is horrible … Even the sound of him clearing his throat in the morning irks me.'

'Whatever you say, Zaza. You're running both shows.'

When my headaches worsened, I felt that I deserved every ounce of pain for what I was doing to Theo and to our family.

CHAPTER TWENTY-FOUR

THE DAILY POST

Monday, February 3, 1997 | We are the news! | Since 1952

Doctors and Young Ladies by Theo Avoka

I met with Courtney and her friends about two months after our encounter at the American ambassador's house, after I'd committed to working for the Doctor. Even though she was being mysterious about our meeting, my first conversation with her had awoken a sort of mad euphoria in me, so I accepted her invitation. It's hard to explain this euphoria, but the best explanation I can proffer is that she exuded an essence of youth that incited a foolish kind of optimism even in the heart of an old fox such as myself. A kind of excitement I hadn't felt in a long time.

Courtney invited us to her house in East Fair, a part of town noted for its schools that kept out locals, flashy cars, and scotch-drinking expats. I never had any reason to go to East Fair, and as I did that day I had very few expectations of the meeting. Courtney's house, with its mahogany French windows and terracotta roofing, looked more like it belonged on an island than in our little West African country.

Three others sat in her living room, which smelled citrusy. And I thought it was how she planted the optimism bug in me, through smell. The scent was light and fruity and made me think of the first time I fell in love.

I was twelve, spending the holidays in my father's village. I'd had my eye on a twenty-year-old woman we called Sister Afia. I didn't tell anyone about my crush and didn't know if the other boys were as intrigued as I was by her. She was not slim or fat, but her chest and backside were so perfectly globular I didn't know which I'd choose if a gun were cocked to my head. One day I saw Sister Afia all dressed up in a lace dress and white gloves. She looked so angelic, I just had to have her hold me. As she ambled down the path that would lead her out of the village, I ran and flung myself onto the red soil in a perfectly staged fall. I was surprised when she scooped me up into her lap and rubbed my head, occasionally pressing it to her chest. She smelled like fresh lemons. Later, when rumours went around the village that my father had had his way with her, I refused to believe them. The smell of Courtney's home, the suppleness of her features, brought back the memory of being massaged by Sister Afia's delicate hands.

The three others in Courtney's place were a man called Diouf, one called Zibrim, and a Miss Olympio. Most of you already know what happened to William Sangare, then using his pseudonym of Diouf. He looked nondescript, which I suppose is what allowed him to return to the country without getting noticed. His hair was an inch overgrown, tufts of grey sprouted from his ears and mid-brow, features which would lend another a semi-distinguished air or at least make him memorable. But William Sangare could be passed over in a room, over and over again. Zibrim was equally unimpressive, with a nervous handshake and sun-bleached, threadbare clothes. Only the women inspired confidence: Miss Olympio was a petite, pretty woman who seemed competent. Altogether, though, something about the group felt uncooked, yet I tried to be as civil as possible.

'I'm glad you could make it today,' Courtney said, settling on a cowhide pouf. She wasted no time in letting me know why I was there. She and her friends wanted to get the International Criminal Court to try Doctor Karamoh Saturday for crimes against humanity. My role: to find evidence. Letters, faxes, books he was reading. Anything that would create enough of a paper trail to open up an investigation.

William Sangare aka Diouf had served in the army with Karamoh Saturday, and had helped him organize the coup. 'I was his right-hand man,' he later said to me. He went into self-exile in 1983 because he and the Doctor stopped seeing eye to eye. He was granted political asylum in America, but decided to return after the elections. Miss Olympio was getting her PhD in political science, studying how revolutions start. The Doctor executed her father when he came to power. Zibrim was a journalist. Extremely stupid, was my initial thought. But Courtney assured me he was there to bring perspective.

The meeting was short. Then, after everyone left, Courtney told me to stay behind. To feel out my thoughts, she said.

'What makes you think I want to have anything to do with this?' I said. 'I could go straight to the Doctor and have you arrested. This is ridiculously stupid. Excuse my honesty.'

Not smiling, she said, 'You could do that but you won't. I

took a big risk inviting you over, and I know that even if you choose not to join us, you're not going to give us away.'

'That's presumptuous.'

'I know all about your past. You'd be surprised about some things.'

'Well, if you were thorough with your homework you'd find that I have nothing against Karamoh Saturday. Besides, there's not much to read about me.'

'You'd be surprised,' Courtney said again, fluffing the pillows that had been squashed behind Diouf. 'Your father was Minister of the Interior. He was executed a few years before Saturday's coup. Of course there are files and files on you.'

'You picked me out of the crowd at the American Embassy,' I said. 'You already knew about me before we met?'

'You could say that.'

'What are you?'

'That's not important.'

'I don't think I can help you.'

Courtney was quiet. She stared at me for a long time, then said, 'All right.' She didn't beg, didn't ask me to keep what I'd heard secret, she just thanked me for my time.

I left her place totally confused. Should I report them to the Doctor, even though I actually believed he had to account for the atrocities he committed in the eighties? If I did, I would be made a hero of the nation. I was in a real pickle. I never thought any part of me would want fame or notoriety, but there I was, trapped. Either way, this was my big chance to do something: to prove to my dead father that I could be great, too; that I could make the wrongdoers pay;

to show Zahra that I could be more than the man she wanted me to be. For the first time in my life, a proper door was being opened for me.

CHAPTER TWENTY-FIVE

Family Time

I couldn't just accept Dr. Mamby's claims that my symptoms were in my head. The headaches hadn't subsided, my vision was making an impressionist painting of the world, I could hardly eat, and I was feeling highly unattractive. I needed a second opinion.

The day before I went back to the Teaching Hospital, I stood in the bathroom of Obi's master bedroom, where he'd installed a bright light fixture above the mirror that I called the truth-teller. I reached forward and pulled on the light's string. My whole body—moles, scratches, and all—lay before me. My face looked the same, my breasts were flatter than they'd ever been, though still bulbous at the tips, still large-nippled, and my belly hadn't lost its fat after I gave birth to Kojo. My hips were smaller than they'd been earlier in the year. Before England, I was rail-thin, but when I came back my hips had thankfully filled out. Under the truth-teller that day I found myself sickeningly boyish. Minutes later, when Obi pawed at my breasts, I told him my headache was worse. He lay back on his side of the bed (we'd already begun to form routines on whose side was where) and pulled my body to his chest. I was beginning to lie to him, too.

The Teaching Hospital, teeming with sickness and death, was the last place I wanted to be. I sat in the ophthalmologist's chair, my hands shaking as I stared at an eye chart: a blue-and-red network of threads, crossing a sea of orange, which I found both terrifying and inspiring. The ophthalmologist dilated my eyes, making the world a rainy day. I told her about my vision problems and winced as she pressed her latex-covered fingers on my eyeballs and shone piercing light onto them. After half an hour of letting me wait, she told me she couldn't find anything wrong with my eyes.

'But with your symptoms,' she said, 'I suggest you get a brain scan as soon as you can. They are expensive and the wait list is long, but you look like you have connections.'

'Do I have cancer?' I blurted out, too nervous to respond to how politically incorrect she'd just been, too nervous to express how I didn't appreciate being tossed from one doctor to the next, and too nervous to say my connections did nothing for me.

'It may be a growth pressing on your optic nerve. But I can't make that kind of diagnosis.'

'Where do I do this? How much am I looking at?'

'I'll link you with that department. And make an appointment sooner rather than later.'

What would you do if you were handed a death sentence? True, I hadn't received mine yet, but all along I'd known something had gone wrong in my body and had been too afraid to face it. I had to start being honest with the people I cared about the most. I rounded up the family to deliver the bad news, or the possibility of it. I told Theo to pick up Kojo from school (he had a day off) and take us to the beach, just like the old times. Theo fussed about driving *all* the way to Kojo's school and then *all* the way to the beach, and the only way I could coerce him was making it seem as if this was the first of many mini-vacations to come. The next one would be just the two of us.

Kojo was chatty on the drive to the beach. He told us about how the headmistress of a rival school was involved in a scandal. First, the woman had taken money from a parent to let a boy into the school, and then she'd accepted more money to slot the child into the top ten even though his grades were abysmal.

'I heard about that,' Theo said. 'Appalling. What people do these days for money.' He was doing something appalling, too, writing for the Doctor.

'We know the kid,' Kojo said. 'He played basketball against us. And he was very good. We all thought he was African-American.'

'Because he was good at basketball?' I asked.

'No, he's tall and he has this *look*.'

'What look?' I had to laugh.

'He looks fresh. And always has this faraway expression in his eyes. I can't explain it.'

Theo and I laughed.

We sped on the Beach Road, windows down, past kiosks with crude cartoons advertising treatments for diabetes, hypertension, cure-alls for every ailment under the sun. Would they have a cure for me? Billboards of the Doctor flew by, one of them so faded that his moustache looked white.

'The Doctor is something else,' Theo said. I guess the billboards were hard to miss. Sometimes, even if something was terribly obvious, I thought I was the only one who noticed it. Part of my narcissism, I suppose.

'That's a first, Daddy,' Kojo said. 'I've never heard you say a good thing about the Doctor.'

'Say that again,' I said. 'Now the Doctor can do no wrong. What has His Highness done that's something else?'

'I'm still figuring him out, but the man *is* fascinating. Will you two let me land? You know how superstitious everyone from my village is. Same with the Doctor. He says when he was a boy he broke his arm after falling from a tree. He stayed in bed for a week, sweating, until the medicine man set it. It's funny that the same thing happened to me.'

This anecdote had been repeated so often, each time with a different embellishment. Sometimes Theo's father found him in the grass, other times, the medicine man was the one who sensed the fall happening and rushed over to find him in the grass.

'The Doctor stretched out his arm to me. I swear it was scarless. You couldn't tell it had ever been broken. He then says the medicine man gives him these leaves to prevent him from getting hurt ever again, and since then, he's had a clean bill of health, hasn't been hurt, and hasn't had malaria. Nothing can touch him. Then he says he will show me. He calls Pape—his assistant. Tells him to bring a razor blade, a fresh one. At this point I'm doing my best to protest. It's okay, I believe you, sir. That kind of thing. Even though, of course I wanted to see him cut himself and not bleed.

'Pape brings a fresh pack of razors, the Doctor unfolds the packaging and hands me the blade. Asks me to cut him. To stick this sharp thing in him. I'm holding the blade, saying, I'm sorry, sir, I really can't do this. The Doctor is screaming 'Cut me! Cut me!' and so I jab the blade into his forearm and of course blood comes gushing out and the Doctor swears and gives me the look of death. Luckily Pape has the presence of mind to have gauze and cotton wool on hand, and disinfects the cut. Needless to say I was sent off early. But can you imagine?'

'What a madman,' I said. 'Of course he would get cut, the fool.'

'I was hoping he would be right.'

'Was his blood red?' Kojo asked.

'You're so silly,' I said.

Theo laughed and said, 'So much material to write my book with.'

'Tell us the horror stories,' Kojo said. 'Is it true that he only eats raw meat? Or that he sleeps in a coffin?'

'Some of these stories are so ridiculous,' Theo said. 'Surely you don't believe them. Do you, Kojo?'

'Leave the child alone,' I said.

'Well, I've seen him eat. Real food. But as to the other rumour, I have no evidence to prove or disprove it. I actually have no horror stories for you.'

As we pulled into the Beachcomber's Resort, just before midday, Kojo asked what the occasion was. I had to think fast because I could sense them both focusing their attention on me. This wasn't the time to break the news.

'What's wrong with us spending time together?' I said. 'Last I checked we were still a family, and that's what families do: spend time together.'

Theo rented out three chaises longues and a giant umbrella, and we headed to the beach. The sand burned my bare feet, but it felt good. The beach wasn't as pristine as I'd hoped, though. Ice-cream wrappers were scattered all over the sand and crabs scuttled in and out of evaporated-milk tins. The muzzle of a toy gun had been stuck in the sand. A rotary phone lay a few metres ahead of me and I wondered whether a jilted lover had come all the way here to dispose of it.

I slipped into my bathing suit and, peeking through the slits in the palm-fronded enclosure that had been provided for changing, I watched Kojo and Theo. Kojo dug out a hole in the sand, and Theo stuck the umbrella into it. Suddenly I wished Obi were with me, and I felt bad that, given a choice, I would honestly rather be with my lover than with my family. I sucked in my stomach and walked out. They were still trying to get the umbrella stable, and I still couldn't break the news.

The first time I saw the ocean was with my father, when I was eight or nine. We had driven for two days to get from the north to the south, first taking a ferry and then we'd twisted and turned on laterite roads pocked with a million potholes. Mma never made those trips with us. My father was meeting various rice distributors, and I spent most of the time sitting in receptionists' rooms, fending off questions about my mother's existence and then requests to put in a good word for them if my father desired a new or second wife. To make up for what had become a boring trip, my father took me to see the ocean. The sand was slightly off-white and bordered by beautiful coconut trees that provided shade for beach-goers. And the sea! I remember describing it as filled with all the colours of the world: blue and green and even red. Yet as beautiful as it was, I found it frightening in its infinity. It was like the sky, like space, like God.

This sea was light grey, calm, and almost waveless. I put in a big toe, then my whole foot. It wasn't warm, but I splashed water on my arms, belly, and back and then threw myself into it. Once I overcame the shock of cold water, I felt better. I needed that shock. Like the sand under my feet, the water was telling my nerves they were still alive, in spite of whatever was growing in my body. I wanted to be able to forget, to forgive myself for everything I was doing to my family, everything I was doing with Obi. I hoped the sea would cleanse me, but it was too cold to linger in. I shook off the water and went to lie on the chaise by Theo. Kojo was digging another hole.

I tried to comb through work—anything to delay my telling Kojo and Theo that I was sick. Halfway through reading, my eyes drifted to the cloudless sky, shaded every so often by birds flitting crazily by. For a minute I could forget everything and stare at endless blue. I drifted off into a doze, and when I woke up Theo was staring at me.

'What? Was I drooling? I drool. So what?' I said, wiping the corners of my mouth.

'You're so beautiful,' Theo said.

I couldn't remember the last time he'd said that to me. It was bemusing.

'Thank you.' He seemed to be regarding me with eyes so tender I wanted to throw something at him. Maybe that telephone I saw when we walked in. He made me feel bad with his affection. He hadn't done anything wrong to me and I had gone and had an affair. Then I conveniently remembered a conversation I'd had with Anna a couple of days before. She told me she'd seen Theo with the same woman on two separate occasions. The first at the woman's photo exhibition, then when she was shopping for a rug for her living room. I hadn't encouraged Anna to give me details because it seemed unlikely that we'd both be cheating, but mostly because I would have caught him. He would do something to slip. For instance, he had remained friends with the girlfriend before me, and apparently used to go to her house to eat, sometimes before he came to my place. Then one day, when I'd surprised myself and all around by cooking a decent meal, he called me by her name. He broke down and confessed those visits, which I promptly put an end to. Theo wasn't wired to cheat, I was sure of this.

'Anna tells me she's seen you around town with some white woman,' I said, and watched for his reaction.

'We're doing work for the Doctor,' he said.

'I thought he loathed white people.'

'Haven't you heard all the talk about his white mistress?'

'Is that her?'

'I don't think so, but really, we need to lead more interesting lives and stop peddling gossip.'

I was sure that there was nothing sexual happening with the woman, but in the way his voice trailed off, I knew he wasn't telling me the entire truth. And after that exchange I decided to keep my illness to myself.

'I can't tell you some aspects of work,' he said, as if he'd read my thoughts. 'This is the Doctor we're talking about, after all. I have to protect you.' I pursed my lips and nodded. 'Is the water cold?' he asked. I shook my hand—*comme ci, comme ça*—and he headed for the sea.

Theo swam gracefully and went farther than I would let myself go. Kojo plonked himself on the chaise next to mine.

'Can I ask you something? It's a bit embarrassing.'

'Shoot.'

'How did you know when you were in love?'

'You want to know what love feels like? Huh. I guess I don't think it's in your heart at all. It's more a feeling you get deep in your belly. Right here at the base of your stomach, almost like an immense wall of pressure is pushing against your pelvis and it can overwhelm you, flood you with wild emotions. When you feel like you want to hold someone forever and, as cheesy as it sounds, never let go. Or at other times you want to smother them to death because they're the only ones who can get under your skin. That, my child, is what I think love is.'

I'd thoroughly confused the boy. I'd confused myself. I couldn't tell if I was talking about Theo or Obi.

'Close your mouth, Kojo! This thing you do is going to stick.'

'Sorry, I was thinking about what you said.'

'Why do you ask? Everything okay with Inaam?'

'Wait. How do you know?' Kojo said. Obi had told me, and we'd laughed at what an odd quadrangle we'd formed.

'Mother knows all. Aren't you going to swim?'

He said no and went back to his hole. He dug and dug, his long, skinny body as graceful as his father's. I watched Theo taking long strokes parallel to the horizon with a sense of freedom I desired. I stared at Kojo again. I wondered what would become of us.

CHAPTER TWENTY-SIX

Visitors

One month since English classes started, and Atsu has suffered days when she's felt like the teacher was talking to everyone but her, and experienced others when she's been on top of the world, like when she read her first sentence. She struggles with pronunciation and phonetics. The *th* sounds and *sh* sounds were and still are not easy for her. But what she's found the most difficult is life outside the classroom—her relationships. Since they went out together, she hasn't talked to Nasar or to Ndeye. Her social life went from blossoming to non-existent in one night. In class, trying her very best to ignore Nasar hasn't been easy. The first class after the dance, he came over and asked her how Ndeye was doing, which only added kerosene to her anger. Instead of asking about her health, he was asking about her friend. She eyed him and, for the first time, sat in the back. She's stayed there ever since, which is also why she's struggling to understand what's going on.

After a surprisingly good class, Atsu's on her way out when Nasar stops her.

'Stranger,' he says.

She ignores him, but doesn't act fast enough, and soon

they are the only two left behind. She tries to squeeze out through the gap between him and the door, but he moves nimbly and blocks her way. She tries to weasel out the other way, but the same thing happens.

'Nasar, let me go,' she says, trying to see if there's anyone else in the courtyard. Beyond the door is a bluish silence. She can hear the night market, but all those people are outside the school walls. 'If you don't move, I'll scream.'

'Atsu, what's wrong?' he says, grabbing her arm.

'Don't touch me.' Their lack of communication seems to have had only one effect on her: she's constantly thinking of him.

'What happened? I thought we were friends and then you stopped talking to me. Did I do something wrong?'

His voice is so quiet it stops time and leaves the two of them facing each other. His words are making her wonder if her anger was unwarranted. He is right; he really hasn't done anything wrong. She leans against the wall of the classroom, feeling the substance of the concrete, of the room, of the whole building, without whose support she would fall. She's ashamed of her behaviour, petty and ungrateful, since he's been nothing but nice to her since their first encounter.

'So?' Nasar says, unblocking the door, which he might as well have filled with cement, because now, out of shame, she can't move.

'Sorry,' she says, stealing a glance at his face. 'I can be very stubborn about my beliefs. I shouldn't have come to the club.' His eyes are looking down at her feet. His nostrils flare ever so much, and his lips are slightly turned up. She doesn't understand the expression on his face. Suddenly he reaches forward, it seems to kiss her.

'What's wrong with you? What are you doing?' She can't ignore the growing warmth in her chest and between her legs. She likes this attention, but she's also scared to death.

'I'm sorry,' Nasar says.

She should tell him to leave her alone, but that's not what her body wants.

'You have to do this the right way,' she says finally, exhaling. She feels as if she's been sent around the world and back, but she's happy with her answer. She scuttles out of the classroom, hurries past the line queuing for fried plantain, and stops where her lorry will pick her up. Her heart is racing, and when she turns around, she's disappointed that Nasar isn't right behind her.

The bell rings, startling Atsu as she's hanging Mr. Avoka's shirts to dry. Washing has become one of the most relaxing activities for her. Annoyed at the interruption, she wipes her hands on her dress and heads for the gate.

'Who's there?'

'Me.' Ndeye's voice.

Atsu's relieved and happy Ndeye is being the bigger person, and swings the gate open to find Ndeye standing there with Nasar. She doesn't know where to rest her eyes—definitely not on Nasar, so she glares at Ndeye.

'I'll leave you two alone,' Ndeye says.

'No, don't go,' Atsu says, pulling the gate closed so Nasar

doesn't see the house. She's embarrassed that he's seen her look like a housegirl, that he'll put one and two together and realize she *is* a housegirl, though that fact is probably not news to him if he tracked down Ndeye.

'What are you doing here?'

'Doing it right.'

Ndeye turns around without another word and heads back to the Freemans's house. Women! Just when she thought Ndeye was being the bigger person.

She wipes her hands on her dress and debates whether to let him in. Her stomach twists in knots because she knows if she does, it will be the start of something and she won't be in control anymore. Just that seemingly insignificant act of letting him in through the gate could, and probably will, disrupt her life.

'Aren't we going in?' he says and grins.

She inhales deeply, then says, 'I'm not one of your easy girls.'

'You don't have to let me in. I promise I'll do this right. Let me take you out after class one day. Tell me when you're ready.'

He tries to hug her but Atsu holds her body rigidly, and he backs down. As he disappears around the corner of the Freemans's wall, she shuts the gate. It wouldn't have killed her to offer him a glass of water. Basic decency, Mama taught her. When someone visits, you offer water.

The bell rings. It's early evening, and both Madam and Mr. Avoka are uncharacteristically at home. Maybe they were expecting a guest. When she answers the gate, she almost screams in fright. Mama is standing there in a red, blue, and yellow cloth (one of her Sunday bests), her breasts powdered, an orange scarf atop her head.

'I've come to get you,' says Mama. Atsu's not sure if this is a joke or a dream.

'What are you doing here?'

'I would have done it earlier. But I had to save for this trip.'

Mama, who seldom leaves the village. Atsu laughs. This is a dream. She leans against the gate and pushes her palm into a nail poking through the gate. It hurts. She's very much awake.

'We can catch the last bus back and be fine. Get your things.'

'No,' Atsu says, beginning to feel hot and cold. In a way, a big part of her is flattered—this must be Mama's way of showing love, fighting for her. Yet this is the last thing she was expecting. She'll have to turn her away, her own mother. 'I'm not going back.'

'Ah Atsu, at least offer me water,' says Mama. 'I've been travelling.'

God, why do you test your children? Atsu thinks. She can't leave her mother outside, but what is she going to tell her bosses? She grabs the red-and-white jute bag from Mama and leads her in. It's heavy, filled with metal objects clinking against one another. They walk through the garden and then into the kitchen, where Atsu offers her a cup of water.

In the living room, to Atsu's disappointment, sits Madam, not Mr. Avoka.

'Who was that?'

'Madam, please,' says Atsu, 'my mother's here from the village.'

'What a surprise,' Madam says. Her tone seems genuine. 'Bring her in.'

Mama is taking in everything. The blue-tiled walls of the kitchen, the fridge, the electric stove, the sleek frying pan, the tap and sink. Now she must understand why Atsu doesn't want to come back. Village living is time travel to the eighteenth century. Atsu impatiently shows her into the living room.

'Mrs. Akakpo,' Madam says, getting up to shake Mama's hand. 'We had no idea you were coming. Welcome. Let me get my husband.'

Now Madam is being too sweet, and when she returns with Mr. Avoka, he is just as cordial, if a bit flustered. He must have figured out Mama is here to take Atsu back.

'So what brings you to the city?' Madam asks. 'Please, sit. Atsu must be happy to see you.'

'Business,' Mama says. She can't meet Madam's eyes. How the formidable lion has fallen! Mama intimidated? It's not possible. Why didn't she tell Madam the truth? Or was that the truth? Mr. Avoka asks how the boys are, Mama says fine. The room goes quiet after all possible inquiries have been made, and Atsu begins to feel uncomfortable and embarrassed. Mama is out of place in the room, seated behind the dining table, her orange scarf too bright, her feet dusty.

'Where are you staying?' Madam asks.

'I'm catching the lorry back tonight,' says Mama.

'No, no, no.' Mr. Avoka leans against the living-room wall. 'The way these drivers behave at night is atrocious.'

Madam agrees. 'Our son's room is empty. Atsu, you'll prepare it for her?'

Atsu can't believe they're being so generous, and she's confused about her mother's motives. 'She'll sleep with me,' she says. Her tone is snappy, but Mama must be working some juju on her employers.

'I'll drive you to the station in the morning,' Mr. Avoka says, and returns to his room.

'Why are you really here?' Atsu asks her mother in the privacy of her room. Her strength must come from God because in the past she'd never have dared ask Mama a question like that.

'Business,' Mama repeats. 'I came to buy farm tools. They are cheaper here.'

'And what about taking me back to the village?'

'Ah, these people have poisoned my own child against me, so what can I do?'

Atsu rolls her eyes before she can stop herself. Her mood is so destroyed she turns over on her side and stares at the wall. She wishes she could tell Mama about her classes, about this man who's pursuing her, and get Mama's advice. But she can't even bring herself to have a normal conversation with the woman. So they'll both lie there, each staring at some spot on opposing walls, and then at dawn, Mama will return to the village without Atsu.

CHAPTER TWENTY-SEVEN

Sed Games

Inaam keeps cancelling our math sessions and our dates. These dates usually consist of us standing in front of the dining hall, catching up, and sneaking in hugs or holding hands when no one is looking. Serious Open Display of Affection. But lately it doesn't feel like we're boyfriend and girlfriend. I have a few theories, and the strongest is that she's scared I'm stealing her thunder. Here's why: for the first time in the history of the ISS, of the world, ladies and gentlemen, Inaam got an answer wrong in math class and guess who got it right? It's not like I raised my hand or anything, but after Inaam got the answer wrong Mrs. Diouf called on me and I said the right thing. It was a probability lesson. I think I'm just naturally gifted at probabilities and hypothetical situations. Inaam glowered at me like I'd done something horrible to her. What did she expect me to do? Act dumb?

In front of me is my biology textbook. I'm on the same page I've been looking at since lunch ended and siesta began. My plan was to read through notes before sports, but that's not happening. I'm distracted.

Kunle groans in his sleep, then wakes up. He's dating a middle two girl whom all the boys have been drooling over. She's cute, but I don't know how she got into the ISS, considering the exams and interviews we jumped through. Obviously her parents have money. I'm happy she's around, because since she came into his life he's cut me some slack.

Kunle slurs, 'What are you doing for the Sed Games?'

'The what?'

'Saturday's games?'

Groan. How did I forget? Every school in the country must, once a year, throw these Olympic-style games from Ancient Egypt. Somebody of importance from the government is going to be there, and our parents, too.

'I'm doing the javelin, high jump, tug of war, and the 100-metre relay,' Kunle says.

'Don't we just have to pick one sport?' I ask, half-wishing he could do mine for me. Every student has to take part in the games, and now I'm going to be stuck with stupid long-distance running, and goodness knows I don't have the lungs for that, or annoying tug of hoop, which is the stupidest game ever invented. No disrespect to the Ancient Egyptians.

'How are you going to prepare for your midterm exams?' I ask.

'I'll worry about that on Sunday night,' he says. 'Besides they're midterms, not final exams.' Failing is a poor-person problem, I suppose.

We have to be on the field from morning to evening, chasing each other like moronic monkeys, flinging sharp objects in the air, and throwing our bodies in ways I don't believe our bodies were meant to be treated. All this to gain points for our dorms. The dorm with the most points wins something—what, we do not know. The big-shot government person will reveal the prize at the end of the day.

The football field is crowded with boys and girls and teachers, and it's not even the day of the Sed Games. The teachers are talking to themselves and ignoring us, and boys are happily helping girls do the high jump. I scan the field and see Inaam and Ngozi. Inaam, armed with a javelin in her right hand, shoots forward and lunges the thing and it goes an impressive distance. I thought we could suck together. I walk to Mr. Ba and Miss Bola and I'm told all that's left for picking is the 6,000-metre run, or wrestling.

D-Day. I actually woke up at dawn, hauled myself over to the field, and timed how long it'd take me to run a kilometre: ten minutes. Ridiculous. What ten minutes means is that, at best I'd be on the field for an hour, at worst, what could be worse than an hour of running? I'm walking with Kunle to the field, and he's stopped at least four times to do jumping jacks and run on the spot. You'd think I'd mimic him, given that he knows what he's doing, but really. Really? His parents aren't coming, and for the first time I feel sorry for him. I've actually never met his parents. A driver picks him up and when his father visits, Kunle is back in the room in fifteen minutes, although not without a pair of new sneakers or a Chicago Bulls basketball jersey. Kunle is taking part in a thousand and one games and there'll be no one here to see him win gold.

We're almost at the gate to the field when Inaam runs to me, panting. She scowls at Kunle and says, 'I need to talk to you, privately.' Kunle walks away.

'Is it important? I need to concentrate. To prepare for my marathon.'

'Kojo, it's not a marathon,' she says and opens her eyes wide at me, pushing her glasses up.

'I know, but it feels like one to me, and I have to …'

'I might be going back to London,' she says. 'We're not sure yet. My dad is interviewing for this job there and he's in the final round. He says it's highly likely we'll be going. And that it'll be easier for me to get into Oxford or Cambridge from a secondary school there.'

'You're leaving?' Is my voice cracking?

'I know. I don't want to go back, but there's no one to stay with here.'

'Is that why you haven't been helping me with homework?'

'No, of course not,' she says and looks away. My theory was right. It's because I'm stealing her shine. If she's so worried, it means that the exam on Monday is probably going to be good. I'm better than I used to be. 'Can I still be your girlfriend when I move?'

'If you move,' I say. 'I need to get ready, Inaam.'

She runs off and I look at my palms, now filmed with sweat. I wipe them down my shorts and move onto the field, where groups are gathered. Parents are sitting on plastic chairs arranged by the field. I see *the* Theo and *the* Zahra, then I recognize Inaam's father, currently my least-favourite person. Because of him I'm losing Inaam.

Miss Bola blows her whistle and Mr. Ba wields a megaphone. Why do all the teachers in this school have names that start with *B*?

'Good day,' Mr. Ba's voice crackles. 'Welcome to our first annual Sed Games at the International Secondary School. We would first like to acknowledge the Member of Parliament of Kita West, Honourable Mr. Saidu. We are most honoured at your presence. And then we welcome all the parents, the guardians, and caretakers of these very talented children.' Mr. Ba never ceases to make me laugh, even when I feel like hurling out my insides. Miss Bola is twenty times more eloquent, but Mr. Ba's always the one doing the talking.

'In our Sed Games today, we are featuring high jumps, long jumps, shot puts, javelins, 100-metre dashes, relays, long distances, wrestlings. You name it, we have it. So without much further ado, I would like to introduce the honourable headmistress of our distinguished school, Mrs. Gertrude Bobole.'

Mrs. Bobole goes on for a little too long, by which time I'm beginning to feel like a roasted animal. Am I going to survive this?

First is the 100-metre dash, then the long jump, which Kunle wins for our house. I am so proud of him I actually throw my hands in the air and applaud. And somehow that makes me want to win, too. One by one people win and lose. And then, before I know it, it's time for the 6,000-metre run. Lined up are five of us. I don't want to look at anybody's face to discourage myself. I've heard rumours that two dorms are tied at first place in the boys' games and I'm sure our dorm is one of them, but I won't think about it; I don't need the pressure. Now it's just me and the track. Mr. Ba's voice screeches, 'Ready, steady, GO!' I start fast but remember that I'm circling the track a good fifteen times, so I slow down and two racers overtake me. I can hear faint voices, faint conversations. Is that Mummy telling me to speed up?

After I've done three loops around the field I'm still in third place. I thought I'd be last. I peep at the parents' area and Mr. Theo Avoka, looking stiff and unimpressed, is sitting by Inaam's father, my mortal enemy. I look behind me and another racer is gaining speed. My muscles tense up, the gravel under my feet crunches non-stop.

As we get into our tenth loop, people gather around a racer ahead of me, so I slow down as I approach them. The boy is lying on the ground, his face contorted in pain. People shove their hands at me, 'Go! Go!' And I continue, feeling bad that I have to go on. The other racer is half a field ahead. I try to keep that space between us on the eleventh, twelfth, and thirteenth laps. On the fourteenth, I am drained. I want to stop. Every part of my body aches. But I force myself, tell myself to increase my speed. I trip and fall. I hear a loud, collective 'Ohhh!' but pick myself up. I'm not in my body anymore. It's someone else's and I'm begging it to just keep on moving.

I'm catching up. The racer ahead turns around and gives me a menacing look, but I don't care. Another stumble, but my body keeps going. I'm an arm's length away, and we're maybe three metres from the finish line. He keeps turning to look at me, and that's the problem. He falls. He falls! And I'm at the finish line and I can't hear, not because of the crowd shouting, 'Kojo, Kojo, Kojo!' but because my heart is beating so loudly, my eardrums can't handle it. A whole crowd whooshes and descends on me. I feel all sorts of bodies sticking to my sweat.

The member of parliament says our Sed Games were the most organized he's seen in the country, and that the winners of the games receive washing machines and vouchers to Chez Madam, one of the most expensive restaurants in the country.

I walk to the parentals, and Inaam and her father come to join us. Inaam stands by me, slips her hand in mine, squeezes tight, and then lets go of it. She'd stopped showing me any affection, but now she does it around both our parents? Girls must like boys who win things. No wonder Kunle is popular.

'Congrats, Kojo,' Uncle Obi says and pats my back. Why is he with us?

'Kojo the star,' Daddy says.

'You made me so proud,' Mummy says.

'Your mother was quite the sprinter in school,' Uncle Obi says. 'We called her daddy-long-legs. You must take after her.'

'Obi!' says Mummy, and she looks away.

I look at Inaam and suddenly feel extreme sadness. I'm losing her. The happiest day of my life at the ISS is now bittersweet.

CHAPTER TWENTY-EIGHT

THE DAILY POST

Monday, March 3, 1997 | We are the news! | Since 1952

Unexpected Advice by Theo Avoka

My friend Zea invited Zahra and me over for dinner. When we were younger we lived for such events, sampling beverages he and his wife Mabel had brought back from one trip abroad or another. In those days Zahra and I made just about enough to take care of ourselves and a very young Kojo, so we lived vicariously through them, listening rapturously as they brought us up to speed on new art and films hot in Europe and the United States. Invariably the conversation would steer towards politics after we'd imbibed one too many drinks.

We hadn't come together in a while, mostly because Zahra said the whole thing was like pulling teeth. She had nothing in common with Mabel, and she didn't see the point in spending hours yapping and yapping and not coming up with anything concrete to effect change in the country. We'd always make some convenient excuse when they invited us over, reserving our visits to big celebrations, when other people would be present to act as a buffer for Zahra. On this occasion, I told Zahra it had become too obvious—Zea was, after all, my best friend.

Zahra and I schlepped over a basket of fruits and Mabel welcomed us with flutes of bubbly, plum-coloured liquid. 'Kir Royal,' she said, 'all the rage in Paris.' Zahra rolled her eyes as if to say, I told you so, pretentious. I couldn't tell if she genuinely disliked Zea and Mabel's ostentation or if theirs was the lifestyle she'd have wanted us to have. She did like the finer things in life.

Zea stuck a cigar in my pocket. When I visited them by myself, this was usually the point when he and I would retreat to his study, light up the cigars, and he'd show me something he'd read in the papers that had riled him. But this time we stayed in the living room, and he proceeded to flip through his expansive record collection. Zahra asked for upbeat music and Mabel excused herself and went to the kitchen. Zahra never followed Mabel the way most women did when they went to other people's houses. No matter where they were, the women I knew quickly jumped into the domestic role, helping the host lay a table, finish a salad dressing, or provide moral support by just being present. Zahra never did any of that. I'll be in the way, she said. I can't cook.

Mabel prepared a wonderful spread of *cocoyam* fufu and groundnut soup, complete with crabs, snails, dried river fish, and heaps of beef. Everything was deliciously flavoured, and I asked Mabel if she'd done everything herself—which I already knew—and that was apparently a big mistake.

'Yes, of course,' said Mabel. 'I leave the fufu-pounding to the girls, but the soup I won't have anyone touch. Even when we travel abroad, that one likes to have his fufu and soup. I'm telling you, I know where all the African markets in the major cities are located.'

Mabel hadn't worked a day in her life, hadn't been educated beyond secondary school, but carried herself with a rich woman's air and flair. Zahra would say, 'I like Zea. But that nouveau-riche wife of his, couldn't he do better?'

Zahra glared at me as Mabel went on to list the markets she'd frequented to find snails and crabs to make Zea's soup.

'In fact,' prattled Mabel, 'my father was even worse. I mean, sometimes the girls cook and Zea can tell the difference, but he won't not eat. Not my father. He wouldn't have anyone but my mother, not even his own children, cook for him. And my mother loved that. She used it to keep him in check, as you can imagine.'

Zahra barely touched her food, excused herself to go to the bathroom, and when she came back decided she and Zea should have a conversation, because clearly Mabel and I were excluding them from ours.

'Do you think this Karamoh guy is ever going to relinquish power?'

Zea laughed. 'Why don't we ask his right-hand man over here?' I said nothing. Then Zea bellowed: 'Never! He's going to hold on to power for dear life. And since he controls all the State institutions, he's going to make sure he wins every election.' He turned to me. 'Respectfully, your man is just like the rest of them: a power-hungry African dictator.'

I turned to Zahra. 'Why do you ask?'

'It seems to be the debate du jour everywhere I go. The office, farms, wherever. There's this feeling that the transition was a farce and nothing is going to change.'

'We did draw up a constitution,' I said. 'Each president will be given a two-term limit.'

'Avoka, you've always been too diplomatic and optimistic,' said Zea. 'The man is simply going to rewrite the constitution in his second term.'

'I don't think he'll last,' Mabel said. 'He's lost his military strength, which was what kept him in power. His boys are still around, but they can't do anything or we'll lose all our international funding.'

'I agree,' I said. 'Besides, the man is old. I get the sense that he'll want to retire in peace after the second term.'

'I still feel vestiges of the military era,' said Zahra. 'I honestly don't think much has changed. Ordinary people have more of a voice than before, but we have no power at all.'

'Isn't that power in itself?' I asked. 'Having a voice?'

Mabel announced that she'd baked a plantain cake for dessert and began to clear the table. I helped stack the dishes and took them to the kitchen as Zea and Zahra continued talking. I was placing the dishes in the sink when Mabel touched my back.

'You two are going through a rough patch,' she said, and I almost broke down crying. 'Just hang in there. We all go through this.'

'She's slipping away from me,' I said. 'And I don't know what to do.'

'This sounds simple, and it's always hard to put into practice, but people always want what they can't have. Give her plenty of space and she'll realize that she's taking you for granted.'

On the ride back home, I completely ignored Mabel's advice and asked Zahra why she was so sour, if it was because I'd complimented Mabel's soup. She shook her head and said she had no reason, and asked me just to drop the topic. And so I did.

CHAPTER TWENTY-NINE

Math Teacher

'And even though we hate to be losing her, we have to congratulate our own Inaam Majid for getting all As in her exams. She will be leaving for England to continue her education.' Bobole's voice.

So many things wrong with that sentence. Now it's officially official. But that's not the problem. We don't have to write our bloody exams until the end of the year. That sneaky girl must have known from day one that she was leaving, because you don't just study for and take exams overnight. That's why she's always been shifty. It's fine. I'll get a new girlfriend. I've seen some of the lower girls checking me out since the Sed Games. In fact, one group was blatantly talking about me as I walked by. I could ask one of them out. No big deal.

After we're dismissed from assembly my anger grows claws, really sharp talons. Who knew Inaam, 'the sweetest person' in the whole school, could be this sneaky? She could have told me she didn't want anything serious. I would have been fine with a casual thing. I'm so preoccupied with the Inaam thing that I don't realize how slowly I'm walking, and by the time I arrive in Mrs. Diouf's class she's already written an awful lot on the board.

I sit far, as far away from Inaam as possible, because I don't know what I'll do with my blood boiling this hot. I've bunched up my fists, ready to strike even Mrs. Diouf if she terrorizes me today.

'Who can tell me what seven factorial is?' Mrs. Diouf says.

Predictably, Inaam can answer the question, and two others. Why does she even care? She's already passed her exams. I do my best to block out her voice. And when she's done, from across the classroom, she turns to look at me. I don't smile, I don't frown. She doesn't exist.

'Kojo, before I forget,' says Mrs. Diouf suddenly, 'see me after class?'

That completely destroys my plans of asking to go to the sick bay because I might be running a fever. My forehead is cool against my palm, but the way things feel inside, I should have a temperature.

'Kojo, how would you go about solving this?' asks Mrs. Diouf.

I wasn't paying attention and I could say I don't know, but not in front of the evil girl, I won't admit that. On Mrs. Diouf's board is a ten with an exclamation mark dividing a five and another exclamation mark. The curse of the small class! I can't just disappear.

'Two?'

'I didn't ask for the answer,' she says. 'Come up and show us what you would do.'

You know what? I've just figured it out. Women are evil.

And they start learning their evil ways when they're thirteen, so by the time they are sixty, or however old Mrs. Dioufy is, tormenting boys is something they do with every breath. I take the chalk from her crusty, evil fingers and face the green board, and I feel all the stares burning into the back of my body. People are coughing, someone yawns. The horror—tears are building in my eyes. Today I don't need the humiliation. Wasn't Dioufy at assembly? Doesn't she know about me and Inaam? Isn't she supposed to be on top of the gossip on student relationships?

I turn to Mrs. Diouf. 'I'm sorry. I don't know how to do this.'

She grabs the chalk from my hand, disappointment so clear in her eyes. I've disappointed her so much that, she doesn't ask anyone else to come forward. She scribbles numbers, more exclamation points, and then says the answer is 30,240. What in tarnation?

After class I linger, ready for a talking-down. But Dioufy admits that she's heard about me and Inaam. Inaam told her she couldn't tutor me anymore, and she wanted to make sure I'd have help. If I was already feeling small at the beginning of the class, I am now a tiny red ant, ready to be squashed by a baby's foot.

'I want you to do well, Avoka,' Mrs. Diouf is going on. 'Let me know how I can help you. In fact, tell me how I can help you.' She puts her fat hands on my shoulders and stares at me like a mother hen.

'Okay,' I say.

'Tell me. Your exams are coming up and I know you're

a scholarship student, so it's important you do well. Your father has become a good friend, so I want to help you.'

When did they become good friends? Teachers can be such liars. Mummy is the one who came for Open Day. I suppose she'll say anything to encourage me.

'You know?' Mrs. Diouf says. 'Skip sports. I'll get permission for you to come to my house. We'll go over what we did in class today. You'll find it very interesting, not difficult.'

'It's fine. I don't need the extra help.'

'Don't be silly! Okay, let me rephrase. You are required to come to my house this afternoon instead of sports. You're here for academics first.'

Just as I'm walking out the gate Inaam corners me. Jezebel. The only thing I can think to do is turn back, but that will be silly. I have to descend the stupid hill with her. People start racing down because the sky's suddenly darkened above us, but I'm not going to speed up. Maybe Inaam will leave me alone.

'I want to talk to you, but can we walk faster?' she says, drops of rain plopping on us.

'Do what you want,' I say, focusing on the soaked shirts of the people running ahead. I glance at Inaam and notice her black bra underneath her wet shirt. She catches my eye. I shouldn't have looked, because now I'm sure she's thinking, poor Kojo still wants me.

'Why are you being mean?'

I stop, feeling the thick drops of water seeping into my hair, my skin, everywhere, then I bend down, unlace my sneakers, and tie them again.

'I didn't think we were going,' Inaam says. 'That's why I didn't tell you earlier.' I'm still on the ground, relacing my shoes, because this morning's anger is back. A burst of light flashes above, followed by a long, low rumbling. She rubs her arms.

'We'll get sick. Come on!'

'Just go. If you don't, I'll say something nasty. And I don't want to do that.'

She is drenched in rainwater and little rivulets run down her face into her clavicles and she looks so pathetic, but all I can feel is anger and pity, not for anyone but myself.

'I'm sorry Mrs. Bobole had to announce it in front of everyone,' she says.

'Inaam, go away.'

I look down the hill and almost everybody has arrived at the dining hall. By the time Inaam makes it down there, they'll be saying grace. And I'll loiter in five minutes later, looking so pitiful.

'I'm sorry, Kojo,' she says, still lurking.

I can't take it anymore, so I spring to my feet and march down, leaving her behind as the rain pounds harder. I want to look back and make sure she's okay, but I force myself to keep walking down. There's this itchy, biting feeling that's gripped my stomach and my insides. Am I crying?

By the time I get to Mrs. Diouf's, the sun is shining like it needs to compete with the rain from before. I knock on her door, an elaborate black rectangle with artificial flowers on it, and step back so I'm not right in her face when she answers. Her husband opens the door and shakes my hand.

'Avoka?' Mr. Diouf says. 'Jenny, you're right. Spitting image. Come in.'

Mr. Diouf is skinny and not much taller than me. Inside, Mrs. Diouf waddles over and instructs me to sit at her dining table. She disappears into another room and returns with a Fanta and biscuits. She smells like camphor, reminding me of Mma. Her husband sits down and stares at the TV and images of the Doctor. I can't hear any sound coming out of the TV screen.

'Look at him,' the man mutters under his breath. That must be pure hate right there. Kind of scary to watch. It's almost like in James Bond or one of those spy movies, when the evil character watches the hero and chuckles evilly while plotting. Not that Mr. Diouf is evil or that the Doctor is the hero.

Mrs. Diouf drags a chair close to mine and one by one she explains those exclamation point things. They're like puzzles. I look on the wall above the dining table. There's a picture of Mrs. Diouf, her husband in military fatigues, and two daughters I've never seen. In America, is the story around school. I watch Mr. Diouf still staring at the TV screen and Mrs. Diouf shuffling back and forth between the dining room and kitchen and wonder if this is what life is like for the parents when I'm not around. Just spending all the time with each other and watching boring documentaries? It has to be more exciting than that.

'Your father is a great man,' Mr. Diouf says suddenly.

'Let us work, Willy!' Mrs. Diouf says.

'No, I have to tell the boy.'

That came out of nowhere. I nod and hope Mrs. Diouf will release me. Strange to hear him say these things about Daddy. It is surprising in a rather unpleasant way.

'And since you look so much like him, I'll say you're also destined for great things,' the man goes on. Mrs. Diouf sucks her teeth and writes down more problems for me to work on.

Later that night falling asleep is impossible, and as Kunle snores I hear Mr. Diouf's voice saying how Daddy is great. When I do sleep, I see Daddy looming above everyone. He becomes a huge man and Mummy and I are tiny. I wonder if this means anything.

CHAPTER THIRTY

Madness

In six years of working at Duell and Co. I had never received a bad review. I had even stopped getting reviewed (this may have happened just after Somto came on to me), and Emma and I spent the time making fun of Somto and his wife, whom he'd married only because he'd knocked her up. This year I knew it would be different, especially because one of the bosses from our London office had flown in and was sitting in on employee reviews, a pasty man with grey hair combed over his bald patch. My bosses flanked him and seemed to have dressed identically for my dressing-down. Red trousers on Somto, a red skirt on Emma. Blue and white stripes on top. As if they'd escaped from a Dr. Seuss book.

'Explain exactly what happened with our biggest palm-oil producer, Mrs. Avoka,' said Comb-over.

I wasn't greeted, wasn't offered the tea they were swirling in their mugs. He went straight to the point: why had I lost the company money? It was then that I figured out that Mr. Sullivan had been summoned because I had messed up big time.

'They were in breach of contract,' I said.

'I see, Mrs. Avoka,' said Comb-over, 'but did you consider just checking in with Mr. And Ms. Thomas before making such a drastic move?'

'Well, in my role as public-relations officer—and as an employee who wears several hats—I've been, on several occasions, given responsibilities and the clout to make executive decisions.'

I could have implicated my bosses. There were countless times when Emma and Somto had told me to forge their signatures or to make big calls in the name of the company because they were just too lazy to investigate anything further. I tried to catch Emma's eyes but she wouldn't look my way. She and Somto shifted in their seats. If they'd told Mr. Sullivan that they hadn't okayed my decision, what were their signatures doing on the document? Had they told him that I had faked their signatures? The silence in the room grew oppressive.

'I didn't ask them,' I said, swallowing the words painfully. Emma and Somto wouldn't meet my eyes. Somebody needed to pay for the company's loss and it had to be me. Now I was going to be punished at the worst possible time in my life. I needed to get the MRI scan as soon as possible and if I lost my job I didn't know where that money would come from. Theo's new job was bringing in more money, yes, but nowhere near enough to pay for whatever expensive disease it was I had.

Mr. Sullivan said, 'Well, that's solved, then. I'll leave it to Somto and Emma to come up with the appropriate retribution. Thank you, Mrs. Avoka.'

He nodded, and like a chastened pupil I left the room. I went straight into my car and drove away from the office, but didn't get far because my hands were convulsing in anger and shame. I burst out crying two houses away from our office and prayed that no one would pass by. It was a terrible crime in the grand scheme of things—forging a signature—and I could be suspended indefinitely. My salary could be slashed. I decided to take the rest of the day off and go see Obi. Might as well start my suspension early, because that was inevitable.

My first stop was the pharmacy, where the woman dispensing condoms kept looking at me, her eyes filled with judgment. I wanted to ask her, 'Why? Don't you have sex with your husband?' She could keep her disapproving eyes off me and save them for somebody who cared. Maybe she knew they weren't meant for my husband? Perhaps I was in a sick TV show—the way I used to think the world was one giant TV program with me as the sole actor—and everyone was in on my life. I smiled sweetly and asked her to include two packets of gum and a painkiller while she was at it.

My next stop was Auntie Rokia's Wine Shop. I don't know why I was spending money when I needed to save, but it was as if my auto-destruct button had been turned on, making me do each thing clinically, as if my life depended on it.

'I was beginning to think you'd found somebody else,' Auntie Rokia said, lifting her hefty body off a plastic chair. She enveloped me in warm folds of flesh. 'I didn't see you at Christmas, nor for the new year. Why?'

'Oh, Auntie, I didn't have a big party this year.' Even though ours was a small city, it was true that we could go for months and not see the people we held dear.

'Well, I'm happy you're here now, and I have many new wines I know you'll love.'

'Something tasty,' I said, lapping my tongue against the roof of my mouth.

'*Ei*! What's the occasion? Wait, wait! Let me guess. You and Theo are having your anniversary?'

I wanted to lie, to say yes, but the moment the word came out of my mouth, the universe would drag Theo here for some reason and the woman would congratulate him, baffle him, and lead him onto my trail. Instead, I thought of the worst possible excuse, given the circumstances: 'It's for a celebration at work, and we need good wine for a change.'

'Very well, then,' she said, her smile not as effusive as before. 'I have this 1989 Merlot. Straight from France, if you like. Or—'

'Perfect!' I said, paid for the wine and didn't stay for our usual chitchat. Five minutes with her and I'd be spilling my guts about Theo's work with the Doctor, or my affair. And if Aunty Rokia wasn't a gossip, I don't know who was.

Obi let me in and welcomed me with a kiss on my forehead, and I told him about the meeting with Mr. Sullivan.

'I'm sure Emma and Somto will appreciate that you stuck your neck out for them,' he said. 'You're not losing your job.'

'You should have seen that horrible man. One of those English farts who hate to be doing anything with Africa.' I settled on the couch in the living room. 'What am I going to do?'

'Sometimes you have to look on the bright side.'

'What bright side, Obi?' I was shouting. 'I might have cancer or God knows what. I'm really just damned.'

'What happened at the hospital? Cancer? Slow down, Zaza.'

'I haven't done the scans yet, but my ophthalmologist thinks I might have something.'

'Get a diagnosis from a real doctor.'

'She *is* a real doctor. Besides, you know I haven't been well for a long time. We've all just been in denial about it. I'm going to die.'

'Can you stop being morbid,' Obi said.

'Oh my God, Obi. I'm so sorry,' I said. 'I've been going and going non-stop. And all of a sudden stuff is out of control. What's happened to my life?'

'Breathe,' said Obi, settling by me and resting my head on his shoulder.

'What are we doing?' I said, springing up. 'Maybe that's why everything is going wrong. I don't know anymore.'

'Shhh,' he said. 'Is that really how you think the world works? The worst tragedies have happened to saints.'

I fell sick even before Obi came into my life, so that couldn't be why I was being punished. It had to be something else. 'I know. Juvenile. But I can't help it. We need to make sense of the bad things that happen to us, and my way is to think that if you're bad, you bring bad onto yourself.'

'It's going to be all right,' Obi said, lifting my chin so our eyes would meet.

'How did she do it?'

'Who? What?'

'Your wife.'

'Overdosed on pills.' He said the words coldly, and his gaze drifted from mine.

'I'm sorry,' I said.

'She'd been depressed for a long time. After she had Inaam. We thought we could deal with it ourselves. We did the religious thing, talked to imams. And she just got worse and worse. She started seeing shrinks and that didn't help either. 'We don't need therapy. That's for white people,' she'd say after every session. 'Such a waste of time.' She forced me to take a session so I could see what she was going through. And she was right. Therapy was such a drag.'

'What would have helped?'

'I still don't know, Zaza. Maybe we should have moved back here?'

'Look at me!' I screamed. 'I'm a mess.'

'Stop with the melodrama.'

'I should go.' And despite his protests, I got up and took out my keys.

'I'm going back to England.'

'Good!' I said, trying to tamp down the hysteria that was rising in me. I wondered about his timing, and if he was telling me this despite the bad day I was having, or if he did it because of the bad day I was having. He figured that I was already down, knocked out, so one more blow wouldn't hurt.

'You don't mean that?'

'No, I do. Go! It will be better for both of us.' I fought back tears. 'Wow, this day just keeps improving, doesn't it?'

'This fantastic opportunity has opened up in London, and Inaam can take her A levels there. All around, it's better.'

'When did you decide this?'

'The day I saw you at the kids' school. That's when I had to decide if I was going or not. It was so hard, near-impossible, for me to stand by Theo and not feel rotten, Zaza. He doesn't deserve this.'

'Great!' I said. He walked over and held me. 'Great transference. Now I feel just peachy. Let me go!'

'I won't let you go until I'm sure you're okay.'

'I'll survive.'

'I'm sorry,' Obi said.

I thought age would alleviate the blow of a break-up. That this time it wouldn't be the same as when I was seventeen, because I had already been through the motions. But it was worse. At seventeen, I felt like my world had ended, but with time school took over and the world didn't end. As an adult I just got crazy. I would have to pinch myself hard to stop myself from scheming: showing up at Obi's house or office and putting on such a show of charm that he'd regret ever leaving me.

I was so used to pretending to be perfect, to be above it all, that I couldn't understand my feelings, which seemed so base, so low, so common. I was jilted and filled with raging jealousy. Theo and I attended a play, and after the lights came on I thought I saw Obi with another woman. I couldn't really be sure that it was Obi, but my chest constricted and I felt like the walls of the amphitheatre would start moving towards each other and crush me to death. I ran out under the pretence of going to the bathroom (lying to Theo), under the pretence of getting air (lying to myself), and staked out a position by a giant Akwaaba doll with multicoloured beads around its nude waist. I watched everyone who exited the amphitheatre, and of course Theo came out before I had a chance to verify if it had been Obi. Then the madness really took over. I called him not long after, begging him to confess that he'd found someone else. It would make the split easier for me. He said he didn't owe me any more of an explanation because we weren't together, and suggested that I fix things with my husband. I proceeded to call him several times a day, hanging up before he picked up, and, I'll admit it, I drove by his house a few times, try as I might to stop myself. I fell into weeping fits in the bathroom, crying so hard that I would retch. It was as if Obi had planted a huge chasm in me, and I wanted it out before it swallowed me whole.

It also didn't help that I didn't have a job. Emma and Somto suspended me for the rest of the fiscal year—not the indefinite suspension I had expected, but just as bad. I would forever be the one they couldn't trust. Before I left the office I received a call from a women's collective I'd been trying to woo for a while. I snagged all the paperwork and decided I was still going to check them out. I needed something to do or I'd go insane.

CHAPTER THIRTY-ONE

Lan-come

After what seems like forever, Atsu has worked up the nerve to invite Nasar over. She would have met him at Gloria's, but she's not ready to be alone with him in one small room. She figures she's too scared of her boss lady to even think of getting up to no good in the house. The house will serve as a deterrent.

Her invitation was for one in the afternoon but he doesn't show up till three, and she's so annoyed that when he finally rings the bell, she takes her time, noticing how wild the grass has grown (a job she'll tackle later) and how the power and phone lines criss-cross messily above the house. Even though she's sure he heard the gate whine he ignores it and keeps walking away. Everyone from here to Addis Ababa can hear the gate when it swings open.

'Nasar!' she shouts, and he turns around and her chest grows warm and heavy. 'Are you annoyed?'

'I rang twenty times.'

She can't help but smile. 'What if my madam or her husband had come back? Eh?' she says. 'I told you one because there was no way they'd be home then.'

'They're there?'

'I said what if.'

'Sorry, Atsu. Don't be angry. I thought I didn't have to work today, but the security company came for me at dawn and disturbed the whole area with their four-by-four pickup because one of the other security guards is sick. I wanted to call but didn't know how to reach you.'

'You can't stay long. Hungry?'

'You can't imagine how much! Did you cook for me?'

'It's for my bosses, but I made plenty.'

'Oh, Atsu, I should marry you.'

She laughs and leads him inside through the kitchen. As she watches him observing the place, it begins to feel like the house is disappointing. He was probably expecting a more important edifice, one of the sort found in the magazines on Madam's dresser. Big chandeliers, five storeys, swimming pools, ten bedrooms. This house stands at only one storey high. It's not even *her* house, so she doesn't know why she's worrying about its appearance.

She serves him and then picks a lump of yam off his plate.

'You like your bosses?' he asks between bites.

'Yes. They are good to me,' she says, but doesn't want to talk about them, because it will make their ears prickle and draw them back home. She reaches for his plate again.

'Get your own!' he says and taps her hand. She eats slowly, savouring each bite, then catches herself and is ashamed—this must be what is called lust. 'Atsu, this is more delicious than anything I've eaten. I wish you could cook for me every day. Why don't you just marry me?'

He's said it twice.

She quickly washes the dishes so her bosses don't come back to find evidence, then she goes back to Nasar and turns on the TV. They sit quietly before images of a lion mauling an antelope. Nasar isn't as chatty as he usually is.

Then he says throatily, 'A tour?'

She figures a quick look won't hurt. No lingering. In and out. She points to Mr. Avoka's sound system and music collection. Racks and racks of cassette tapes. He reads out the names of their labels, and even though he is slow and unsure, she's envious. She can't read without sounding out the letters first. Next, she shows him Kojo's room, then Madam and Mr. Avoka's bedroom. He asks her why she knocks before entering these rooms, and she points to the stern Linus Avoka looking down on them, which makes him laugh. If any of the rooms is worth seeing, it's the master bedroom. The bed, with its solid dark wood frame, is always immaculate with sheets she has to keep white and spotless. Then there's the room's pièce de résistance—she calls it the treasure chest—a five-foot dresser with all sorts of textured and colourful whorls etched on its surface. Nasar doesn't seem to care about the chest's intricate exterior. On top of the chest rest perfumes and photos of Mr. Avoka's father, of Mma and Madam's father, of Madam, Mr. Avoka, and Kojo. He picks up a frame of Madam during her days abroad.

'Your madam is beautiful,' he says. Her hair is combed into an Afro and deep-red lipstick stains her full lips. Atsu feels a twinge of jealousy. She would like to snatch the picture from his hands and put it back, photo facing the wall. He sets down the frame, picks up a bottle of perfume, pops off the pink plastic top, and smells it.

'Okay, enough. Let's go,' she says.

'Wait,' he says, then scrunches his nose. 'Too old-womanish.' He picks up the next and doesn't seem impressed by it, either. On the fourth bottle he says, 'Lan-come. That's better.' He walks toward her with it.

'No, no, no! I beg you, Nasar, No! You want me to kill me?'

'We'll wash it off,' he says and sprays it on her wrist. 'Rub them together.' He takes her right wrist and lifts it to his nose. Atsu holds her breath as his skin touches hers. He caps the bottle, returns it to the dresser, and says, 'Now, the most important room in this house. Your room.'

Mr. Avoka's desk is littered with paper, and her mattress lies on the floor, covered with a blue-and-white cloth, looking half-presentable.

'You didn't tell me you were writing a book,' he chuckles, and sits behind the desk. 'Have you been lying to us? You just come to class to see the rest of us suffer?'

'I beg you, don't touch anything,' she says just as a sheet flutters to the ground. She picks it up and is ready to stuff it in the middle of the pile when Nasar says he knows where it goes. He puts it on top of the pile.

'It's a nice house,' he says, leaning back in Mr. Avoka's tattered cane chair.

She asks Nasar to tell her about himself. He says he grew up with his grandmother and had an uneventful life until he became a security guard. He takes her hand and she becomes very aware of the hand, of his fingers around it, rough and firm. He pulls her toward him and sits her on his lap and everything slows down. It feels good to have him so close, but this isn't the place for her to be doing that. He wraps his arms around her torso, pressing his nose into her back. Her thighs press together, exuding heat and sensations she's never let herself feel. His hands travel up and down her arms, massaging and rubbing. Why hasn't anyone told her this feels so good? It must be why the whole world is fascinated by sex, what with all those condom advertisements on TV. He turns her head so they are face to face, and fear and excitement clump in her throat.

'Has anyone told you how beautiful you are?'

She's giddy, but the feeling instantly evaporates as a honk cuts through the room. Then a second, then a third. She lands on her feet, staring in wide-eyed horror at Nasar.

'Oh, God!' She smells of Lan-come or whatever it's called and is entertaining a strange man in her room. 'Stay here!' she barks, straightens her dress, and goes to let Madam in.

'I've been so sick, Atsu,' Madam says. 'How are you?'

'I'm fine,' she says, trying to keep her distance. Madam is going to smell the perfume.

'I was so ill today I had to pull off to the side of the road to throw up.' Madam is never this open. In the living room she plops onto the sofa. 'Please make me a glass of ginger juice. Keep the skin on. No sugar.'

Atsu's heart is pushing out of her chest. She can't believe she has a man in her room. She goes to the kitchen, takes out the ginger from the fridge and returns to the living room.

'I left the small knife in my room,' she says. The worst excuse she could come up with—especially since she was told not to peel the ginger—but Madam's unstrapping her sandals and twiddling her toes and thankfully doesn't care.

Nasar is still where she left him, but has some of Mr. Avoka's papers in hand.

'I told you not to touch anything,' she whispers, looking at the door. Madam could just barge in, and that door doesn't lock. 'You can't even read, so what are you doing?' He looks hurt. 'Sorry, you've put me in a lot of trouble.'

'I know.' His voice is too loud, too deep.

'Shhh. What are we going to do?'

'Just wait?'

'I'll be back. Be quiet. Don't move. *Don't* do anything.'

Madam is no longer in the living room. If she went into her room she must have heard their voices. Walls in this house aren't thick. Back in the kitchen, Atsu hears Madam retching outside. This is probably the best time for Nasar to escape. Too late. Madam clears her throat and comes back into the kitchen.

'I thought I could do this,' she says. 'But it's getting bad, Atsu. It's getting really bad. Is that my Lancôme?'

The question is said more like a statement, and is so unexpected it leaves Atsu speechless. Then she stammers, 'When I was cleaning, I pressed too hard on it.' Madam says nothing. After that lie, if Nasar is discovered, Atsu will instantly be homeless and jobless. Atsu scrubs the ginger under a stream of tap water, then grinds it as smoothly as she can on the stone slab. She wonders if she should say he's her brother from the village, but Madam's already met them. Or her cousin. But why didn't she say so earlier? After being caught wearing Madam's perfume, she better not risk anything.

Atsu takes the ginger juice to Madam, and even though the bedroom door was wide open, she plucks up the courage to shut it behind her. She tiptoes to her room and signals for Nasar to follow her. As they're walking down the corridor, Madam's door clicks open. With reflexes she didn't know she possessed, Atsu shoves Nasar into the living room and turns to regard her employer.

'What was that?'

'I almost fell.'

'Hmmm. Please make me soup, too.' She's wearing just a bra and underskirt, and Atsu hopes Nasar can't see her from where he is.

'Yes, Madam.'

Atsu opens the front door slowly and drags Nasar out. If Madam looks through her bathroom window she'll catch them, but it's a risk Atsu has to take. She doesn't exhale till they're out of the gate, where Nasar bursts out laughing.

'It's not funny.'

'I want you to come to my house next time,' Nasar says.

'I won't.'

'Fine. I'll come back next week, then,' he says. 'See you in class.'

She walks back into the house and looks in the direction of Madam's room, where the thick curtains are drawn.

CHAPTER THIRTY-TWO

THE DAILY POST

Monday, April 7, 1997 | We are the news! | Since 1952

Bush Doctor by Theo Avoka

My father's village, unlike the capital of our great country, was underdeveloped, with no electricity or running water. We were left to our own devices, succumbing to poverty, river blindness, bilharzia, and all manner of preventable diseases. Even after Independence, when the euphoria had died down and the real work of nation-building was supposed to begin, nothing changed. I kept watching, waiting for change to happen, but year after year, people in power got richer and the poor were thrown deeper into the abyss of poverty.

We had nothing, growing up. My mother bore ten children. My father married three women and educated all the boys with whatever money he made from his small pharmacy. He would sometimes disappear for days, returning emaciated, with strips of Paracetamol, small bottles of half-used cough syrup, and bits of other medicine he could find at the large dispensaries. He was what was known as a bush doctor, and he lived up to his name, stocking local roots and herbs in addition to proffering his diagnosis of peoples' ailments and conditions. It was because of him that I wanted to study *medicine in school, though I stumbled on psychology along the way, which was unheard of in those days. My father was initially disappointed I didn't become a medical doctor, but when I sat in his room and told him of the power of his mind, like how the brain could stop the heart from functioning, he was astounded. 'Psychology, Karamoh,' he said, 'is modern-day witchcraft.'*

We sat at a different part of the Doctor's house one afternoon, not the patch of grass that had become my de facto office. And before we began, I wondered what the Doctor thought about when he revisited the humbleness of his youth. Whether he looked upon it with disgust, his poverty a disease, or if his retrospection was tinged with nostalgia. I pondered these things because it seemed to me that a person who clung to power in the way he did must have suffered a traumatic childhood. And perhaps he thought relinquishing control of the country would mean a return to his stark beginnings. As if he knew I was looking for clues to understand him better, he wore green-tinted aviator sunglasses during our sessions.

The new writing spot was set up in the middle of a garden blooming with flowers I'd never seen before. 'The Mrs.,' the Doctor had said when I complimented him on the beauty of the landscaping. The house was even bigger than I realized, the lawn stretching off for metres, and for moments I forgot that we were on top of a hill. I also noticed that even though the building was constructed with a new shell—in the shape of the Ashanti stool—it still bore traces of its former glory as a Portuguese colonial fort: solid stone fortifications, a lone cannon jutting from the seat of the stool. Not far from the flower garden lay a Grecian pool with water glistening under the mid-afternoon sun. We'd left our Third-World country and had travelled to a Mediterranean resort.

'She visited Greece a couple of years ago and wanted to recreate everything,' the Doctor said.

I could only imagine what had been there before. Another of Mrs. Saturday's flights of fancy? Maybe a Japanese cherry-blossom garden. Or a Mayan ruin. My stomach doubled over. How much money had gone into construction? Mrs. Saturday's family was old and established, but I was sure they didn't have that much money. My head reeled. The country was still dealing with huge inflation. Buying milk was an issue in my house, because Zahra thought one tin of Carnation milk should get us through a week, not just two days.

Pape came out of the stool-shaped house cradling my typewriter, his face fraught with anxiety and fear. If he dropped it, surely a new one would be sent for immediately, so I didn't understand his worry. He set it on my table without incident, then returned with a glass of tea, the Doctor's tobacco, and a photo album.

'Pape,' the Doctor said, lighting his pipe. 'Tell your aunt her gardenia tree has some strange rings on its leaves.' Then he muttered, 'We need more practical trees.'

As I stared at the reflection of palm trees in the pool, I decided to finally take on Courtney's offer. It was a crime that, while he had put the country through twenty years of misery—inflation, famine, travel restrictions, endless curfews, public beatings, allowing his thugs to loot from market women, devaluing our education system—he could sit on top of his hill and continue to enjoy life and worry about gardenia trees. I decided, before I looked at the pictures, before the Doctor showed me his sentimental side, that I should make up my mind and stick to it. I would be Courtney's mole.

'I was ferreting through the house and found those pictures,' the Doctor said. 'I'm sure you've noticed how spotty my memory has been for the last couple of chapters. Old age. Don't laugh. You will get there soon. The pictures should jog things.'

He passed me the album. Most of the photos were sepia-toned, some spotted with water damage, others torn and taped together. In the first picture was a man stuffed into an elaborate smock, similar to what the Doctor liked to wear, but with guns strapped across his chest and talismans draped like chains.

'My grandfather,' said the Doctor. 'He was a chief and hunter. It is said that the talismans he wore made him invincible. He was out hunting one day and didn't have them on and never came home. No one knows if he even died.'

I bet if the Doctor had his way, he would pillage the entire country in search of his grandfather's talismans. I could never forget the day he asked me to slice him with a blade to prove his juju worked. The next photo was of a woman in white—a white scarf, white skirt, and a huge white bead necklace, bare-chested. The Doctor flipped the page. He stared at the next picture, a small naked boy, then he shut the album. The pictures probably reminded him too much of his humanness, his frailness, the past he was trying to rewrite.

'Shall we write?' he said.

I fed a sheet into the typewriter.

'Let's call this chapter ... What are we on now?'

'Chapter Three: Work in the Ministry.'

'No, I don't want to ... Look, let's call this 'An Inheritance.' We'll come back and iron out the order of the chapters later on, eh?' After a pregnant pause he said, 'Okay, write: My paternal grandfather was called Etse Red Hunter Karamoh. He fought in several battles, but hunting was where his heart was. Where his heart lay. I see myself as a man after my grandfather's heart ...'

'Sir, if I may?'

'Of course, Theo. If I could do this myself you wouldn't be here, so please, make suggestions.'

'I think you should first focus on your grandfather and his life.'

'Very good. What was the last line we wrote?'

'"... hunting was where his heart lay."'

The Doctor narrated the Red Hunter's mystical birth, how his grandfather had been born an *abiku*—a spirit child who couldn't make up its mind and kept dying immediately after birth—and how, after the sixth time, when he was about to be buried, scars all over his tiny body, the baby had burst out crying. After that point, the Red Hunter didn't go back to his spirit world.

The Doctor recalled his maternal ancestors—a family of traditional healers. On both sides he was gifted with the power of healing. That was why he took control of the country: he hoped he could heal a scarred nation.

After I had typed the last word for the day, the Doctor invited me for dinner with his family. How cruel the universe was! After I'd decided I'd betray the man, it was doing everything in its power to prove that he was a kind soul. I didn't decline his invitation. For two reasons: I was sure the interior of the house would exude even more disgusting grandeur, and I needed to feed my newly discovered renegade spirit. The second was that I was just plain curious. I won't lie—I, too, wondered if he slept in a casket.

We ate in a room modelled on the Abundance room in the Château de Versailles, complete with framed photos of the Doctor à la Louis XIV. The Doctor, his wife, their son Joseph, and I sat in the room with its velveteen upholstery. Joseph was taciturn, and Mrs. Saturday was surprisingly bubbly and welcoming.

I used the bathroom twice during lunch, which went on for hours. The first time I was too scared to linger. I did my business and hurried back to work on the lamb on my plate. The second time, I took note of the gold-plated faucets, the art nouveau-framed mirror, then I opened cabinets but found them empty. I don't know what I expected to unearth.

On my way home I slotted a cassette into my car stereo to calm myself. My emotions had been worn thin. The classical-music tape wouldn't play, and as I tried to extract it the stereo spat out the tape, loops and loops of it. One tug and the tape tore. In my frustration I banged on the stereo and a piece of the dashboard fell onto my lap. The Doctor had enough bedrooms to house the whole city. I was working for him and my life was still falling apart. I went straight to Courtney's.

She was home by herself, and it took so much strength of will to keep myself together. She touched my arms when she talked, holding her gaze on me for long stretches of time. At this point things weren't going well with Zahra at all. She'd been suspended from work, and even though I thought it would mean spending more time together, I saw less of her. I could have succumbed to Courtney's advances, especially because she'd grown on me. The sun had baked her skin to a lovely golden brown. The way she wore her *boubou* seemed natural, like she'd been born wearing it. And her smell—a rich coconut-shea butter infusion—reminded me so strongly of Sister Afia. Maybe the larger task is what kept me on the narrow path. It's hard for me to say, even in retrospect. I told her I would do whatever it took to indict the Doctor.

I stayed at my spot by the pool for a month, until Pape informed me I'd be moving into an office in the house. I couldn't place the Doctor's madness, but I suppose the more I proved myself trustworthy, the more of the house was revealed. Soon I was a full-time worker at the Doctor's, and I didn't return to the MoFA.

My office was a cold room with drapery that fell from ceiling to floor, pastel curtains reeking of dust and camphor. The furniture, sturdy and ancient, filled most of the room, and what space was leftover was stacked with piles of paper and folders. Pape told me I had to keep the door open at all times, except when I went to the bathroom. No other staff member was allowed into my office. It was the classic rabbit-with-the-carrot-stick situation. Those piles were my carrot, and I was constantly being monitored. I worked with the Doctor sometimes, other times on my own, with Pape hovering. When Pape finally relented and went back to whatever he spent most of his day doing, I'd nick sheets from the bottom of the pile and take them home with me.

I made copies of everything and returned the originals to the Doctor's. I read minutes of meetings from various ministries, reports of every boring correspondence that took place in interior offices, registries of arrests made at police stations. Every day, the results were thankless. Nothing to implicate the man I knew was responsible for our great country's demise.

Many have accused me of being involved in black magic, juju. And that's what I'll address in this chapter. Some went as far as suggesting that I was behind the ritual killings that plagued our beloved nation starting from 1989. Their theory was possible, though unfounded. They said I had young women killed so I could instil fear in people, knowing that I would have to give up power in 1993. They insisted that the fear I was creating would make people vote for the continuation of military rule. To all those people, I ask, why do the killings continue?

Did I dabble in our natural medicine? Yes, I did. In the same way the churchgoing woman who has prayed and prayed to God for a child to bless her marriage decides to finally consult a fetish priest, in the way a man who has suffered from diabetes for years and has been driven into bankruptcy with hospital bills chooses to see a herbalist. In that way, then, yes, I am guilty. I come from a long line of healers, and my father always told me not to forget about the bark of the tree, the little green shoot, a tortoise's shell, and how these things of nature can serve us just as well as modern medicine. And even though I studied Western psychology, at the end of a long, stressful day, it's with a glass of warm bitters that I put myself at ease, not talking things out, not with manufactured drugs. If this makes me guilty of juju, I rest my case.

CHAPTER THIRTY-THREE

ANR 246

After Mrs. Diouf's generous offer to tutor me I conveniently found myself making excuses every time she asked me to come over. One time I bribed Salif to tell her I had a stomach ache, which cost me a plate of fried plantain. The next time, I saw her in the dining hall and told her I had a big chemistry test the next day, which I did, and it was great not to deal with her strange husband staring at the Doctor on TV. This time, though, I have decided to be a good student and go see her, even though when she saw me in class she didn't extend the invitation.

Why am I being a good student? Two things: Mrs. Bobole called me into her office and told me my grades in math were bringing down my average. If I continue like this I'd have to score 95 per cent or higher in all my other subjects to keep my scholarship. She was smiling as she said this. Smiling, the Wicked Witch of the West. Then Inaam. After she went behind my back in cowardly fashion to tell Mrs. Diouf she couldn't tutor me anymore, she's still trying to be my friend. She had the nerve to ask me if I'd come if she threw a going-away party. I was probably rude, but I couldn't help it. I asked her what she'd do if she were me, and left her in front of the dining hall. She needs to know I don't need her.

But now, as I approach Mrs. Diouf's house, I see good Old Faithful, the battered Mazda, and I'm not sure whether still to ambush Mrs. Diouf. What in tarnation is Theo Avoka doing here? I want to make sure it's the same car with dents galore on the driver's side, and when I see the number plate ANR 246, it's confirmed. It's none other than *the* Theo's car. I see there are other cars that aren't Mr. or Mrs. Diouf's parked next to Old Faithful. Are they all parents of people failing math?

I sneak into the courtyard and make for one of Mrs. Diouf's windows but realize my shoes are some kind of squelchy, so I'm forced to tiptoe instead. The Sed Games did a number on my sneakers and I should ask the parentals for a new pair for sports, but I feel bad asking for things like clothes, because Mummy's out of work for now, and although Daddy's job is prestigious, Mummy says his is the riskiest position on the planet. Worse than the man who digs a pothole in a perfectly fine road as his way of making money. Even though he could get run over, Mummy says, at least he's self-employed. So: no new sneakers.

I hear voices but they aren't coming from inside, and a peek through the slits in Mrs. Diouf's outer wall shows me three upper two boys strolling by with buckets. Do we not have running water? Is that yet another thing to worry about? If the uppers catch me, I'll be carrying buckets of water for their showers tonight.

'Dioufy is throwing a bash,' one of them says, and they laugh.

When they're a safe distance away, I continue my creep forward. I look into the house through the first window at the back, and it's a small bedroom stuffed with a giant bed. Whatever space is left is taken up with a huge dresser with teddy bears on it. Stuffed animals should be banned. The door to the room is open but I can only see a wall, nothing more.

The next window isn't any better. I can barely even reach it, and I'm not a short person. It's the bathroom or toilet. Two more windows to go. The one farthest from me will give me the best view, but it's also the one most likely to get me caught, so I tiptoe to the second. I'm so curious about what Daddy is doing here. He's never taken an interest in my schoolwork.

I have a slim view of the living room, and even though most of it is blocked by Dioufy's dining table and stuffy old chairs, I can see Daddy, a white woman sitting by him, Mr. Diouf, and another woman. Some man I can't see is talking, and there's no sign of Mrs. Diouf.

Their voices are muted and Daddy looks worried. Mrs. Diouf finally surfaces, balancing a tray of fried chips of some sort. Daddy greedily reaches out and stuffs his face with, like, ten of them. I'm embarrassed for him.

'Delicious,' he says, mouth full. Observing him like this allows me to see him in a new way—he's not putting on a show for me or Mummy. This is how he shows himself to the rest of the world when we're not around. He seems less closed. As if, when we're around, we suffocate the life out of him.

'I honestly think it's enough to build a case,' the white woman says.

'Just one woman's testimony?' says a man I can't see.

'I've looked everywhere I could,' says Daddy. 'He doesn't keep anything in that house. As far as his house is concerned, he's clean.'

'I think we should present this,' the white woman says.

'Well, you know best,' Mr. Diouf says.

I have no idea what they are talking about and it sounds insanely boring and has nothing to do with math.

'I think Theo should look some more,' says the man I can't see. His tone is angry. 'Where you least expect things to be.'

'Do you want us to switch roles?' Daddy says.

'It's all right, Theo,' the white woman says.

What a dry party. And, honestly, Daddy is kind of spineless. His voice softened, like he was going to cry. Why did he let whoever that is talk to him like that? All I know is that this is one strange combination of people.

On my way back to the dorm I almost collide with Kunle walking downstairs with an empty metal bucket. I start to smile but he thrusts the bucket in my face, and there's nothing I can do but to take the nightmarishly heavy thing. That will be two buckets of water coming right up.

When I return with the water (I spilled so much of Kunle's water that I had to empty half of mine to fill his bucket), I ask him if anyone's come looking for me.

'Like your girlfriend?' he says. 'Sorry, no. But I heard you two were finito. No?'

As annoying as he is, the one thing I'll give Kunle is he doesn't lie about things that don't concern him. He'd have told me if Daddy had asked to see me. I can't believe the man drove all the way here and couldn't even write me a note. This is exactly why we have issues.

After studying in the evening, the sting of Daddy shunning me is so strong that I call Mummy. She's sure to have answers. She always does. Her voice is tired, however, and she sounds like she's been crying.

'Daddy was here today,' I tell her, after she's asked me over and over about how I am. Somebody has graffiti'd breasts near the phone booth.

'He didn't even come and say hello.' A lump is growing in my throat and it needs to go away. There are other people gathered behind me and I'm sure they can hear this conversation. I need to keep things together.

'I don't understand,' she says, after a long pause.

'He came to see my teacher and didn't even drop a note.'

'Which teacher? Slow down. I can't hear you properly.'

'My math teacher. Mrs. Diouf.'

A girl and boy pass by with buckets. Isn't it too late for them to be fetching water? They're definitely up to mischief. I miss Inaam. I feel like I'd get more from talking to her than I am from this current conversation.

'These bloody phone lines, Kojo. Repeat that?'

'My math teacher. MRS. DIOUF!'

'Oh. Maybe she called him in to discuss your math.'

'There were other people there. A white woman, Mrs. Diouf's husband, another woman …'

'Avoka, stop hogging the phone,' someone says in a faux baritone. He deserves to be ignored.

'They kept talking about things I didn't get,' I say.

'Sorry, hon, hold on. Put the glass there. Thanks, Atsu. I'm sure he was just busy. And it wasn't like you could receive visitors, right?'

'Yes,' I say. That isn't what I wanted to hear. I don't know what I wanted to hear. *Yes, your father's horrible*? Maybe something like that? I expected anger. I thought we were a team. Me and Mummy against him.

'We'll see you after your exams. Pass, and pass with flying colours!'

I hang up without saying bye.

CHAPTER THIRTY-FOUR

THE DAILY POST
Monday, May 5, 1997 | We are the news! | Since 1952

Life's Purpose by Theo Avoka

At first it was easy living my double life. I would write for the Doctor during work hours, and then in the evenings and on weekends I would sneak into Courtney's house, or whatever decidedly seedy hideaway the group had chosen. We were slowly plodding along, peeling away at the Doctor's sinister and very elusive past. In my day job I persuaded the Doctor to invest in cassette tapes and an Aiwa tape recorder so he could save his ideas when I wasn't around. I was hoping he would slip, give me some nugget to hand over to Courtney, but the man kept his secrets highly guarded.

My two worlds contrasted terribly. Karamoh Saturday was a man who tended proudly to hyacinths in his greenhouse, yet Diouf, his former right-hand man, was showing us abandoned shooting ranges where this same man's political opponents had been executed. I struggled not to cry as imaginary echoes of bullets riddling my father's body reverberated through the range. When I told Courtney—ever the conspiracy theorist—about this, she asked if Saturday didn't have a hand in my father's death. She'd hinted at it before, but for years I'd wondered what the true story behind his death was, and it was a rabbit hole that sucked me in, so I didn't entertain the thought. The terrible contrast was also made worse by the state of my domestic life: a shambles. Zahra was passing out in strange places, barely talking to me, and more alien by the day. My solution: do what I did best—bury my head deeper in the sand and take my two jobs very seriously. When I worked with the Doctor, I wrote with passion, praying he would soon open up about the atrocities he'd committed.

The day we landed our biggest breakthrough was also the day I began to question the point of everything we were doing. Courtney, a videographer, an interpreter, Diouf, Miss Olympio, and I drove up to a village in the westernmost part of the country, a day after a flash flood had converted most of our journey into a mud-filled, crater-pocked experience. After being cooped up in Courtney's Land Rover for eight hours, we got to know each other quite well. When Diouf wasn't obsessing about the Doctor—'To think I used to shave the hair on his head!'—which seldom happened, he prattled on about American politics, how he'd watched Clinton's inauguration on the telly with his wife and wished we had someone like him for president.

'The ladies love him,' Courtney said, 'and he *loves* the ladies too.' She and Miss Olympio laughed and then veered into a conversation about good-looking politicians. The interpreter was quiet, speaking up only to buy boiled eggs along the way. Courtney had made him jump through several hoops, including going to his house and recording the names of his family and neighbours, photographing his room and every belonging, and telling him that if he talked about this to anyone, the CIA and FBI would be on his tail. He seemed shifty through the entire affair, and to this day I'm convinced he was the one who exposed us.

We arrived at a raging red river and parked the Land Rover at its bank. Canoes lay half in the river, half on the wet soil, and three men lazily sat under a tree. One of them, quite portly, recognized Courtney.

'Madam!' he said, picking himself up faster than I thought possible, given his girth. We told him where we were headed. 'The river is very rough and full today. But we can go.'

'Baku, you're sure it's safe?' Courtney asked. She explained that she'd been there once to take photos and hadn't realized she'd return for entirely different reasons.

'Yes, yes. We just have to row carefully. Two of us will take you.'

We wobbled into the canoe, our escorts scooped river water with their thin paddles, and soon we were gliding down the wide river. The view was breathtaking, and if we weren't going to discover the Doctor's gruesomeness, I would have enjoyed the trip thoroughly. It was a cool afternoon, and the bush around the river was verdant and resplendently rain-washed.

When we arrived at the village, its inhabitants were re-thatching roofs that had fallen in after the rainfall. The hut of the old woman we were meeting had suffered a fallen tree, and her grandchildren were hacking the tree's trunk into firewood when we arrived.

'Come,' she said, leaving instructions for her brood, her

irises shaded grey, half-covered by the folds of her eyelids.

The videographer turned on the camera and we followed the old lady down a winding dirt path. Grey-and-white guinea fowl darted in and out of our way as we ascended and descended. At one point we could see an expanse of savannah, acacia trees in a sea of red sand and patchy grass. I imagined this was the idea of real Africa to Courtney and it's why she'd been there to take photos. We continued walking until we arrived at a small forest area, where the faint, sulphury smell of human excrement hung in the air.

The old lady took us to a clearing with several mounds of sand.

'They are scattered all over the forest,' the old lady said. 'Graves.'

'How do you know it was the Doctor?' Courtney asked.

The old lady extended her index finger into the air and drew circles. Helicopter.

'When did this happen? How often?' Diouf said. I was surprised even he didn't know about this. I suppose he was privy only to military affairs.

'It's stopped now,' the old woman said. 'Before, every week.'

'Before when?' Courtney said. Such keenness. I wondered why she was so resolute on impeaching the Doctor. She hadn't suffered under him. What did she stand to gain? A Nobel Prize? What about the rest of us? If she reached those heights, would we be remembered? Why did it take a foreigner to dig up our own truths? Is it because she had money? What was this 'save-Africa' syndrome that clutched at the hearts of foreigners? Or was she really a scorned lover seeking revenge?

'I haven't seen the helicopter in two years,' the old lady said.

'Bingo!' Courtney said under her breath. 'How do you know it was the Doctor?' she asked again.

The old lady gestured the shape of a pipe. That was his iconic feature. Hitler's moustache, Bokassa's regalia, the Doctor's pipe.

'When did you see him?' I croaked. Nothing about the woman suggested she would make up such a story. She probably never left her village. Money didn't motivate her. Probably had never told a lie in her life.

'We used to carry night soil here,' she said, 'because we didn't want our sewage and food mixing. Someone came to warn us to stay away from the forest, to find a new place to throw away our night soil. We were told that there was powerful juju in the forest, and the people in the helicopter were trying to fight it. They said whatever lived there was causing our floods and poverty. But me, I wouldn't just believe that. I spent two days hiding in the forest to see the helicopter. I don't know why I wasn't scared. For two days I inhaled stinking shit and saw that we had been lied to. They were throwing two bodies into the earth that day. Bloody things. And the Doctor stood not too far off, watching the men at work. I saw blood dripping into the soil.'

Miss Olympio gagged.

'Why didn't you tell anyone?' Courtney said.

'Would you?' the old woman retorted.

'Did you come back?' I asked.

She shook her head and said, 'Only when we stopped hearing the helicopter. I came, and all over the forest were heaps of sand, like anthills. Bodies everywhere. Maybe you are even standing on some.'

'How do we know it's not just the burial ground for the village, or that she isn't just making this up? Can we open one of the graves?' said Courtney.

The old woman threw up her hands, brandishing them at Courtney. 'No, no, no!'

Courtney turned to the interpreter. 'Don't repeat this to her. We have to know if she's telling the truth. This could be a ploy for attention. We need to know that there are bodies in there.'

'Courtney ...' Diouf began. 'I think we'll have to take this woman at her word. Can you imagine her fabricating this story?'

Courtney turned to me for my, I presumed, more rational opinion. Efo Komla kept popping into my head, which I heeded as a warning sign.

'She reminds me of someone I know,' I said. 'He never lied.'

Courtney muttered something under her breath, and I'm quite sure I heard 'Africans.'

'Okay, you all stay here. Give me the camera,' she barked at the videographer. 'Is it on? Make sure it's on.'

The old lady backed up and left us in the forest, and I felt horrible. The video never made it to the light of day, so I don't know if Courtney managed to film her bones. The videographer would have nothing to do with the camera after that. It was Courtney's, anyway.

I considered myself the progressive African man, yet when confronted with superstition, I was immobilized. Courtney had come to a place that was sacred, and was ready to defile it to achieve her goals. And yet we'd just found evidence that would bring justice to everyone who'd suffered under the Doctor. For the first time, I realized my life's purpose: I had to tell this story. Not Courtney. And even if I only got an audience of one, at least one person would know the truth about Doctor Karamoh Saturday and the other bloody architects of our country's history.

CHAPTER THIRTY-FIVE

Picnic

Atsu's first proper date with Nasar. Outside the classroom or the comfort of the Avokas's house, she finds herself unable to relax. She's bashful again, and even though she wants to hug him, to feel that physical intimacy they shared in her room, she shakes his hand instead.

'Yeah, yeah! This is DJ Onesandtwos, live from the nation's capital, bringing you the hottest beats from around the world. But first, a note from our sponsors,' blasts from the car radio.

Nasar begins the story of a half-crazy woman who tried to get into his office building the day before.

'How can anyone be half crazy?' she asks. 'Either you're crazy or you're not, no?'

'She looked normal, beautiful, even. She was wearing a bright-green dress and red lipstick and said she was looking for the Pan Am offices.'

Atsu wants to ask if the woman was more beautiful than she is, but doesn't. It's madness. Getting jealous over a madwoman. Although his tone allays her fears. He's just narrating a story.

'I tell her Pan Am closed its offices years ago. I wasn't

even born then. But she insists that she's supposed to meet a man there. After I say over ten times that the office she wants is not in the building, she decides to be smart. She walks out and charges back in. I had to chase after her and carry her outside.'

'That's funny.'

'Not the smell coming off her body.'

'Sorry.'

'Love can do things to people.'

She pictures being in that woman's shoes, Nasar leaving her, and she, distraught and love-crazy. The thought isn't pleasant, so when Nasar slots a cassette into the tape player and Bob Marley croons, 'Roots, Rock, Reggae,' she closes her eyes, swaying her hips in the seat to block any more negativity. The dread that had filled her before has abated somewhat, but a hint of it remains in her belly. She likes that it's still there, watchful and cautious.

'Can I surprise you?' says Nasar. She is tempted to say yes, but what if he leads her to a place and takes advantage of her, asks the pit in her belly. 'You trust me, right?' he says, as though he heard the lump of fear. She nods reluctantly and watches as he steers the car effortlessly.

'Whose car is this?'

'Ah. That's all part of you trusting me. It's not important whose car this is. It's about where we're going. Let me get some things first.'

He stops outside a red-and-blue kiosk, with the words 'the,' 'sum,' 'of,' and 'parts.' Pride swells in her chest. One day reading won't be a thing she has to think about. It'll just be as natural as breathing. Nasar returns with two fat plastic bags and places them on the back seat.

'You're going to love this place,' he says.

'I'm already very happy,' she says. 'Thank you.'

They drive up the hill that leads to the Doctor's mansion, and Atsu is not sure if she should be comforted or scared. Buildings below grow smaller. Only a few houses remain the higher they go. Are they going to the Doctor's? Just before the high walls of the Doctor's home become visible, Nasar veers left and they arrive at an open field dotted with royal palms. Below the hill she sees the road that leads to her hometown, the stone hills that line the road, and the thick forest that starts beyond it.

'This is a small slice of paradise in the city,' he says. 'Not a lot of people know about it.'

As she's dragging out the mat from the car's boot, she panics. No one else is in sight.

'How did you find this place?' she asks, ignoring the tightening in her chest. Even though they aren't strangers anymore, she can't quite relax around him.

'When we were going through guard training. We had to run up and down the hill. You see that pole? We'd start there, run downhill and climb back up. Not easy.'

'Why did you decide to become a security guard?'

'Haven't you seen these muscles?' He pulls up his sleeve and flexes his arm.

'Seriously.' She spreads the mat on the grass and settles on it. Nasar spreads out a tin of sardines, bread, box wine, margarine.

'It felt like the only thing I could do. And it pays well. But I'm going to start my printing press. And you, why did you become a housegirl?'

'A woman brought my boss to my village to look for a housegirl. I decided to take the job so I could send my mother money. My dream was to go to catering school. I thought if I started making my own money I could eventually pay to take cooking classes and then open a restaurant, but here I am.'

'It's not too late,' Nasar says, sitting on the mat, his body inches away from hers. 'First you learn English, then you take cooking classes.'

'Why are some people luckier than others? I don't think my madam has ever struggled for anything.'

'She's not *that* rich. And you don't know where she's going to be in ten years. Who knew I'd have this car? Who knows what's …'

'It's yours! Why have you been hiding it all this while?'

'I just got it. A man in one of the offices sold it to me.'

'It's nice.'

'Your boyfriend doesn't play around.' Nasar smiles and stares at her. She breaks the gaze. The palm tree in front of them is less threatening. His eyes were too intense. Are they boyfriend and girlfriend? 'Atsu,' he says and grabs her hand. It's a firm but gentle grasp. She tries to picture what he sees: her hair, curled last night; her eyes lined the way Ndeye showed her when they were on speaking terms; lipstick. The make-up she did in the lorry on her way to meet him. No way she was leaving the Avokas's house all made up. People stared, but she'd seen women do it before, so she ignored their disparaging, judgmental looks. He should know that she's made an effort to look nice.

'What are you afraid of?' he says, his eyes softer.

'Nothing.'

'No. Really.'

'You're a stranger.'

He laughs and says, 'Still? Will you let me prove to you that you can trust me?'

She didn't realize her fear was so palpable. She's not sure if it stems from thinking he'll leave her, like her mother's men did. Or it's just the newness of this interaction, of being with a man.

When she nods he releases her hand and caresses her arm. She feels his hot breath, inhales the mint of his gum. He's looking at her deeply, pressing his nose to her cheek. Slowly his mouth settles on hers, then his tongue wets her top lip. He pulls back, stares at her intensely, and presses his mouth on hers again. They kiss deeply.

CHAPTER THIRTY-SIX

Paradise

I couldn't believe I had stolen documents from Duell and Co. after my suspension, but that's the thing about madness—things just spin out of control. I decided to scope out the collective even though I didn't exactly have a plan. Truth is, I think it was more that I was looking for help, and on the phone, Auntie Adisa, the head of the collective, sounded like a woman who had taken care of hundreds of children. I needed a mother, and Mma was the last person I could speak to. I would go to the farm, establish a relationship for the ungrateful people at Duell, and hopefully find a way out of my messy situation with Theo and Obi (even though he wanted nothing to do with me).

That morning I woke up more woozy and nauseous than ever, but I wouldn't give up on my need to see Auntie Adisa. I sat in my car, light-headed and foolish but unstoppable. I drove for three hours, and from the moment I laid eyes on the place I knew my foolhardiness was warranted. It was market day, and a flamboyance of girls was seated behind plush tomatoes, garden eggs, plantains, and a host of other vegetables pyramided on long wooden tables. It reminded me of farmers' markets in England, which I couldn't afford to shop at but which I loved to frequent because of the burst of colour and freshness. The girls beckoned me over seductively, and in my dizzy state I went from stall to stall.

The young women smiled even when I didn't buy from them, although I could see the disappointment etched in some of those smiles. Still, it wasn't like other villages, where friends were in constant competition with each other, where five women sold the same thing and jostled over customers. Here, everybody specialized in their own product. When I got to the last girl I snapped out of my daze and asked for Auntie Adisa.

'I'll take you to her,' the girl said and asked her friend to mind her table. She walked me on a dusty path that snaked along small neat adobe huts until we came to a bright-blue house. As I waited outside, she skipped inside and returned with four stools. She offered me one, and I sat and looked at the peaceful village. The houses were arranged in straight lines, and before each was a little garden with tomatoes and herbs. It felt magical and yet unsettled me slightly, because it made me wonder why I'd chosen to live the way I did. Constantly running up and down, chasing the next thing, when at heart I was a farm girl.

Auntie Adisa came out, a tall woman with hair braided in a cornrow that grazed her back and silver earrings that glistened. She shook my hand and lowered herself next to me.

'Adisa,' she said. Something in her demeanour—maybe the timbre of her voice, or the way she held herself, shoulders high—told me I wasn't going to be working with an uneducated farmer. I would have to put on my best selling game. Yet I couldn't summon my cojones. It wasn't my place to talk to her, and I had nothing to offer. I introduced myself and she listened quietly as I brought her up to speed with the history of our company—headquartered in the UK, offices in ten countries, our branch was started by a brother-and-sister duo, exporters of palm oil, cocoa, and shea butter. I started my usual spiel on how working with us would be mutually beneficial, and she looked at me with an expression not dissimilar to Mother Superior's when I was seventeen and had been called into her office for staying in the dining hall too late with Obi. I kept talking but kept my head low, cursing the chipped nail polish on my toes. Three others came over and Auntie Adisa finally spoke.

'Welcome, Zahra. We usually start with an introduction of ourselves, and what our mission is, and then we let you tell us how we can work together.' I was a bit peeved that she hadn't stopped me earlier. She introduced the other women, and nodded gratefully at the girl who'd brought me over as she placed cups of water at our feet.

'We're a cooperative of women that started in 1980,' she said. 'Our mission is to grow our own food, to be as self-sufficient as possible, and to sell what we don't use. We're from different walks of life. I was once a schoolteacher. Some of us are nurses, housewives. We even have a bus driver.'

She explained how each of them focused on one crop to cultivate, how they were learning to process their raw materials, but wanted me to know that they weren't isolating themselves. Some women held other jobs in the cities or went to trade there, some were married and lived with their husbands and children, and others lived on their own and it was fine.

'We're just trying to live peacefully and productively,' she concluded. 'Some people say this is paradise, but we still have problems. We're not immune to the larger goings-on in the country. And now, tell us about yourself.'

I fumbled through how I was excited to be possibly working with them, because my organization's goals were aligned with her cooperative's. We also worked with women, helping them add value to their raw material by teaching them processing techniques and then exporting their semi-finished products to other countries and companies.

'You're the middlemen?' one woman said.

'Not really,' I said, not sure how to counter that, because we were.

'I'm not saying it's a bad thing,' the woman said. 'It's just good for us to call a spade a spade.'

I hadn't realized what I was up against. Maybe I should go back to the ignorant, illiterate farmers.

'Several of the cooperatives we've worked with haven't had the money, tools or wherewithal to get their material from raw to presentable,' I said. 'What we do is provide the training, capital, and equipment, and then help them get their material out there.'

'What's your commission?' Auntie Adisa asked.

'It depends on what we provide. If we train and equip

you, we get 50 per cent of the earnings. If we work with a cooperative like you, you know, where all we're doing is providing exposure, it's 30 per cent.'

I was expecting some response, but they just continued to stare at me.

'Okay!' Auntie Adisa said and clapped her thighs. 'Thanks for coming out. Seeing as you've come all the way, we'll show you around the farm and the rest of our village.'

I couldn't protest but didn't like the feeling of being rejected, which is what had just happened. Most people balked at our high rates, but the money went into paying off crooked customs people and the rest trickled down afterward. If she hadn't cut me off I would have told her so. Who was I kidding? I could only carry off the lie this far and I didn't have the energy to keep it going. Auntie Adisa sent for a boy, who looked not much older than Kojo. She and her friends stayed seated. What would they say about me? Had they looked at me and seen, deep in my soul, that I was dishonest, unfaithful, and rotten? Could they see the disease eating at me? And even though that was hardly to blame for my actions of the past year, would they forgive me on account of that?

The boy, David, walked shyly ahead of me, and I tried to make small talk with him. He was applying for universities in the city, he said, and wanted to be an agricultural engineer. His current job was managing the huge composting plant the cooperative had set up. He showed me the deep well they pumped their water from, then we ended the tour on the palm-oil plantation, where red bunches of kernels gleamed at me. I needed Auntie Adisa more than she needed me. I was being interviewed. It wasn't the other way around. They didn't need the middleman.

I turned to David. 'Will you move back here after university?' I asked.

'No,' he said, staring intently at one spot. 'It's boring. I'll come visit and come here to get my food, but go back to the city. I want to manage a big office in the city.'

His answer was honest, and perhaps he didn't know better, but I was heartbroken for Auntie Adisa. What was it about youth that made us want to rebel and have nothing to do with our parents? Even though I loved my father's farm, when I went off to school I didn't even consider agriculture. And now here I was, desperately wanting back in. I stared at the palm kernels again and they'd grown blurry.

'Okay,' I said to steel myself, but my guide took that to mean we should get going. Unsteadily I followed him, watching the white of his shirt blur into the grey of his shorts. 'I think I need to lie down,' I said.

To this day, that's all I remember before I woke up in Auntie Adisa's house. I don't know how David got me there. Did he carry me there, his adolescent hands fondling places they shouldn't? Did he call out for help?

In the dark room my vertigo was stronger than ever, so I pressed my eyes shut. I couldn't fall asleep even though I wanted to. My head felt like it was spinning on top of the pillowcase. I pulled my thighs to my chest, inhaling and exhaling, and soon the bed, too, was spiralling. It went around and around while my body floated somewhere. I didn't feel pain, just airless vertigo.

I woke up with a cold press on my forehead in a small sparsely furnished room, and across from me, a photograph of Auntie Adisa in a black graduation cap and gown. She walked in as I was trying to lift myself up.

'You're not well,' she said.

'What happened?' I asked.

'Shhh,' she said. 'You can't drive back to the city today. There's no way I'm letting you do that.'

'Can we call my husband?'

She nodded and mopped my forehead. In walked a girl carrying a tray of something soupy. She set it before me but I didn't think I could stomach anything, not with the way I was feeling. Auntie Adisa asked for my number.

My confusion cleared and I remembered why I was there. I needed her. 'Are you going to work with me?' I deliriously asked.

'We have to sleep over it.'

'You can trust me,' I said, trying to believe the words myself.

She helped me sit up, propping two flat pillows behind me, and fed me spoonfuls of tomato soup. I could taste the earth in each bite. I pictured Auntie Adisa bending over to pluck the reddest tomato, could see her lovingly washing it and telling her daughter, or whoever that girl was, how to make the soup. It was divine.

'When you're feeling better I want you to tell me all about yourself,' Adisa said. 'We only work with people with whom we have a connection. And to be honest with you, I haven't felt one.'

The girl came back in and said no one answered the phone. I slept again and woke up fuming. They still couldn't get through to anyone at home. Where was Atsu? Was she being a coward and not picking up the phone? After nine months of working with us, she should know better. As for Theo, I just didn't know what he was up to. We would have to talk as soon as I got back. I would come clean about Obi, and he'd have to tell me what was going on. Kojo wasn't so young anymore that a divorce would be damaging, if it came to that.

I walked outside the room and found Auntie Adisa reading. I was envious of the peace that surrounded and radiated from her. She looked up from her book and smiled.

'You look less ill, but I'm not going to let you drive to the city.'

'Thank you for everything,' I said.

'You were running a very high temperature. You should go to the hospital as soon as you get back. Make sure it's not meningitis. Are you hungry?'

'No. Thank you,' I said and sat across from her. The room was no larger than half our living room, yet it seemed bigger, roomier, and less stuffy.

'I arranged for our driver to take you back to the city tomorrow.'

'Thank you, but you shouldn't have. I feel much better now.' Auntie Adisa watched me in that quiet way of hers. 'How did you find this place?' I asked.

'My husband found it,' she said, laying the book on the side table. I made out the brown skin of a muscular young man wrapped around a small body with flowing hair, and I almost burst out laughing. The pillar of morality reading a romance novel.

'Where is he?' I said.

'He was a lawyer and owned a lot of land before the coup, but after that a lot of his property was taken away. He started to get vocal about the way things were running, and then he disappeared. I moved here the year after. Never found his body. I had to get far away from all that.'

I was surprised by her candour and fearlessness. I could be a Saturday person, and here she was telling me all of it.

'Similar thing happened to my family,' I said. 'Except no one disappeared. How come they didn't seize this property?'

'Ah! It was useless to them. They wanted to distribute the land in the city among themselves and build their three-storey houses to parade about town with. But I'm not bitter. I've met the most interesting women through this cooperative. People tell me not to say this, because it makes me sound callous or cold, but I'm a genuine believer in things happening for a reason.'

'My husband is writing the Doctor's memoirs,' I said, unsure why I said so. She looked taken aback, so I added, 'Not that he had a choice. Though, every now and then he tells me how hard it is for him to connect the man he's writing about with the man who committed all these atrocities. For instance, the Doctor is soft-spoken when he's not behind a microphone. Can you imagine?'

'That's one book I won't be reading,' she said and smiled. 'Do you have children?'

'A son. In secondary school. You?'

She adopted a daughter late in life. 'Are you in love?'

Her question jarred me. I knew I was being interviewed, but that was too personal. Was I in love? With two people. Who did I love more? Theo? But I had never stopped loving Obi. Being around Auntie Adisa made me feel hollow. And whorish.

'I think I am,' I said.

'I mean, are you still in love with each other?'

'Oh, I don't know. We're different now.'

'What's different? Who changed?'

'I don't know,' I started. Why was she probing so deeply? Her chest heaved up and down in her indigo *boubou* and a smile puckered her lips. A naughty smile, not malicious. 'Theo's always been good,' I said. 'Not overly ambitious, but caring, very loyal.' She was staring at me intensely. 'I think I changed. He's too good. I think I want more excitement, and maybe he doesn't have that.'

'Excitement? Darling, you're not twenty anymore. Can you see yourself growing old with him despite this lack of excitement you speak of?'

'Ye-e-es. I suppose. But couldn't you grow old with anyone, really? I don't know. I'm more concerned about the quality of time spent together.'

'Just something to think about. Some of us didn't get that opportunity.'

When I got home Atsu was holding vigil in the living room. Theo was on the phone. I wanted to ask them where they'd been the day before, but I saw the bags under their eyes and realized I'd given them the scare of their lives.

'I passed out,' I said. 'The woman I was with didn't think it was a good idea for me to come home. We called. Several times, then it got too late.'

'What woman? Where were you?'

'Working.'

'Working where? You've been suspended,' Theo said. 'Unless you've miraculously found a new job.' Atsu was still in the living room, lingering. I didn't want her to see me getting dressed-down, and wished she would disappear, but she just stood there staring at her feet, probably relishing this moment she seldom got to experience.

'Exactly where were you?' Theo said.

'I told you. I think I've found our next big producer.'

'Have you lost your mind? What if your Somto and Emma don't take you back? Then what?'

'Atsu, get me some water,' I said. Why couldn't she take a hint? She shuffled into the kitchen and I turned to Theo. 'Look,' I said, 'I know if tables were turned, you'd be happy to sit on your ass the whole day and get nothing done, but I'm not you. That's the fundamental difference between you and me. I do. I act. I am not acted upon. And if I have to break some rules to help us get food on the table, why not?'

The muscles in Theo's jaw flexed, and if I'd been standing closer I don't doubt that he'd have hit me. He wasn't the hitting kind, and had never laid a finger on me, but I'd pushed him.

'Woman,' he said, 'don't ever talk to me like that. Not in *my* house.'

He picked up his car keys and left the house.

CHAPTER THIRTY-SEVEN

Saturday's Boy

Atsu's never really had to yearn after anything, learning, as she did from Mama, to swiftly pick up the pieces and move on. But now she has to deal with anticipation, and after a couple of days apart from Nasar, it's built up in her chest so strongly that she's ready to explode. She didn't realize it would be so physical, this love thing. Her body craves being with Nasar, similar to the way it wants ice cream or a good fried bean cake, but stronger, an almost insatiable thirst, quenched only when she sees him. But Madam has started making her life difficult, like asking her to stick around the house even on her days off. Nasar says she should tell her bosses she has a boyfriend—after all, aren't housegirls human too? Don't they deserve love? But her bosses will think she's not serious about the job because she wants to get married, and sack her. And then where will she go?

    He's asked her to come home with him several times, but she's had to turn down his requests, so he's stopped asking. Imagine her surprise when he brings it up again after class, after not talking about it for weeks. This time she says yes. Besides, this time, he tells her, it's highly important, without a flirtatious light in his eyes. She's heard that men get serious about marriage proposals, and although she thinks it's too soon for a proposal, one never knows.

After class, she calls the Avokas' from a communication centre and tells Mr. Avoka that Gloria isn't feeling well. He's understanding and tells her to take all the time she needs. But just as she's about to hang up, Madam's voice cuts in, like a mosquito thirsty for blood.

'Is that Atsu?'

'Her cousin is sick.'

'Again?'

Mr. Avoka's voice grows softer. There are words coming through, but they are muffled. Madam must know Atsu is lying.

'Zahra ... Atsu, sorry, Mrs. Avoka needs you,' Mr. Avoka finally says.

Atsu's heart breaks. What if Nasar takes back his marriage proposal because she's spineless? She looks at her reflection in the dull grey glass of the booth. Life is a road filled with people blocking her happiness, and she needs to fight back, the same way she fought Mama. She tries to find the energy, the words to tell Mr. Avoka, Madam, that she can't come now.

'She's very sick,' she stammers. 'Please.'

'Hold on,' Mr. Avoka says, and the mumbling starts again. Nasar peeks into the window, gesturing with his hands, 'What's going on?' She shrugs.

'Atsu.'

'Madam?'

'The idea with these classes was that you'd finish your housework first and then, as a bonus, take classes. Now, this cousin business of yours ... The next thing I know you'll be telling me you're pregnant.' Is Madam on to her? 'I need you around the house.'

'Okay,' Atsu says, unsure if it means, Okay, I'm coming, or Okay, but I'm still doing what I want.

She hangs up. Outside, Nasar is talking to the old man who runs the communication centre.

'I think they know about us,' she says as they leave the kiosk.

'They don't. And so what if they do? They're having problems and using you as bait.'

'What if I lose my job?'

'You won't. Besides, what I have to tell you is about them. It's important.'

Her heart feels heavy. What has a marriage proposal got to do with her bosses?

'Tell me.'

'I can't tell you here.'

'I'm going home if you don't tell me here.'

'Is that it? You're going?'

'Then tell me now. Right here.'

He looks about. 'I can't.'

Nasar lives in a one-bedroom bungalow in a courtyard enclosed with small, colourful chalets. He keeps the place with a soldier's neatness, not a shoe out of place. A two-seat sofa is flush against the wall, a centre table holds a few newspapers, and a small TV sits on a wooden shelf. At the other end of the room is a kitchenette with dishes stacked from red to blue.

'Your house is nice,' she says. Even though she's hardly placated, she feels like she shouldn't be rude.

'Thank you,' he says as he pours her a cup of Coke.

On the blue walls are posters of Bob Marley and other Rastafarians she's never heard of. He disappears for a while, and she wants to tell him to speed things up. It's not like there isn't a lioness at the house waiting for her, ready to shred her to pieces.

Nasar returns dressed in a singlet and shorts—almost naked. Although his body is not unblemished, he's fit, and his skin is rich, like an iroko tree.

'I couldn't tell you this anywhere but here,' he says, peeking out through the curtain-less windows. She would put up orange curtains in the living room if she had to give it a woman's touch. 'At least I know no one is around to hear us. There could be a recording machine in the car.'

The last serial killing happened on the day she was with Nasar. Unless there's more than one killer and he's standing in front of her. Has she been fooled all along? She sees Nasar's expression become grave and her fingertips grow cold. She's suddenly aware of how rough the sofa feels under her palms. She can't show any fear, so she places her palms under her thighs.

'Tell me,' she says, her throat dry. 'I have to go soon.'

At this rate she'd rather take a lorry home than have Nasar drive her to the forest to do away with her. The room plunges into darkness, and Atsu feels a lump of fear constrict her throat. Nasar groans.

'This country will never progress!' he says. 'Every day, no power!' He sits next to her and grabs her hand from under her body. Did she miss all the signs earlier? Human beings are blind, until it's too late. 'I haven't been entirely honest with you about who I am.'

God! Atsu thinks. He's going to tell me, then rape and kill me. What's happening? She's not sure whether to bolt out of there or whether to hit him, then run. Truth is she's paralyzed, too scared to act. No one trained her for this kind of situation. He clasps his fingers in hers. To free herself, she's going to have to undo the hand grip, which seems to be growing tighter.

'I used to be a Saturday Boy,' he says. Atsu hears him, but it doesn't register. She can't see his face to read what his eyes are saying. Is he joking? Does this mean she's out of the serial-killer zone or not? A: Isn't nobody supposed to know who Saturday's Boys are? B: People say they are the ones killing women in the city. He continues, 'And even though I haven't worked for the Doctor in a number of years, I made some good friends. And one of them told me something about your boss.'

The bulb above them lights up. Finally able to exhale, she sits back in the sofa. It really isn't about her. And in that instant, she's not sure she cares about her boss, whichever one it is. She thought she was going to die. Nasar looks sad or sorry. Not menacing.

'What is it?' she says.

'My friend was talking about a coup plot that's being investigated. He said one of the plotters was a government official, an Avoka. And then I remembered the day I was in your house, when your madam almost caught us. I read some of the papers on your boss's table and saw his name on the sheets, and because it's not a very common last name, I started asking the guy for more. Also, because the papers had information about President Karamoh.'

'Wait. A coup, meaning what?'

'Meaning they want to kick President Karamoh from power.'

'My boss?'

'That's what I've been asking myself. But he's been blacklisted, so if you could warn him, it would be good.'

Her fright has gone and left something empty and unfeeling. She wishes she could feel bad for Mr. Avoka, but her emotions are spent. Besides, isn't Mr. Avoka working for this same Doctor? The Avokas never told her, but with the thin walls in that house, she was able put it all together. It would make sense for him to have papers on the president in his study. Then it begins to sink in, who Nasar is.

'What's the worst thing you did?' she says. 'As a Saturday Boy.'

'I can't tell you.'

'I can't be anything to you, not even your friend, if you won't be honest with me about this.'

'Atsu, I can't. I'm not proud of my past, and I'm not the same person. Please, let it be?'

She picks up her bag and walks to the door. Going home from this neighbourhood is going to be a nightmare. She'll have to switch lorries at least three times.

'Wait, I'll take you.'

'No. Not if you won't tell me the truth.'

'Fine. But I'm not the same person. Remember that. I did a lot of things. But the one I still get nightmares from is … I beat up a pregnant woman.' A part of Atsu is relieved that he didn't kill or rape someone. 'She begged and begged us to stop. But we kicked at her belly hard. The louder she screamed, the more violent we grew. There were three of us. She cried out until blood stained her cloth. Our boots kept going. We'd been trained to punish greed, and it didn't matter if you were man, woman, or child. The woman had stockpiled boxes of provisions, selling them at four times the normal price. Women like her, we believed, were the root of the country's inflation and economic problems. We didn't stop until an older commander saw us and ordered us to cease. Two boys dragged her into her own store.' He pauses. 'I don't know what happened to her or the baby.'

When they're parked in front of the Freemans's house, he says, 'I understand if you don't want to be my girlfriend anymore.'

She doesn't know what she wants. She's so confused she starts opening the Freemans's gate by mistake. The watchman answers it and seems surprised. It's just as well—she needs someone to talk to. Ndeye lets her in without a word.

Atsu says, 'I really need a friend. Will you forgive me for whatever I did to you?'

Ndeye stares at Alejandro and Ernestina, about to kiss, and doesn't respond. This cold treatment is beginning to feel worse than everything she's been through tonight. When an ad pops up, Ndeye finally acknowledges her.

'Foolish girl,' Ndeye says, her tone caught between playful and serious. 'Why did we drag this out for so long?'

Atsu rushes to Ndeye and breaks into sobs as they hug. It turns out Ndeye already knew about Nasar's past because Harry told her, which makes Atsu resent Nasar even more. Ndeye suggests that Atsu not tell her employers. Either way she's in a bad situation, so it's better to stay quiet.

And once she goes through the Avokas's gate, she realizes Ndeye is right. How exactly is she to inform Mr. Avoka that she brought a former Saturday Boy into his house, walked him through every room, and because of that the Saturday Boy knows that he's in trouble? She can't begin to find the words. She goes to Madam, who, after trying to get her home, has nothing for her to do. Atsu goes to bed, guarding what she knows will change their lives in the coming days.

CHAPTER THIRTY-EIGHT

Shutting Down

It was late afternoon. Atsu sat behind me, her knees brushing my shoulders, lightly spreading shea butter on my scalp. I frightened the poor thing. I wanted to grab her finger and press it down on my head, but even that I couldn't muster the strength to do. I would have oiled my hair myself, but the slightest effort I made exhausted me. I needed her more than ever because I sure wasn't asking Theo for any kind of help. So, as she parted rows in my hair, I wondered what went through her mind. I'd always thought of her as the maid and had never pictured her as her own person with desires, wants, needs, passion. Who was she when she went to sleep? What did she dream of? What made her cry and what made her laugh? She was always pleasant with me, never pulled a face, and I wasn't always easy to be around.

The TV was on and Auntie Florence was frothing eggs with a whisk. I liked cooking shows, but watching the same programs every day was getting to me, and Auntie Florence was beginning to remind me of Mma. Constant, always there, thought she was funnier than she actually was. I hadn't seen or heard from Obi and I missed him terribly. The house was too quiet, and anytime the TV screen darkened I caught our reflection, Atsu's and mine. I don't think we'd ever had this much physical contact.

She began to loosen up. Her toes uncurled, her muscles weren't as taut as before, and I closed my eyes. Before long I was wrapped in a quick nap.

I woke up with Atsu's knees still next to my head because she was too terrified to wake me up. Was I such a monster? I thanked her and stood up, too quickly. So suddenly that I crumpled to the floor and hit my head against a side of Atsu's chair.

'Madam!' she shrieked and rushed to me, her fingers grabbing the undersides of my arms. I couldn't get up yet, so I signalled for her to hold on. I touched my head and I wasn't cut or bleeding, but I still needed to get to a doctor. The spells now came too often.

'Get my keys, please,' I said. She didn't move, and I was sure if I could extract the words hidden in her mouth, they would be 'stupid woman.' 'Atsu, I need to get to the hospital.'

'Madam, let me call a taxi,' she said.

I could pull myself together enough to drive to the hospital. I wasn't concussed, I wasn't bleeding, and driving was really not that strenuous. I'd had whatever was eating at my insides for so long that it wasn't going to kill me in a day.

'Lock the back door and let's go,' I said.

She disappeared into her room and returned wearing a dress I'd given her. She filled it out better than I ever had. When we stepped out of the house, the sun was already on its way down, shaded with wisps of purple clouds and birds flocking in Vs. My left temple pulsed violently. It would be good to pull over, park the car, and call a taxi, but I'd already convinced myself it would be fine.

Night descended on us the farther we drove from home, and soon the side of the road was lined with lighted-up kiosks with piles of roasting meat and corn drinks. These vendors were preparing for the men and women who lived for the night. I used to be a night person. I used to be invincible.

My vision grew hazy. This wasn't the time to pass out. I was endangering our lives and more, but it was too late to stop now. If I parked the car in the middle of nowhere, it could get carjacked and I'd have to pay back Duell and Co. (they surprisingly hadn't taken my keys away from me).

'Madam,' Atsu said as we approached the Bakoy Market.

'Uh huh?'

'Madam!' she screamed just in time for me to steer the car away from a lorry parked on the side of the road.

'I'm so sorry,' I said, pulling over to the side, shaken. 'I'm so sorry. Sorry.'

'Madam, a taxi?'

'Yes.' Nausea rose, pressing against the walls of my gullet. 'God, I feel sick.'

I opened the door and heaved out everything I'd eaten that day.

'Jesus, Jesus!' Atsu muttered under her breath. She got out of her seat and came to my side. She was talking very fast, and it took a moment for me to realize she was praying quietly and quickly. Her voice was tiny, and I appreciated that she wasn't shouting down on me to cast out my numerous demons, but it was sweet of her to pray for me.

'Thank you, Atsu,' I said when she went silent.

She stuck her hand out at cars zooming by.

'Teaching Hospital,' I whispered, every system in my body saying, this is the end, Zahra.

In the back of the taxi Atsu rested my head on her thighs and smoothed my hair. I wanted to be sick all over again, but I inhaled and exhaled, trying to think of a better place. Auntie Adisa's farm. In and out I breathed, as the taxi driver warned me not to vomit in his car.

At the hospital people were squashed on benches, others were sitting or lying on the floor. I wanted to sit badly, but not a single inch of bench space was available. Big hospitals had a way of equalizing everybody. I couldn't get a seat, and would probably have to lie on the floor in the state I was in. I wanted to call for Dr. Mamby, but I didn't have an appointment and would still have to wait like everybody. I lowered my body to the ground, banishing thoughts of whatever liquids had been spilled there.

'Madam, no!' Atsu said, roughly grabbing my upper arms.

'It's okay,' I said, pulling myself down.

'I'll beg someone to let you sit,' she said.

It was a nice thought, that Atsu wanted better for me, that she thought I deserved special treatment, but truth is I was nobody. Even worse than a nobody. Nobodies lived on the zero-axis, barely existing, not troubling anyone else, and they definitely weren't horrible to people they loved. We walked to the mass of people. Old, young, dressed in

African print, dressed in suits, the people there all deserved seats.

'Please,' Atsu begged, 'she's very sick. Will you let her sit?'

A number of people sucked their teeth. Several times.

'Everyone is very sick here,' said a woman. I didn't look up. I focused my eyes on my feet, ashamed Atsu was doing this for me, but part of me feeling entitled to a seat. I was better educated than three-quarters of the people there, I spoke better English than them, and I'd been to more countries than they even knew of. My husband worked for the Doctor, goddamnit! I deserved a seat.

I sank to the ground next to an old woman who smelled of rosewater.

'Atsu,' I said. 'Please fill out my hospital information and come back.' I rummaged in my purse for my hospital card. She hesitated and I realized why. 'You've been taking classes for months now, you can do it. Just copy this and ask the nurse for help. Also, tell them to call Dr. Mamby. Beg them.'

A woman broke into song, then burst into prayer, asking God to deliver her son from his typhoid fever. My nausea rose again. I didn't want to throw up in front of all of these people, in front of the crowd. I didn't need to feel smaller than I already did. Where was the bathroom? I tried lifting myself up but the room looped in wild circles, so I sat back down. I gagged and caught eyes with a sickly child whose hair was the colour of straw, her skin as dark as mine.

Atsu returned triumphant. I thought it meant Dr. Mamby would see me, but she said she was able to write my information down without a mistake.

'And Dr. Mamby?'

'He's not working today.'

Great. There was no way to call Theo. He hadn't given me the number he was using at the Doctor's. Atsu would have to go home, tell him what happened, have him drive my car back home, and then come back for me. She slid down and rested my head on her shoulder.

'What would I do without you?' I whispered.

She smiled sadly and sang into my hair. There was no rank odour coming off her. Anna had a theory that all maids stank. And here Atsu was as fresh as a hibiscus.

People came and left, and night enveloped the waiting room with its damp smell and distant echoes. When a doctor finally saw me, it was close to midnight. I sent off Atsu with instructions for Theo. The doctor, a young lanky man, apologized for making me wait so long. He probably felt the need to apologize because of the British accent I'd heightened.

'I'll have to admit you tonight.'

'Is that really necessary?'

'Based on your recent history, I have a strong feeling it's a tumour.'

'What does that mean? I mean, I know what the word means, but how can you just tell by looking at me?'

'I can't just tell. But your symptoms, especially the eyes blurring, suggest a growth of sorts. I can run other tests in the morning and make arrangements to get an MRI scan done. It's not the cheapest procedure, and there's a long line of patients.'

'I know. I'll come back tomorrow,' I said, all the while feeling like my stomach and its contents would erupt from my mouth. 'My husband's returning for me.'

'You're in no state to go home. Let's prepare a room for you, and I'll leave a note for your husband at the triage.'

He stepped out of his office and a nurse came for me. She put me in a room painted the same sickly green as every other space in the hospital. I was hooked on IVs and left with a deeply asleep neighbour. If Theo or Atsu came into my room that night, I didn't hear them.

CHAPTER THIRTY-NINE

THE DAILY POST

Monday, June 9, 1997 | We are the news! | Since 1952

When it Rains, it Pours by Theo Avoka

Dear readers, please excuse the length of this column. To do justice to this part of my story, I felt it would be better told as a whole, rather than in instalments.

I'm convinced one of our human survival instincts is being able to sniff out trouble before it lands on our doorstep. Oh, we know when trouble is coming. That's how we know to place ourselves *in* its way. Rarely do we listen to or trust that gut feeling that tells us to run in the opposite direction. Some say this survival instinct is not innate at all, but rather external, that it's the universe or God trying to warn us ahead of time. Whatever it is, I can't think of a single person who hasn't known when they are getting into trouble. Young girl meets charming, tall, handsome man. Every part of her is telling her to split, yet she gets swayed and stays and finds out he's a wife beater when it's too late. I could give a long list of examples. In my case, I knew my work with Courtney would not go unnoticed. The universe sent me the biggest sign before everything came crashing on my head. My wife was admitted to the hospital. It was a signal to stop, to put my family first and not my dreams of grandeur, to get as far away from Courtney and Diouf as possible.

But I did the opposite. I ran straight to Courtney, convincing myself that it was because I had to raise enough money for Zahra's MRI scan. Only Courtney with her American dollars could save us. And after ransacking cupboards in the Doctor's house, bedrooms smelling of dust, mothballs, and age, and stumbling upon fetishes, feathered sculptures, shells and cowries piled in corners, talismans said to guarantee its owner immortality, idols that would make you run for cover, after doing that all for her, surely she would help me out with a loan.

As I spelled out my sob story—I was seated on the cane sofa in her balcony—I felt myself shrink in size. What a cliché I had become: the African with cap in hand. She wrote me a cheque without blinking. The problem was now how to explain to Zahra where the money came from. She still had no idea about my radical activities.

I left Courtney's, heading for the hospital where Zahra was admitted, and right before the Bakoy Market, an unmarked black van overtook me, and I almost crashed into it as it suddenly screeched to a halt in front of me. I barely had time to prepare my usual litany of insults because armed policemen swarmed out of it. I stuffed the cheque into the hole in my dashboard, thanking God that I hadn't had it repaired. Before I could figure out what was going on, I was completely surrounded.

'Get out, get out!' one of them shouted, hitting the butt of his rifle on my window.

'He's shorter than I thought,' one of them said.

My keys were snatched as I stepped out of the car, and with no time to think or react I was shoved into the back of the van. Too shaken to ask what was going on I sat quietly, growing increasingly aware of what this was about. This wasn't a kidnapping or hijacking. It was a proper arrest, just minus handcuffs.

The policemen made small talk that had nothing to do with me. An internal scandal that hadn't wound its way into the civilian world was the topic du jour. The Inspector General of Police's wife was sleeping with a junior officer. And her 'toke' of a husband had found out about the affair but hadn't done anything about it. Toke. Their word, not mine.

We pulled into the police station near the Bakoy Market, the smell of rotting fish and fruit, sounds of a thousand people exchanging money, trading insults, and selling goods. Everything in the station was sweet, fetid, stale, salty. Was this the taste of fear?

In the blue reception area a sprinkling of journalists loitered about, and when they saw me they whipped themselves into a frenzy, snapping their cameras in imitation of the paparazzi. On the east wall, a photo of the Doctor stared down on us.

'Sir, how do you feel?' one of them asked.

'Is it true you were plotting a coup against His Excellency Doctor Karamoh Saturday?' I should have known that's the way it would be spun: a coup. It was worse than I thought. I didn't have an attorney, though I was sure Zea could arrange for one. Or Courtney could. Of course, Courtney. She got me into this mess. What was going to happen to her?

'Two of you have been arrested so far,' said a woman's

voice. 'Who are your other accomplices?'

I almost laughed. Journalists really had to be optimistic, thick-skinned people who would never take no for an answer.

A small knot of people—probably marketgoers—gathered in front of the station, gawking. The policemen seemed to enjoy putting me in the limelight. Word must have spread fast for a throng to be already in place.

'That's the main man,' I heard someone say. It sounded like it was supposed to be a whisper.

'No, the main man is older.'

'Can you see his face? Let me see him!' a shrill voice shouted, and the crowd grew crazed. People pushed each other, stopping short of entering the station, to get a better look at me. I wasn't sure if I should be afraid of this crowd—did they think of me as a hero, or an enemy of the State, or were they just satisfying their curiosity? The volume of people and noise grew higher and I couldn't hear any distinct phrases anymore. Suddenly the policemen decided they'd paraded me enough and one of them shoved me deeper inside, until I was in a cell with a lone, swinging light bulb. The stench of urine overpowered the room, and I prayed I wouldn't have to spend more than an hour there.

I was left alone for over two hours, by which time my bladder was bursting.

'*Massa*!' I shouted. No one came. 'I beg. Someone!'

An older gentleman strolled over.

'Please, I have to use the bathroom.'

'Ah, everyone urinates in the corner.'

'I beg you.'

He chuckled and let me out of the cell to an acrid toilet with a broken seat and stains that had probably been around since the sixties.

'Boss, you should know we 100 per cent support you,' he whispered while closing the door behind me. 'If you need anything, let me know.'

I stepped out of the bathroom and thanked him, didn't correct him. Maybe I could pretend to be proud of something I hadn't done or would never even have the balls to do. He led me back to my cell and repeated his offer.

'Boss. Anything. Cigarette, booze, woman. Just tell me.'

I sat down on the hard bench in the one-windowed room, overhearing a conversation about a boxing match taking place on Sunday evening. Sounds from the market: trucks revving up, bells tinkling, medicine men screaming their wares. I stared at the yellowed ceiling, oscillating between panic and calm. No one I cared about knew where I was. I had to get word out to Zahra. My arrest would come as such a shock, but she would say she saw it coming. I whistled for my new friend, who came laughing and holding his sides.

'What foolishness,' he said to someone in the front room. 'Yessir, boss?'

'I need to tell my wife I'm here. She's in the emergency room of the Teaching Hospital. Zahra Avoka. Tell them to tell her I'm okay. I'll explain everything when I get out.'

The policeman scribbled down my message and saluted me as he walked away.

My panic receded and sadness took its place. If I made it out of this situation alive I would do everything to be the best husband. My father and stepmother had a distant relationship, and I'd hoped my marriage would be different. Overnight I had become my father, in the thick of a political scandal. Trapped in my cell, I thought especially about our son Kojo. I'd hoped to take a different approach from Linus Avoka, letting the boy decide what his life should be, but I didn't realize I'd become just as distant, if not more. We were strangers who shared the same roof.

When I fell asleep and woke up, my reality was completely different. A man in a black turtleneck and army-green combat trousers was seated across from me.

'I didn't want to wake you up,' he said.

I couldn't get a good look at his face. Poor lighting.

'I'm going to ask you some questions, and if you cooperate, we'll both be happy.'

He inhaled, as if he needed to invoke the questions from a box in his brain.

'How do you know William Sangare, now calling himself Diouf?'

I chose not to answer. That would be my MO. The man stood up—a real thug, that one. His sleeves barely covered his biceps and he had no neck. I wanted to tell him we weren't conspiring to overthrow the government, but I figured that I should maintain my silence.

He asked me three or four questions: Who was the American? Where did we meet? How did we meet? Was William Sangare the mastermind behind the coup?

With each question he drew closer to me, and when five minutes of silence had passed he lunged at my left side with his boot. I heard my ribs cracking and pain tore up my throat.

'We'll try this again. This time you'll answer.'

A barrage of questions. Silence. A kick, on the same side. He shoved his boot into my body until I coughed up blood, and then left me. This must have been around 5 p.m. No one came to see me till the next morning, when I was brought stale bread. My stomach grumbling, I grabbed the loaf with my grimy hands, hands that had held the same bars clasped by goat thieves, rapists, and murderers. I swallowed the loaf, barely chewing it, and felt worse than I had before I ate. My friendly elderly police officer must have ended his shift.

The thug returned and we danced to the same song. This time he discovered my right side, and left a wound the size of a teacup's rim on my breast. It rained later that night, a heavy thunderstorm that filled my brain with fantasies of escape, delusions of grandeur. Maybe God would strike my jail cell with lightning or an earthquake and I would be set free, the modern-day Paul or Silas. But none of that happened. I coiled my body on the concrete ledge, spitting out blood and fighting hunger.

On the third day a new set of policemen had taken over. Nobody brought me breakfast or checked on me. I stuck my nose through the bars. I needed water.

'Boss! *Massa*!' I shouted.

One of them said, 'You're all over the papers. You're famous.'

What was being written about me?

'Boss, please, can I read it?' I said. He trudged toward me with *The Daily Post*.

'See you!' It was a big front-page splash with my photo, taken two days before. A red headline: 'COUP MAKER.'

He thrust it through the bars of the cell. 'And *Massa*, I beg you, water.' He nodded.

My story, the paper said, was that I was a fallen hero. A respected civil servant who had chosen to disgrace the whole government and bring instability to the country. Strangely, no mention was made of me writing for the Doctor. Diouf's story was worse. He'd come back under a disguise and had successfully infiltrated several parts of the government to orchestrate this coup. A manhunt was on for our other accomplices. I reread my story, and the last paragraph made me choke. It said, 'We contacted Mr. Avoka's wife for comment, but reports indicate that she has taken ill and is currently admitted at the Teaching Hospital.' Courtney's cheque was still in my car, hopefully safe and undiscovered. Without the money, Zahra couldn't do the MRI. I had to write her a note, have her send Kojo to look through my car—a crazy, dangerous idea, but I was at my wit's end. I called for a policeman but was ignored.

The next day three huge men came to my cell, flung the cage open and dragged me into the brightness of the day. My eyes stung and my whole body ached. There was no crowd as I was thrown into the back of a van, and I was partly disappointed.

They blindfolded me and we sped off somewhere. The van rolled to a stop on gravelly ground. I was hauled out and kicked into a room with the smell of mothballs and perfume. A cold room, probably without a window. Very dungeon-like.

I was left blindfolded for what seemed like days until I heard footsteps going and coming, shuffling, pounding. I'm convinced that the room was in the Doctor's house on the hill. The smell of the room, the cold, the haunting feeling of others having died in this space. Another strong hunch I had was that the Doctor walked in to see me while I was there.

'Your name?' a deep voice said. I heard the strike of a match, a deep inhalation. I smelled a whiff of cigarette smoke.

'Theo Avoka,' I said, trying not to stammer, trying to show them my spirit was indomitable. I was asked my age, my occupation, where I lived. Then my father. His name, when he died, what he'd been accused of doing. I said I didn't think it was relevant to our discussion. Big mistake. The room went silent. I listened for clues of what would come next. Nothing. Nothing. Then the tip of a cigarette searing a piece of flesh on my forearm. I screamed. No, I wasn't that hardened. I wasn't hardened at all. They asked me about Courtney, whether I was having an affair with her, about Zahra, about Obi, whether they were having an affair. They asked about Kojo and his school, and Atsu and her boyfriend. Only one question shocked me. The Zahra and Obi question. I picked at the skin near my burn.

'What about William Sangare?' Deep Voice said.

I said nothing. I felt him approaching with the cigarette, but he rephrased his question. 'Tell us about your accomplice. We know he was the mastermind behind the coup. What did he have you do?'

I was quiet. Deep Voice gouged out my wound with his cigarette. I bit my tongue and tried to flick away his hand, but he was much stronger and I only succeeded in dragging the butt to my wrist.

Was the Doctor watching me? Was he enjoying this?

I held my resolve, not saying a thing. Deep Voice, or maybe someone else, resorted to punching my ribs. They never once touched my face. After hours of being pummelled into what felt like a pulp, they left me.

I lost track of time. Had I been there for two days or a week? I couldn't tell. Death was so near. Would Linus be proud that I was dying a martyr like him? At dawn of day six (Zahra kept count for me) I was pushed into a van, still blindfolded, and after an hour's drive I was let out, hands tied behind my back. I sat on the side of the road and listened. This was a city I knew intimately. I could use my senses to figure out where I was. The swish of cars, cocks crowing. I wasn't too isolated. I listened. Voices floated toward me but they were distant. My stomach was completely empty. I lay on the ground. Sand brushed my face, stones pressed into my cheeks. Cars whipped by and not one stopped. Maybe I already looked like a corpse. Soon vultures would descend. I tried untying the rope around my hands. It was an impossible knot, so I gave up.

Through my blindfold the light changed from a bluish tinge to a reddish one. I sat up and my skin felt raw from the cigarette burns, from the boot wounds. I was on a highway. Standing up was harder than I realized and I almost fell over from vertigo. I tried lifting my arms over my head. Nothing.

An idea: there was bound to be a rock or tree stump jutting out somewhere along the side of the road, which I could use to lift my blindfold. I lay back down and slid on the ground, serpentine. Gravel seemed to slough off my skin.

I stood up, thrashing about. I couldn't believe fellow human beings would just drive by and watch me suffer, but I would have driven by too. Finally, pain. I'd hit something. I knelt and used my torso to feel out whatever it was. It was a stub of a small wooded plant. I bent over, pressing the blindfold to the plant. At first all I did was badly scratch my face, but then, success. I managed to push the cloth over my right eyelid. It took a while to recognize where I was. It could be any highway. But I walked and walked until it became clear that I was on the road between North Odor and South Odor. Atsu's old neighbourhood. The first month she worked for us, Zahra or I would pick her up from her cousin's house until she got used to the city.

By car, I wasn't too far from home, but I had no money and my clothes were tattered and bloodstained. No one would pick me up. I looked like a madman. I walked onto a side road. If I could get to a house with friendly people, I'd borrow money to take a lorry home. I walked as fast as I could, stumbling several times. I passed by uncompleted buildings, giggling schoolgirls trooping to class, and came to a store decorated with Coca-Cola and Pepsi signs: *Everything in God's Good Time*.

An older woman sitting in front of the glass counter shooed me away.

'Every day there's a new madman,' she cried. 'Away!'

'Madam, please,' I said. 'I need your help. Just something small to eat, today's paper, and only ten kowries.'

'And they come making demands, too.'

'Please!' I said.

To pacify her I walked out of the store and tried to make up some story about why I had my hands tied, but came up cold.

'Ask me anything. Let me prove that I'm not mad.'

'Oh, this foolish man, too. Kojo! Kojo!' she shouted.

I lit up. 'My son is called Kojo too,' I said. 'He's at the International Secondary School.'

She looked me up and down and decided I was way past delusional. Kojo stepped out, no young man. He was old enough to be my father.

'Untie this crazy man. Give him water and tell him to stop driving away my customers.'

Kojo patiently worked at the knot until it came undone. He took the rope with him. I wanted to ask him for it, so it could be a trophy of sorts, but I realized making demands might not get me what I wanted—to be back with my family. Kojo came back from behind the counter with cotton wool and TCP antiseptic, which he applied in quick strokes to my burns. I held in my screams. He looked at my face and recognition sank in, but he said nothing to the woman. He brought me a piece of bread and handed me *The Daily Post*. The headline bled: 'Guilty! Prez's Ex-No.1 Confesses.'

Diouf confessed to masterminding the coup and claimed he'd brought me on to take part in a side project: finding evidence that could be used to indict the Doctor, but I'd refused to have anything to do with it. He was working on his own. I sat down on the floor and held my head. I think I cried then, or it could have been later, when I hopped in a lorry with the ten-kowry note old Kojo had given me.

Diouf was the hero (in my eyes, at least), and I crawled back home, tail between my legs. It would have been better if I'd been killed, I thought then. There was so much valour in dying for politics, like my father had. Now I was just a coward.

Another mystery remained. Where was Courtney? She certainly hadn't had the time to close her bank account, because when my car was returned to me, I was able to cash her cheque. She knew too much; apart from my close friends and family, no one knew I was working for the Doctor. How did she know to recruit me to join her bandwagon of dissidents? And then her constant repetition that the Doctor could have had a hand in my father's death. Was she his mistress? Had she framed us? My father's death had begun to weigh heavily on me, especially during my detention. But did I have the strength to open up another can of worms?

CHAPTER FORTY

Atsu

Tomorrow I am taking my make-it-or-break-it math exam. I've tried to study in my room, but Kunle decided to bring in his friends, and they're sitting on his bunk bed, playing cards, drinking alcohol, and making me miserable. Although I suppose it'd be less satisfying than destroying his father's thousand-dollar watch, I could get him in serious hot water.

Ayensu is winning the card game, and every time he throws down an ace or a king, he hops off the bed and flaps his arms like a constipated vulture. Then everybody screams loudly and it's just plain stupid. I walk out, banging the door for effect, and head to the boys' common room.

There, too, upper levels have taken over. The TV is roaring and they aren't even watching it. Someone's made a makeshift ping-pong table and the ball keeps bouncing off the walls. It's ridiculous that these uppers are preventing the rest of us from learning. They already wrote their exams, and the ones left behind are proctoring ours. The image on the TV is black and white with a green line running down the left. Ebenezer Ojo appears, looking as solemn and disturbed as always. Then there's a picture of an arrest.

A man being led into a police station. I go closer, to where someone is sprawled on the couch, drool and all, and sit in front of the TV set.

'... allegedly plotting a coup.' Mr. Diouf's face appears on the screen, a picture of when he was in the army, similar to the one hanging in his living room. My heart skips. Maybe because I imagine poor Mrs. Diouf watching this right now.

'Going by the name Diouf, William Sangare and others, who are still being investigated, were putting together elaborate and sinister plans to oust President Karamoh from power,' Ojo says.

I look around the room and no one is interested. It's so sad. I was beginning to like Mrs. Diouf, but for her husband to be involved in this is terrible. I am about to walk to the dining hall, my last option of a place to study, but I have a sick premonition and keep watching the screen. Every muscle in my body freezes when the premonition comes true: Daddy's picture is on the TV. It's him all right. He doesn't have a dignified photo like Mr. Diouf's, his is a mug shot. Then it all comes together: Mr. Diouf, Daddy, the white woman, and the other people in Mrs. Diouf's house. They definitely looked like they were conspiring. Ebenezer Ojo is talking about Daddy, saying that his father, my grandfather whom I never met, was executed under the First Republic for an attempted coup and misusing State funds. Ojo pauses, furrows his brow, and stares deep into the camera, and I begin to feel like I'm floating outside my body.

'What's this?' An upper two boy, reeking of alcohol, comes and sits by me. I want to throw up.

'My father has just been arrested,' I hear myself saying.

'No! For what?'

I point to the TV, the black-and-white footage of the police station where Mr. Diouf is being led. They keep looping the images—of Mr. Diouf, Daddy, the police stations, and the National Palace.

'I'm sure they've framed him,' the upper guy says. 'It will be okay. Don't worry about a thing. Everything is going to be all right.'

He's singing Bob Marley's song. I leave the room and walk to the phone booth. No one answers my call at home. I can't think of anyone else to call. And when I get to the dining hall I find Inaam chatting with Ngozi.

'Inaam, can I talk to you?' I say. She hesitates, but Ngozi tells her to go with her lover boy and we head outside, where the lights of the girls' dorms appear as fuzzy oblongs instead of sharp rectangles. I tell her what's happened.

'I would hug you, but you know these crazy uppers. Try to put it out of your head tonight. Write your math exam tomorrow, then get permission to go home. They'll be wicked not to let you go.'

'Nothing is beyond Bobole,' I say, almost laughing. 'I can't write that exam. I couldn't find a place to study, and now with this, there's no way I can focus.'

'You have to try.'

'No, I can't. I will fail horribly and that's worse than not showing up.'

She grabs my hand, then sighs.

'When my mother died ... When my mother killed herself, I was writing exams, too. She decided to swallow pills the night before I was to take the exams that would get me into a private middle school in London. Can you imagine what that did to me? Still, I locked myself in my room, cried like a giant baby, then crammed English, math, and general science, and I got into the school. As I was writing the exam I kept seeing her vomiting blood. Sorry, it's disgusting. It was the hardest thing I've ever done in my life. My dad was going to ask them for a different exam date but I just did it. And even though I'll never know why she chose that day, I hope she's proud of me.'

I don't know if it's self-pity or if it's the picture of Inaam's mother killing herself, but before I can stop myself I start sobbing. I feel so lame. She hugs me.

'Awww, Kojo,' she says. 'I could go with you to Mrs. Diouf's ...'

'*She* definitely won't want to talk about anything.'

'Let's get another teacher to give you an extension.'

'I'll do it,' I say. 'I'm going to try to study.'

After an almost sleepless night I make like I'm heading to the dining hall, but instead trot to the basketball court, to the gate I saw during midterm break. I find out it's padlocked, which throws a huge dent into my plans. I was hoping to just walk out. I'm no good at picking locks, and the wall is not low enough for me to climb over. I see students walking on the path toward the dining hall and crouch by the milk bush so I'm not spotted. I take a big stone and hit the lock repeatedly. Nothing happens. I peek through the fencing on the basketball court and people are still marching by obliviously. I resume knocking on the padlock harder, like a carpenter hammering a nail in. I hit the lock again, and the back of my neck prickles when I think I hear someone sneaking up on me. False alarm. After a few more attempts I notice that the padlock is barely scratched and I wonder if I should have just asked for permission to go home. Mrs. Bobole and the other authorities would have understood. Suddenly two figures approach, one looking like Bobole with her big wig. I chuck the stone to the side and take to my feet, keeping to the wall and feeling the concrete, hoping there'll be an opening, a small crack, anything.

'Wait,' one of them shouts. I continue running and it feels like a high-speed movie chase, Antonio Banderas-style. How am I going to escape? 'Avoka, stop!' It sounds like Ayensu.

Someone else rushes toward me. I should have known they'd have backup. Whoever the person is, he's sprinting like Carl Lewis at the Olympics. There's no way I'm going to make it. I return to the secret door and kick at it with all I have and stub my toe. Still I kick harder. It's pointless. The door isn't budging, and before I know it Ayensu has grabbed my shirt and Bobole catches up to us.

It's a blur, how I get to Bobole's office. But now I'm sitting by her, on the sofa she interviewed me on before I came to the ISS. I can see her icky neck meat and it seems like her weak point, her Achilles heel. I should bite it and then scram. When she starts talking I burst out crying pathetically, which makes her pull my head to her chest. She smells of dusting powder and Quaker Oats. She presses my head deeper into her chest and I can't breathe or think. I need a clear head to get out of here. It's actually better that we're in the admin building. It's a longer escape route, but those gates are always wide open and I already know the path. I'll ask to use the bathroom and then book it. Bobole squeezes me tighter, then thankfully peels herself off me.

'Better?' she asks, and I nod. 'You've heard some horrible news, but running away from school is not the solution. One of your teachers checked on you last night, but you were sleeping. I made a few calls, and your mother will arrange for someone to pick you up this weekend.' I sweetly ask to use the bathroom. 'Tell Vincent to show you where it is and come right back. We have to talk about rescheduling your math exam.'

'Yes, Mrs. Bobole.'

Crazy Bobole thinks she can trap me into staying. I walk out of the office and close the door behind me. I don't say a word to her secretary, who I've heard likes boys. He's about to answer the ringing phone when I fling myself out of the office and begin a sprint down the hill, sticking to the road even though I know I'll be easily caught. I doubt that Bobole is up for more of the high-speed chase. It's also the easiest way to get a taxi. And thankfully, before long I spot one and hop in it.

At home, no one answers the bell after I've pressed it several times. I'm about to give up when Atsu finally opens the gate.

'Were you sleeping?'

'No. I thought you were someone else.'

Who? I wonder, but I have other things to worry about. We go inside and I ask about Mummy's whereabouts. What does she have to say about all this? Did she know what he was up to? I'm sure. Parents love to keep secrets from their children.

'Oh, Kojo!' Atsu says and hugs me. Are all these women hugging me because Daddy's been arrested? I'd take Atsu over Bobole any day, except when Atsu's been cleaning and cooking. I feel her breasts, much softer than Bobole's, pressing into my stomach. We stay pressed together for a long time until Atsu breaks away and asks me if I've heard about everything.

'I saw it on the news.'

'Hmmm.'

'Where's Mummy? I need to talk to her.'

'Two troubles, one God!' Atsu says. She goes to the curtain and straightens a crease at its base. 'In hospital.'

'Because of Daddy?'

'Are you hungry? No. Before. She went to the hospital and they admitted her.'

'What happened?'

'I'm coming,' Atsu says, and disappears into the kitchen.

I throw my school bag on the floor and she returns with a plate of rice and forces me to sit and eat. I didn't touch breakfast and I can't eat anything now. Staring at the blank television screen, I wonder what's happening to our family. We're falling apart.

'I'll eat this later.'

'Kojo, you have to eat. Keep your strength up.'

'I can't. What hospital is my mother in? I need to see her.'

'Eat, rest, and you can come with me. I'm taking her food in the afternoon.'

'I want to go now.'

'Let's go together. I haven't cooked yet.'

I lie on my bed, trying to slow down the racing of my mind. I know Mummy's at one of three hospitals, but I'm running out of cash and can't go searching in all of them. I don't even know what unit she's in. I turn on the radio and it's all about Daddy's attempted coup, even on DJ Onesandtwos's station. I slot in my hardcore hip-hop mix tape and turn up the volume three times louder than Mummy allows me.

When I wake up from a nap I hadn't planned to take, I find Atsu sprawled on the living-room carpet, the TV on and flashing Mr. Diouf and Daddy's pictures.

'… there's no information as to their release,' Ebenezer Ojo says. 'The President commissioned the building of a new latrine system in the …' I switch off the TV, and Atsu stirs awake.

'Sorry, you were sleeping so I sat here waiting and fell asleep too.'

'They're both guilty,' I say. 'I saw them with my own eyes. Plotting.'

'Don't say that,' she sits up. 'Your father is a good man,

and I'm sure he was doing what he thought was right. Only for the wrong people.'

I stare at her feet, then her legs, then she joins me on the sofa, where she hugs me again, Bobole-style. At first I'm mad at Daddy for everything, then I relax and melt into Atsu's arms. We hold each other for a long time, and before I know what's happening, my arms tighten around her back. She feels good. I rub her shoulders and press her body closer to mine. My fingers inch up her neck and I can smell the soap she just showered with. I sniff harder at her neck, my nose flattening against her skin, and then my right hand clasps her breast.

'Kojo, stop!' she shouts and stands up.

'I'm so sorry.'

'It's not your fault. The devil is trying to take advantage of our weakness.'

'Atsu, there are three troubles, not two. I'm going to be expelled.'

'Oh, why?' She's still standing, not coming any closer to me. I'm too ashamed to think about what just happened.

'I didn't write my exams today and I ran away from school.'

'Can't you go back and take them tomorrow?'

'I don't want to take them.'

She looks shocked. No, worse, offended. 'Kojo, your parents have put you in the best school in the country and you want to intentionally fail? My mother never sent me to school, but if she had, I wouldn't be a house help by now. You need school to get far in life. Go take your exams.'

'Don't be silly,' I say, too strongly. 'I'm not dropping out of school. I just need not to be at the ISS. I'm dying there.' Will I be able to get into another school? What if Atsu is right, and my expulsion means the end of my education?

'All we can do is pray,' she says. 'Let's go see your mother.'

CHAPTER FORTY-ONE

Making Up

Three days before Madam's surgery, Atsu is studying in her room when the bell rings. She's about to pick herself up to get it when she hears the gate whining open and shut. Perhaps Mr. Avoka or Kojo were already outside.

She's startled when, not long after, there's a knock on her door. She was hoping to finish preparing for the surprise quiz Mr. Sy has been threatening to give them. A visitor would mean having to prepare a meal and put studying on hold. It's Kojo at the door. He looks at her shyly and then shifts his gaze to his feet, probably still ashamed about what happened between them. Atsu's forgiven him. Any other man would probably have done the same with such confused emotions, and given that he's still growing up, he was especially mixed up.

'There's someone here to see you,' he says. 'He's outside.'

A sinking feeling fills her chest. He. Nasar. She wasn't expecting this person to be *her* guest. What could he want? She needs room to give him a piece of her mind, but not with Mr. Avoka and Kojo around. She goes outside, where, horror of all horrors, Mr. Avoka is talking to Nasar. She sucks in her breath and approaches the men.

'Let me leave you two,' Mr. Avoka says. She's been feeling so sorry for him that she can't look him in the eye.

'My classmate,' she says by way of clearing the air, should Nasar have suggested anything otherwise.

'Yes, he told me,' Mr. Avoka says and walks away.

On Nasar's face is a smirk she would like to slap off.

'What do you want?' She hasn't spoken to him since he told her about Mr. Avoka.

'I heard about his release,' Nasar whispers. 'He seems to have recovered. I came to ask you if we could try this again.'

'No,' Atsu says, faster than she means to. It was a defensive no. She's more flattered by his persistence and courage. Someone else would have walked away as soon as he saw the boss of the house. She stares at his face, at how what was once strange has become familiar. She knows that before he smiles, the corners of his lips dip down before pulling up. His eyes, sad, almond-shaped things shaded by their lids, stretch up too. His whole face lifts up. His dimples. And his constantly moving jaws! He loves chewing gum. She doesn't want to show any happiness or give him hope by smiling because a part of her holds him responsible for what happened to Mr. Avoka. What if he had been killed? The man lost so much weight and, even though he didn't tell her what happened to him, his clothes when he arrived, bloody and ripped, told enough of a story. He looked like a thief who had been beaten after stealing a market woman's money. She doesn't care if Nasar warned her. She really could do nothing with the information he provided. Did he expect Mr. Avoka to run into hiding? They'd have smoked him out like a bush rat. Nasar is guilty by association.

'Why not?' he says, playing with the button on the cuff of his shirt. It's such a childlike move, she wants to reach over and place his head on top of her breasts. She curses herself for entertaining such thoughts.

'I have work to do,' she says.

'I know,' he says, moving closer. He better not touch her because she'll scream, and that won't be good for anyone. Embarrassing for her, Nasar, Mr. Avoka, and any others who hear.

'What did your people do to him?' she whispers, her insides itching in exasperation. 'Have you seen the scratches on his face? In fact, don't tell me. Ah, just go. You're making my life complicated.'

'Atsu, I swear, on my grandmother. I had nothing to do with it. I found out through some friends and thought I should let you know. Maybe I should have kept my mouth shut, but I'm not that kind of person. I couldn't just keep quiet …'

'But you are. First you don't tell me who you are. Then you watch your friends do this to him.'

He says nothing. A look of disgust flickers on his face and leaves, and for a second she's scared.

'I've done things I'm not proud of. I've told you. When I joined Saturday's Boys, I was a child with no idea what I was getting into. Some people can't leave. Some of them are still my friends, but I came to my senses early. I'm not that person anymore. But I won't waste your time if you don't think people deserve second chances.'

'How did you leave?' she asks—a question that has plagued her since he confessed.

'I started drinking heavily not long after the pregnant woman episode. One night I drank so much that I passed out in my own vomit. The other boys had to send me to the hospital to get my stomach pumped. I was in a coma for days. When I recovered, my grandmother went over to my senior commander and caused such a scene that even if I'd paid him ten thousand kowries, he wouldn't have let me back in.'

The ice block in Atsu's chest begins a fast melt.

'I'll respect whatever you decide, but I want you to know that when I'm with you, I feel like I'm home. You're filled with such inner and outer beauty; you make me want to be a better person. I've never met anyone like you, so calm and strong, and I want to be with you. I know you don't trust me anymore, but if you give me another chance you won't be sorry.'

Nasar looks at his feet and says, 'Marry me.'

'Are you mad?' she says, her armpits prickling so badly that she's tempted to sniff them to make sure she wore deodorant. Stop, breathe, Atsu Nadege Akakpo, breathe. Before she can stop herself, tears gush out of her eyes, and she chokes on words that would have come out as nonsense anyway. This time, she knows he's serious. It's so soon and sudden and crazy.

'Take your time. I'm not going anywhere. Think about it.'

'I'm coming,' Atsu says, walking to the kitchen, deeply confused.

She mops her eyes with her dress, thankfully one of her nicer dresses. It would have been a travesty to get proposed to in a smelly working dress. Her foot is barely in the door when Mr. Avoka and Kojo, both grinning widely, ambush her. She's so embarrassed, she feels like her body's shrunk by half.

'*Ei*, Atsu,' Mr. Avoka says. 'Why didn't you tell us you had a serious suitor?' She chooses to keep her gaze on Kojo. Mr. Avoka's scratches are painful to look at. 'That is a man who is here on business.'

Should she tell them? Kojo is all grins, and it seems like whatever attraction there was on her part (a hint of it existed even though she didn't want to acknowledge it) is gone. Now, he looks like a small boy.

'So?' Kojo says. It was almost as if Madam were standing here. Should she tell?

'He proposed to me,' she blurts out.

Mr. Avoka says, 'Congratulations!' and high-fives her.

Kojo raises his hand too. Then says, suddenly serious, 'Have you said yes?'

Mr. Avoka leans against the wall of the dining room. They both look at her expectantly.

'No, not yet,' Atsu says. 'I want to make sure it's okay.' When the words are out, she realizes she does want to marry Nasar. Even though she's only known him for six or so months, he's been the most consistent, loving part of all twenty years of her life. If they fire her, so what? She can cook, her English is better, and she has basic reading and writing. She can find new work much more easily now.

'Come on,' Mr. Avoka says. 'Don't stretch the man.'

'You want us to come with you?' Kojo says. 'In case you say no and he gets wild and rambunctious?'

'Stop it,' says Mr. Avoka.

Atsu smiles. It feels so right, but she should be having this conversation with Mama, Avah, and Edem.

'I'm going to say yes,' she says.

Nasar is right where she left him on the gravel of the Avokas's driveway, and she's sure Kojo and Mr. Avoka are in the bathroom, eyes trained on them.

She leans in and whispers: 'Yes. But, you have to ask for my hand from Mama first. Now please go and stop complicating my life.'

He hugs Atsu and springs out the gate. She hopes Mama approves.

CHAPTER FORTY-TWO

Rice Farm

The day of my surgery arrived, and like any big day (exams, wedding day, childbirth) I was filled with dread and yearning. Yearning, because I couldn't wait to see the results. Would I come out of this the same? Would I heal? Despite the uncertainty I was in surprisingly little pain. Before the operation, a nurse walked in with a man I hadn't met before. A lanky old thing topped with patches of white hair.

'Madam,' the nurse said, 'Pastor Frank is doing rounds of the hospital and praying for those of you with conditions.'

The old me would have yelled at the nurse first and told Father Frank where he could shove it. But I didn't say a word. I nodded lamely as the nurse let in the man of God. I had been humbled completely, not just by the state of my health, but by everything.

Auntie Adisa, apparently visiting town, had decided to pass by our offices to check on how I was doing. She met with Emma and Somto, who had no idea who she was or that I'd even been to her farm, and had gone on to inform her that I no longer worked with them. They then tried to woo her to work with them, but Auntie Adisa wanted nothing to do with Duell after my deceptiveness. Lizzie, our secretary-treasurer, had come to visit the day before and had told me how Auntie Adisa had huffed out of the office, and how Emma and Somto had broken the news that I wouldn't be coming back.

They hadn't told me I'd been fired, but at that point I couldn't give two hoots about working with them. What I had to do was apologize to Auntie Adisa, a woman who had shown me immense kindness and reminded me about the things that made me happy. I would get Kojo to send her twelve yards of indigo, the latest collection from Silhouette Romance, and two of Auntie Rokia's best red wines. After my surgery I would go see her myself.

The man of God moved to my side and grabbed my hand. His hand felt raw and scarred, he smelled of fried eggs, and instead of my heart filling with joy at his presence he deepened the cloud hovering over me. I'd had time, since being admitted to the hospital, to do some soul-searching: I wanted to say sorry to Theo for considering him a less than ideal husband, which I know I had over the years, taking him totally for granted; for pushing him to the point where he felt he had to do something heroic to get my attention; for having an affair. I needed Kojo to forgive me for being a pushy mother, sending him in a direction that I thought was better for him than he himself knew. To Mma, my list of apologies was too long to even begin to mention. And Atsu I wanted to thank for sticking by me, for bearing my abuse and distance. I had a fifty-per cent chance of coming out of the surgery whole, as the Zahra I was before. I could come out blind, a burden to my family, the people I would need the most, the people I'd been slowly alienating.

'My sister,' Pastor Frank said. 'Let us pray.'

I closed my eyes and the murky pink, green, and grey inside my eyelids fluttered.

'Father God, we're here to pray for our sister,' he paused. 'Zahra.'

'Yes! For our sister Zahra, who is lying sick in bed today. But Father God, we know that she should not despair, because you healed the lame, you cured lepers, the blind, and I know you can do the same for our sister Zahra today. Father God, I pray that whatever iniquities she's carrying, whatever sin she's bearing that has brought this state upon her, I pray in the precious name of Jesus that you wash it away. Heal her! Cleanse her! Purify her!'

Even though a part of me believed that I'd brought on the condition by my behaviour, it was not comforting hearing the same thing from a man of God. His voice grew quiet but not for long. He erupted into tongues and I wanted to tell him it was enough. But I didn't. Here was a man who believed humanity could be saved, that human beings deserved a second chance, even as depraved and terrible as we could be, as I had been to my own family. Expecting nothing in return he was praying for me, rather hoping to add to my life.

The door swung open as the preacher's voice took on a frog-like baritone, and in swarmed Theo, Kojo, Atsu, Anna and family, Zea and Mabel, and Mma, and I almost cried. The preacher man didn't flinch, stop, or even open his eyes, and my family stood by the wall, waiting.

When Pastor Frank wrapped up his prayer with 'amen,' everyone shouted a huge 'AMEN!' in response, startling the poor man.

'*Ei!*' he said. 'I didn't realize you had a whole battalion waiting for you. You are blessed. Be well, my sister.'

One by one my friends and family came to hug me, planting kisses on my cheeks, my forehead, and in Mma's case, tears everywhere. Theo, bless him, must have arranged for her to come down.

'Allah will get you through this,' she said.

They crowded around me, sharing different stories. Some were still talking about Theo's arrest and how he'd lost weight he didn't have to begin with. Zea was the loudest, laughing, calling Theo 'the freedom fighter.'

If any of them was worried, they didn't show it. All but Theo, who, even though he laughed, could not hide his pain from me. I knew him too well. Each movement was laboured, and I could tell that even just rearranging the flowers on my bedside table took such effort that I knew he wasn't ready for what I was about to go through. If he was already in such physical pain, what would he do with the emotional missile I had to drop on him?

'We actually have big news,' he said suddenly, hibiscus in hand. He turned to the group and waved the flower in Atsu's direction. 'She's getting married!'

Wows and congrats worked their way around the room.

'He's a lucky man,' I said, really meaning it, and wondering how that had managed to slip me by.

'Thank you, Madam,' she said, hiding behind Mma.

The anaesthetist came in, an old man in sea-foam scrubs, tailed by my surgeon and his assistants.

'I'm afraid I have to kick you all out now,' the surgeon said.

Everyone trooped out and I wished I could hold someone's hand. Theo's. The anaesthetist prepared vials of his injections and stuck a syringe in my wrist.

'You're doing fine,' he said.

My father wasn't a perfect man, but he only married Mma, even though he could have married three others if he'd wanted to, providing he could take care of them. He was educated in Catholic School, like me, yet initially wasn't accepted into university because in those days people from the northern territories were employed for lower-level work. They were security guards, farmhands, and groundsmen. They weren't sent south, where the good universities were. But my father had seen the world in the books he read in Catholic School. He wanted more than to be somebody's cutlass-wielding houseboy. He smuggled himself into the truck that came up north once a month to collect yam, millet, and beef, and headed to the south, changed his last name to Peters, and continued school. He became a teacher and was sent back to the north, where he restored his name, taught agriculture, and ran a farm until he died. His spirit was limitless, boundless. He died chasing his dream of developing rice that could grow in both dry and waterlogged conditions. He made enough money from the farms to keep our family together, because teaching, especially as a non-European in the north in those days, brought home nothing.

While I was away at university in England, the Senevolta River flooded while my father was planting his seeds. Out of nowhere a deluge of water invaded the farm and swept everything away. He'd never learned how to swim.

When my father bought his first car I was seven or eight—an eggshell open-top car whose make I can't remember because it didn't last very long. He either sold it or it got stolen, I can't remember. He let me ride in the front seat while Mma stayed at home, too scared to join in on the fun. We drove to his rice farms, speeding along dusty roads, telling off farm workers who weren't cooperating, and when we got to the last farm he'd let me off. The farm was expansive, and for miles all I could see was green about half my height. We'd stand there, just us two, marvelling at the lushness around.

The farm was where I felt most at home. The smell of soil, life starting from the smallest seed, growing into a crop that sustained a whole nation. That was paradise.

When I came to, my doctors, hidden behind their surgical masks, hovered above me. Pain shot through my entire head and my body felt so weighed-down, I couldn't move. The room looked unbearably cloudy and I wondered why I had fought so much to stay alive, because in my addled condition I thought the pain was going to be permanent. Every part of me hurt and throbbed.

With a grave face, my surgeon pulled down his mask.

He said, 'We cleared the tumour, but it had already done irreparable damage to your optic nerve. We're afraid your vision is not going to be as good as it once was, and there's the chance that it might get worse with time, but the headaches and nausea should be taken care of.'

I had experienced thirty-something years of being able to capture every single colour in sharp detail—I never wore glasses and had seen some of the world in its splendour. My father's rice farms were probably the most beautiful place I'd been to. I loved beauty. I might not see the man Kojo would become or what Theo and I would age into, but as I absorbed what it meant, I decided it wasn't a death sentence. The death sentence would be if I lost my family.

I squeaked for Theo to be let in to see me. He crept into the room and said, 'The doctors tell me you're doing beautifully.'

I didn't know if they'd lied to him or if he was trying to keep up my spirits. More likely the latter.

'I have something to tell you,' I said, my words warped and distorted, some creature out of a space movie.

'What?'

'I have …' I motioned for him to come closer. 'Can you hear me?'

He nodded.

Breathing was painful.

'I need you to forgive me,' I said. His eyes grew sadder, and I focused on the light bulb hanging on the ceiling, hovering above Theo's right shoulder. 'I had an affair, Theo.' He said nothing, didn't ask me with whom, when, didn't get angry, didn't react like I thought he would. For a long pregnant while, we didn't say anything to each other. Sharp pain, shame. He walked out of the room and I couldn't even cry. It was too painful to cry.

CHAPTER FORTY-THREE

Goodbyes

Mummy's just had surgery. Daddy has entered some weird fifth dimension. And I have some news for them. I need to tell them I'm not going back to the ISS, that they should enrol me in a normal public school. School was bad enough before, but now: no girlfriend, a father with a rap sheet, my shenanigans before I ran away. No way I'm going back.

'What's new?' Mummy says and smiles when I walk into her room. She's giving off a faint disinfectant smell. In all my life, I don't think I've ever seen her look so defeated.

'Not much,' I say. Now would be a good time to bring up changing schools, but I want Daddy around too.

'Tell me more about Atsu's man,' she says. Her breathing is raspy and loud and a tube is running through her nose.

'I don't know a lot. Daddy met him. I only saw him through the window. He looks buff. Very macho.'

She struggles to laugh. And maybe because I'm feeling sorry for her, I blurt out everything that went down with Inaam. I know she'd like that. I start from the beginning and end with the end, and when I'm done she says, 'If it's meant to be you two will meet again. It will work out.'

The door swings open and in walks Daddy, looking

shabby, with Inaam and her father. Mummy must be psychic.

'Look who I found,' says Daddy.

Inaam is clutching a vase of yellow sunflowers, and after setting it next to the already full table, she waves at the room.

'I'll be outside,' Daddy says and leaves the room. Inaam's father walks to Mummy's bed, kisses her cheeks.

'Will you excuse us for a bit?' says Mummy.

'Zaza' is the last thing I hear Inaam's father say as I shut the door. It's strange to hear that. So ridiculously weird. Daddy's pacing in the hallway with the biggest frown creasing his forehead, so I signal for Inaam to follow me to the next hallway. Some privacy would be good.

'Is your dad okay?' Inaam says.

'I guess. We've been through a lot in such a short time.'

'I'm so sorry about your mum,' she says. 'About both of them. How are you?'

'Okay.'

'I still think you should have taken the exam.'

She's beginning to irritate me, and I want to ask her for the umpteenth time why she cares. She's not going to be around to watch me turn into a bum who dropped out of school, a bum she used to go out with. It's none of her business.

'Yeah,' I say and look straight ahead at a splotchy green wall.

'You're still angry with me.'

'No, I'm not.'

'Don't lie.'

An old woman passes by, bent over at the hip and carrying a thick branch for a cane. 'My children, do you have ten kowries for me to buy porridge?' she says.

'No, Auntie,' I say.

'Sorry,' Inaam says, putting on the saddest expression I've ever seen. 'Poor thing.'

'Do you want to go back to England?' I finally ask her. 'Truly?'

She's quiet, looking at a man with tiny Band-Aids plastered on his legs. She stares till he's out of sight.

'No.'

'Why not?'

'So many reasons. This is the first time I'm going back since what happened with my mother. And I'm losing all my friends. You broke up with me when you found out that I was leaving. I like the weather and the food here better. I like you.'

'I wouldn't have broken up with you if you hadn't been sneaky about the whole thing.'

'And I'm just scared,' she continues. 'I don't even know what of, Kojo. I'm always scared. When we left England I was terrified, and now that we're going back, I'm so frightened of what I'm going to meet. Kids there aren't like us.'

'Stay.' I can't believe I said that.

'There's no one to stay with here. My grandmother is in the north.'

'You can stay with us.'

'That *probably* won't work. Oh, Kojo.' She reaches out

325

and hugs me, and I hug her back and I feel this big bubble of sadness expanding in my chest and I wish I hadn't broken up with her. I wish we didn't have to live with parents. I wish we could just be together in a tree house in the middle of nowhere.

'When are you leaving?'

'Day after tomorrow. Daddy read about your mother being sick in the papers and said we had to come say bye.'

'Let's write to each other every day,' I say.

'That's going to be hard.' She laughs.

'Okay, every week. And don't leave out a single detail about what you get up to.'

'I won't.' She pushes up her glasses and dabs under her eyes. 'And what if you find a new girlfriend?'

'From where? I'm a school dropout, remember?'

'Kojo, take those exams.' She sniffles and grabs my shoulders.

'Yes, mother.'

And just then I hear voices raised. A voice. Daddy's almost high-pitched voice. And from where we're standing we are able to catch a glimpse of the hallway through the gap between the doors. Uncle Obi wipes his eyes.

'Sorry,' he says. 'I'm sorry.'

Inaam and I look at each other, embarrassed. It's hard watching her father, a grown man, cry. And it's especially worrisome because my father also sounds like he might cry. Suddenly a finger sticks out. Theo Avoka's. He's jabbing it in Inaam's father's chest.

'You have no right,' my father shouts. 'No right to apologize, to be here, to even talk to me.'

'I know,' Uncle Obi says, and now I can't look Inaam in the eye. 'I am so sorry.'

And with that Daddy marches in our direction. Inaam and I hold each other and try to hide behind the door as it swings open. Daddy storms right past and thankfully doesn't notice us.

I think I know what that was about, but I need a sure answer, so I ask Inaam.

'My dad's in love with your mother.' Bang.

It takes a while to register what she's just said. Wasn't that a thing of the past?

'What's he going to do about it?' I ask, the question absurd to me, but what else could I have asked? I couldn't have asked if Mummy loves him back. She shouldn't. Although she probably does, from the way Daddy reacted. And what makes all this extra-conflicting is that I like Inaam and Inaam's dad likes Mummy. 'Please don't tell me that's why you're leaving.'

'I asked him to admit it, but he insists it's because of the new job. He said, and I quote, "That's growing up. You learn you can't win everything and you have to let go of the things you can't control."'

I don't know if I agree with Inaam's father, that you have to let go of things. I think it's more that life forces you to let go of them. And maybe it's because they're just not meant to be. Like me and Inaam.

Much later, when Daddy returns to Mummy's room, when his temperature is back to normal, I decide there's no time like the present. They both have other things on their minds, so this is the time to get my plea in: 'Can I please go to a normal boarding school? I'll save you a lot of money. And I'll be happier. Please?'

When they say yes at the same time, I can't believe it. My chest feels lighter. I can finally breathe.

'Thank you.'

She's looking at the ceiling. He's looking at my feet.

CHAPTER FORTY-FOUR

THE DAILY POST
Monday, July 7, 1997 | We are the news! | Since 1952

Catharsis by Theo Avoka

I thought my ordeal in the horrendous jail cells of our beloved country would be the most difficult experience of my adult life, but how wrong I was. Getting kicked in my wounds, being left in the cell in my own excrement, eating rotten, maggot-infested food—none of this was more painful than the revelation my wife made to me after fifteen years of marriage: that she had been unfaithful. That drove me to the brink of insanity. Everything began to unravel, different strands of my life stuck in the wrong places, and everything became a hodgepodge of nonsense. Zahra's betrayal was the same as the Doctor betraying my father, a belief I suddenly latched on to.

I became a regular at the Nigerben University library, whose head librarian had graciously filed and catalogued local newspapers on a daily basis for decades. Thanks to her meticulousness, I was able to refer to newspapers from the sixties and seventies, to study their articles from cover to cover, searching for evidence that the Doctor was really my father's murderer. I had nothing else to do, so I would leave home, get to the library, and make notes of anything that sounded relevant.

In April 1962, the Doctor was vetted by a committee of ministers for the Deputy Minister of Health position, but he was rejected after three gruelling rounds. My theory was based on the fact that my father had sat on the panel, which the Doctor thought would find in his favour. They had grown up in neighbouring villages and were acquainted, though not well; the Doctor must have hoped this slightly older fellow tribesman would vote for him. My imagination filled in details the articles didn't provide. I pictured the committee room as small, filled with four other ministers on a dais, the young and hungry Karamoh Saturday sitting across from them on a schoolboy's chair, answering questions to the best of his ability, looking at my father's face every now and then for encouragement. My father, cold as usual, did nothing to allay Saturday's fears. Who was this johnny just come from the village? I imagined that during one of the breaks in interviewing, in the men's room, my father uncharacteristically assured the young man that he would make it through. When the committee finally reached its decision against Saturday, he again looked at my father.

In June 1970, an anonymous tipster wrote to *The Daily Post*, saying that he had very pertinent information about a high-level minister who was using the country's money to finance personal projects. The tipster added that he was an authority himself, so his words were not to be taken lightly. I scribbled violently in my notebook: *tipster = the Doctor*? Again, my mind wove another narrative. The Doctor was going to frame my father. He would be believed; after all, he was now my father's psychologist and had access to his secrets.

He would continue to plant these tips in newspapers, whispering suggestions into the ears of loud-mouthed politicians. The system, broken and opportunistic, was looking for blood, and my father was an easy scapegoat. He was too honest and had no allies, and Saturday knew nobody would launch an investigation.

After my father was executed, Karamoh saw how easily the system could be manipulated. A military man, he buttered up the other lieutenants and soldiers. Then, a year after my father's execution, on a fine day in 1975, he took over the country's affairs.

My mind continued to spin. I would have dreams in which Zahra and the Doctor were co-conspirators. In my waking life, I rationalized that they did have a lot in common. The Doctor relinquished power only under pressure. Zahra's surgery forced her to come clean to me. Confessing her sins would give her favour in God's eyes. The Doctor knew the country was dying and the only way to save it was to allow multiparty elections. And that was how he was able to align himself with the West. Zahra believed that if she didn't atone for her sins, she wouldn't recover.

The Doctor genuinely seemed to think of the country as his: its citizens, you, were his children, Saturday's people. I remember how his face would almost close in on itself, his cheeks falling slack, eyes crinkling and watering, when he heard that we weren't as enamoured of him anymore. I wondered what made him think a whole population of fifteen million people should be beholden to him. Maybe he thought he just could. Same way Zahra thought she could just have an extramarital affair and have things go back to being normal.

I reeled and reeled until I realized I was going to end up in a vortex that would completely suck me in. My father was dead, and even if the Doctor did have a part to play in his death, it wasn't going to give me the catharsis I desperately needed. What I could address, in one form or another, was my marriage. I could do something about my disintegrating family.

CHAPTER FORTY-FIVE

Cat and Mouse

Mr. Avoka's apartment has a mouse in it. This Atsu discovered in the morning, before Mr. Avoka left for the day—where to, she isn't exactly sure. Atsu was mopping the kitchen floor when something dark flashed by in the direction of the garbage can. What it was registered only after a few seconds, then she shrieked and scurried into the living room, which brought Mr. Avoka out of his bedroom in a half-buttoned shirt.

'Ah, I see you've met Karamoh,' he chuckled.

She was bemused. The mouse wasn't around last week or the week before. Not for all the months she'd been cleaning the apartment.

'He showed up over the weekend,' said Mr. Avoka, still smiling, as if he'd heard her mental question. 'I've put some rat poison on traps in there. He doesn't really like people. If he's out, the poison must be working. Maybe I should get a cat. Where there's one, there are many.'

He'd said nothing to calm her nerves—she doesn't like cats—and went back to preparing to leave the apartment. Atsu decided she would do the kitchen later in the day, when the poison had hopefully kicked in and when Kojo was around.

Cleaning for a man is different from cleaning for a family with a woman at its helm, a fact she can state with absolute certainty, especially now that she cleans for two men, although only one pays her. The two men are very different, but with both she has to do more cleaning, especially with the bathroom. With his soldier's precision, Nasar is tougher, mostly because it seems to be taking him a while to accept her presence in his house, and she's often gone home to find her towel removed from the bed railing and planted in the humid bathroom, or to find her shoes shoved, out of sight, under their bed. Mr. Avoka, she has complete control over. She set up his kitchen, buying everything from his forks to the mortar and pestle for fufu from the Bakoy Market. Every time she comes to his apartment there's a different challenge to deal with (today's case in point being the mouse), but he accepts whatever household suggestions she makes without fuss.

As she scrubs his bathtub she prays for her marriage. She empathizes with Madam and Mr. Avoka; entrusting yourself to somebody else is not the easiest thing to do. To think that, after a year of living with them, it had taken an outsider—Ndeye—to break the news of Madam's affair. She'd had no idea! It's true that women are more cunning and better at secrets than men. And it's only now, after being married for under a year, that she's able to forgive her father. Marriage takes bravery, and unfortunately, a brave man it appears he was not.

She swishes the brush in the toilet bowl, pre-soaked with bleach, and her gaze falls on a plastic wrapper in the waste basket. Sanitex, which as a child had seemed forbidden whenever she'd come across it in her mother's belongings, until after she turned twelve, when she returned from the farm and felt wetness between her legs. Blood, it had turned out. Mama gave her a whole packet of Sanitex, and since then she hadn't associated it with shame or as something to be regarded suspiciously, not until now, so out of place in a bachelor's apartment. The kitchen used to be the room where Atsu could sense the presence of Mr. Avoka's lover or lovers. She's not sure if it's one woman or many. Who knows with men? In the fridge, at this very moment, sits a pot of watery chicken stew *she* didn't prepare, with nary a vegetable in sight. The woman is probably desperately trying to win her way into Mr. Avoka's heart via his stomach. Poor thing will need help. Also, poor Mr. Avoka. When she tells Nasar these stories, he seems to envy Mr. Avoka, making silly comments about men needing to spread their seed or it goes bad. But if she feels bad for Mr. Avoka, imagine how much worse her emotions are for Madam! She only sees her in snatches, on days when she drops off Kojo, and that's often through the window. Such longing and hurt fill her chest that such a beautiful family has been rent apart.

Kojo's room, which is more a guest room than a lived-in space, contains a twin bed, a side table, a shelf of Mr. Avoka's political books, and an armchair from the old house heaped with electronic gadgets. It bears not one stamp of Kojo—no posters of Michael Jackson, not even the Eastern Nuggets, which Mr. Avoka likes too. She cleans quickly because Kojo will be in soon. And just as the thought crosses her mind, she hears a car enter the driveway downstairs. She walks into the living room, peers out the window, and sees a taxi dropping off the elderly woman who lives two floors below. If the Avokas' old house had been like this, half her anxieties wouldn't have existed. She'd have been able to see who was coming home and straighten up to the appropriate degree. She hadn't realized how much those honks panicked her. Especially Madam's three.

She moves on to Mr. Avoka's room, not much larger than the guest room. Furnished with a bigger bed, this one has a desk and typewriter, often piled with notes and half-typed sheets. All she knows is Mr. Avoka loves big words! After a few more months of English school, she's going to enrol in typing classes, and even though Nasar insists she doesn't have to work (and cooking is still her ultimate dream), secretarial jobs are easy to find and people will always need secretaries.

She hears the gravelly crunch of a car arriving and looks out the master bedroom's window. Out of Madam's new car—less glamorous, smaller, a Nissan or Toyota—descends Kojo. He goes to the back of the car, grabs a bag, and Madam steps out of the back seat, elegant in a simple white shift. They hug, and Kojo tugs on the handles of his backpack before heading into the building. After the Avokas split Madam hired a new house help, which made Atsu sad for days, because she was convinced she would be the one taking care of Madam. But Mr. Avoka righted things by hiring her to cook and clean three days a week.

Kojo knocks loudly but Atsu is already at the door and lets him in. He waves awkwardly, pulls off his headphones, and asks if his father is home. Atsu says no and apologizes that she hasn't cooked yet.

'You know me,' he says. 'You don't have to worry about me.'

'Well, I'm making your father's food anyway, so you'll get some too. How long are you home for?' The word 'home' doesn't feel right. This situation feels temporary, and Kojo's hesitancy suggests that he, too, thinks this isn't home.

'Midterms,' he says, dropping his knapsack on the cane settee. 'Here for three days and then back to school.'

'Why so short?'

'Three days there, three here. Six in all. Midterms are always short.'

He goes into the kitchen and returns with a big bottle of water, which he sets to his lips. He wouldn't dream of doing that in Madam's house, Atsu's sure. They say nothing to each other, even though she has many questions. She wants to know if he likes his mother's place better. Madam moved out of the old house, and a family of five, the mother an official at the Ministry of Transportation, has replaced the Avokas, Ndeye told her. Atsu wants to know if his mother's new help cooks well, if Madam has a new man in her life.

But all she manages is, 'How's school?'

'Not bad. Math is still math, but it's not the end of the world.'

They are quiet again, and the gulf that existed broadens.

'I'll start cooking,' she says.

She'd forgotten about the mouse, but when she walks into the kitchen, her upper body stiffens, almost as if preparing to run or fight. She opens the top cabinets and takes out pots, and is able to prepare two stews without incident. She's about to start making *jollof* rice when something grazes her leg. She screams, and Kojo hurtles into the kitchen. It's the napkin hanging from the stove's handle. Fear makes people irrational. She tells Kojo about the exchange she had with his father earlier.

'What? He doesn't like pets,' says Kojo, proceeding to open the pots of stew, evaluating them like the head chef in an expensive restaurant.

'Do you like school?' Atsu says, feeling stupid for shouting over nothing.

'You asked me already.'

'Sorry. I forgot.'

'Well, let's just say I'm still working towards America.'

'*Ei*, Kojo, take me with you!'

'I don't want somebody sending macho men after me,' Kojo says, making her wince.

If the Avokas know about Nasar's past, they haven't let on. She herself sees flashes of that violent history when they argue, in the way his jaw clenches, the way he seems ready to strike. But he never does. No one's perfect. And when she's lying by his side, watching TV or slowly slogging through *The Daily Post*, she feels like a baby in the womb.

'How's he, by the way?' Kojo says.

'Fine,' she says.

'Do you like being married?'

She hesitates, then says, 'I do.'

'I am beginning to think,' Kojo says, barely hearing her

answer, 'that life is about trying to find something better, whether you want to or not. But if you find something that works for the most part, you have to fight to keep it, otherwise life will force you to look for better, and a lot of the time it doesn't end up being so.'

Atsu thinks about his words. He speaks truth. She studies him and pictures where he'll be in ten years. Probably in America. People like him have dreams that come true, and fast. He has a beautiful and smart girlfriend, someone Madam approves of. Or maybe he'll never amount to anything. He'll be the person people whisper about, saying, 'He used to have so much potential.' She wishes him the former. She bends over to pull out the sack of rice and has to stop herself from screaming again. Karamoh's left hind leg is caught under the hammer of a mousetrap. He's trying to yank himself free but every effort leads to nothing. She feels so sorry for him.

'Kojo,' she says and points. 'It's Karamoh.'

'He thinks he's so clever.'

'The mouse?'

'No, my father. Naming the mouse Karamoh. Give me your slippers and please get me two polythene bags.'

Atsu slips her feet out of the plastic thongs and hands them to Kojo.

'Only one,' he says, exasperated. And before she can make him reconsider he thwacks the mouse on the head, enough to knock it unconscious. He grabs the mouse, trap and all, with the plastic bags.

'Thank you,' says Atsu.

CHAPTER FORTY-SIX

Paradise Revisited

Two months after my release from hospital I packed a suitcase, hired a new house help, and had a driver take us to Auntie Adisa's. Despite the many gifts Kojo had sent her and my incessant calls, she'd refused to have anything to do with me. Given that things with Theo weren't quite on the mend yet, even if Auntie Adisa wouldn't employ me, my plan was to sweet-talk her, beg her to let me help out as best as I could until I got on my feet.

Then there was the Theo issue. The romantic in her would have to understand. Sometimes space was the balm needed to restore love and healing.

To my relief, Auntie Adisa broke into a smile when she saw me, and quipped that with my dark glasses, walking stick, and suitcase I looked like a character straight out of a film noir.

'You don't take no for an answer, do you?' she said as she let me into her house. 'As soon as you recover you're going to be working for me for free.'

Mma was slighted that I'd chosen to stay with complete strangers for my convalescence, but surprised me by shutting down her business and coming to see me. My eyes hadn't recovered, but the world wasn't a fuzzy abstract painting anymore. Instead, things had taken on a certain precision and geometry. It was almost as if everyone had grown sharp corners. The doctors said things would get hyper-sharp before softening into reality.

Auntie Adisa offered my help and me a room for free, but I couldn't just mooch off her hospitality, and it was only after much persuasion that she accepted my offer of a thousand kowries to cover our accommodation and food.

On Mma's third night over, we ate with Auntie Adisa under a twilighted sky. After the meal Auntie Adisa offered us a bowl of kola nuts, which I declined but Mma took. In the air hung the smell of rain and a faint aroma of cooking.

'I've never understood why your generation likes kola,' I said.

'Everyone needs some stimulation now and then,' Auntie Adisa said as her teeth crunched into the nut. 'These days there are all sorts of unnatural stimulants.'

The sky darkened and a crescent sliver of moon hovered above us. I closed my eyes, thinking life was almost perfect. Not perfect. Almost. I heard birds—probably guinea fowl—clucking towards some destination, and I tried to imagine what it was like for them when they arrived there, at that destination, if they were filled with a sense of accomplishment. Had some of them strayed off course along the way, doing things that could cause harm to the group or to themselves? What would guinea fowl do with free will?

'Auntie Adisa, do you have any regrets?' I asked.

'Zahra,' Mma chided.

'It's okay,' Auntie Adisa said. 'Zahra and I know each other quite well now. Zahra, I see you haven't lost the hippy-dippy trait that been-abroads seem to come back with: talking about feelings in a circle. Don't you know the African way is to bury feelings?' She winked at me. 'Regrets?' Then a pause. 'I wish I hadn't been such a coward. I wanted to do so much: build a school, not just teach in one; travel by myself; have a big love affair with someone exotic.' Mma looked bemused. 'And by the time I realized I should just have taken the plunge it was too late.'

'But you created this place,' I said. 'It's … paradise.'

'I think I would have had more to offer the world if I'd started early. And now I feel like I'm hiding here, just counting down the days till it's over.'

'Oh, Auntie,' I said. 'It's not too late.'

'Don't worry. All's not lost. Luckily, I can now live vicariously through you. That's the only reason I let you stay.' We laughed.

'Mma?' I said. I think the question was meant for her all along, the woman whom I'd avoided becoming because I thought her too dogmatic, too behind the times, too servile. And yet she was a woman who'd borne it all with resignation: a headstrong daughter; a husband who barely showed her he appreciated her; her thwarted desire to be surrounding by lots and lots of children she could take care of.

'Oh, I don't know,' she said, her voice growing quiet. I'm sure she wanted to tell me to stop asking stupid questions.

'Come on, Mma,' I said. 'Indulge me.'

She cleared her throat. 'I wish I'd gone to school. I should have begged to go to school. No, not begged. I should just have done it. Run away.'

'We were less daring,' said Auntie Adisa, then turned to me. 'I could not even fathom defying my bosses the way you did.'

'So true,' said Mma. 'After all, we had free education in those days. Why was I too scared to ask my father? Zahra, you've always been so brave. Even your converting to Christianity ... I couldn't imagine doing such a thing, but your education opened you up to possibilities, and you took them. I am proud of the life you've made for yourself.'

'Thanks, Mma,' I said, surprised.

Doors slammed, TVs and radios buzzed, faint conversations filled in the silence that had befallen us.

'What about you, Zahra?' Auntie Adisa said. 'Don't think you are going to be left out of this. You're no spring chicken.'

'Oh, I have too many regrets to list,' I said, thinking of my affair with Obi, who had still not returned from England, whom I thought of every day. I still don't know if I regretted the affair. 'Maybe that's what being too exposed does to you. Imagine what life is going to be like for Kojo and company. The boy already knows more than I did when I was twice his age.'

'Zahra,' Mma said. 'You're not getting out of this.'

'Fine. I started this, I'll finish it: I wish I'd learned to be a better wife and mother,' I said. 'Less selfish. I wanted to do everything for me, me, and me. Get my degree. Start my family. Be the best at my job. My generation has always been about itself and its pleasure. We weren't so much into making sacrifices, which is what made you both such strong women. Your sacrifices.'

'We made sacrifices because that was the only thing we knew how to do,' Auntie Adisa said. 'We didn't have much of a choice. It was for our survival.'

'But you were fighters. You stood by your husbands' side and won us independence. I'm not sure where our country would be if women like me had been around in your time. Probably still colonized, just so we could get the finer things from abroad.'

'You exaggerate, Zahra,' said Auntie Adisa.

'You made sacrifices, too,' said Mma. 'Some of the jobs you took on to be able to raise Kojo I'd never dream of doing. Selling pharmaceuticals door to door!'

Auntie Adisa's daughter brought us a tray of chewing sticks, her slippers dragging on the floor. 'Lift your feet,' Auntie Adisa instructed.

'Maybe this generation will figure out the secret formula,' I said. 'It's their turn to figure out how to get it right.'

Auntie Adisa slapped her daughter's bottom.

'Did you hear?' she said. 'Enough of TV-watching.'

The next day, as he'd promised, Theo drove over with Kojo and Atsu, who had cooked a mountain of *jollof* rice. We laid out a table under the flame tree outside Auntie Adisa's cottage and spread out plates and indigo napkins next to earthenware bowls. Auntie Adisa sent for palm wine.

Auntie Adisa adored Theo and engaged him in all sorts

of conversations about books and what he was reading, and got a good laugh out of him when she told him of her love of romance novels. After we ate my wrinkly cheerleaders of love, Auntie Adisa and Mma, suggested Theo and I take a stroll. And who were we to say no to them?

We walked toward the palm-tree grove. The day was so clear that everything appeared saturated to my still-healing eyes: the bright cerulean blue of the sky, orange palm kernels, the whites of Theo's eyes that were trying not to meet my gaze. Holding hands, the one bit of physical contact I was hankering for, was out of the question because Theo made sure to keep enough distance between our bodies. I was walking with a cane, and even though I would have given everything to throw it away and have Theo hook my arm, that beast of shame and guilt, that beast of not-wanting-to-throw-out-that-first-word, was wedged between us and kept my fingers clasped around the hook of my cane.

We continued down the stone-lined path and came to an enclosure of grass tapering into a valley of palms, plantain trees, and a brook.

'I now understand why you couldn't wait to return here. One could get some serious work done here,' Theo said.

Thank God he spoke. Yes, he could move here to help me recover, but I kept the thought to myself, instead suggesting that we sit. I felt like I'd aged several years due to my surgery. I wanted to be the spry young thing he'd married, the one who kept him on his toes, the one who was wholly independent. But that person was gone.

'Theo, I don't expect you to forgive me,' I said. 'But I want you to know how sorry I am.'

'Shhh,' he said, creasing his eyes and focusing on the hump of land that sloped into valley. He leaned toward me and laid my head on his shoulder. The air was damp and smelled of earth, and I let my head sink into his flesh.

Doctor Karamoh Saturday died in 1995, before the end of his term, of what we were told were natural causes. The serial killings seemed to go to the grave with him—either he was behind them, or whoever wanted him out of power was satisfied and stopped sacrificing the young women of the capital. After the Doctor was buried and gone, Theo told me he would be publishing articles about his life as the Doctor's ghostwriter and warned me that I featured in a few of them. Each month I bought copies of the newspaper but couldn't bring myself to read them, especially after Anna had said that I came across as cold, calculating, and selfish. But then one evening, with Kojo at his father's (if anything good had sprung from our separation it was bringing Theo and Kojo closer together), I reached into my sock drawer where I'd stashed every single article and devoured them all, reliving moments I'd forgotten. While some facts were distorted, and I'd been stripped naked in front of fifteen million people, I wasn't devastated. If this was his way of healing—just like my surgery and then my time at Auntie Adisa's had purged me of my virus—then so be it.

Acknowledgements

To the ones who read and moulded and teased out and corrected: Natalia Kanem, Mohammed Naseehu-Ali, Baafra Abeberese, Kuorkor Dzani, Zain Ejiofor, Pearl Kyei, Michelle Nee-Whang.

For helping me sow the seeds of *Saturday's Shadows* in the summer of 2010: Anissa Bazari, Max Ross, Michelle Kim Hall, Anelise Chen, Sasha Graybosch, Janet Edwards, Peyton Burgess, Sarah Willeman, Grant Ginder, Grant Munroe.

For those who helped shape the novel at NYU: Junot Diaz, Julie Orringer, Darin Strauss, Matthew McAlister, Makena Onjerika, Cody Peace Adams, Jeff Beardsley, Jill Davis, Jenny Blackman, Maura Roosevelt, Scott Morris, Blair Hurley, Kayla Rae Whitaker.

To the P.E.O. International Peace Scholarship Fund for making my MFA a possibility.

To Marina Penalva, Anna Soler-Pont, and the Pontas family, and to Eric Visser and Corien Ligtenberg of World Editions and Gudrun Will, huge thanks for making this dream a tangible reality.

To Amanda Uprichard for giving me time to write and affording me the luxury of being an artist in New York City.

To Abdul-Rahman Harruna Attah, Nana Yaa Agyeman, and Rahma Harruna Attah for being my biggest cheerleaders.

For more information or to receive our newsletter,
please contact us at: info@worldeditions.org